Chapter 1—Missing Person

It was Sunday morning. Interstate 10 was practically empty, and Slayer made good time. Though the concept of 'good time,' Slayer thought, was meaningless in this context. It would take him another twenty minutes to reach the causeway; ten more minutes to get from there to the island. Thirty minutes in all. Nuclear accidents occurred in milliseconds. That was all it would take for a section of the nuclear reactor's fuel core to melt, reassembling itself into a critical configuration. Then an explosion could rupture the steel dome and release thousands of pounds of radioactive fuel and waste products into the air. The wind blowing off the lake could send intense radioactive clouds rolling over the city in less than an hour. By nightfall a half-million people would be dead. A million more would be less lucky and live out the week. And the entire lower Mississippi Basin would be uninhabitable for more than a hundred thousand years.

Hideous, outrageous events! Slayer's critics would call them preposterous prophecies. And he hoped beyond all reason his critics were right.

The highway veered off from the lake, and once again Slayer could see the grey Pontchartrain and the steel dome at its centre.

The technical term was 'containment sphere.' A geodesic dome of steel alloy and reinforced concrete so huge that immense columes of air could be rapidly displaced within the dome without forcing a rupture in the outer skin. There was also a sophisticated system of fast air pumps to depressurize the dome, in the event that an explosion became imminent, giving expanding gases room to dissipate. The idea was to trap within the sphere all radioactive substances liberated by a core meltdown or chemical explosion. Nuclear explosions weren't supposed to happen.

The city was still asleep. There were no sirens or sound trucks; no mobilization of people into fallout shelters. There was nothing on any of the highways to suggest that an evacuation, however limited, was in progress. The only travellers were elderly or middle-aged couples, on their way to early morning Mass.

Slayer fiddled with the AM radio. He swept the selector needle back and forth over the emergency frequency, finding only gospel singing and a discussion of current trends in stock market investment.

He didn't even see a flashing light till he had exited the interstate and was nearing the approach ramps to the causeway.

Ahead, blocking one lane, was a police car. In the other lane stood a huge, surly policeman. Slayer got out his General Power ID even though the side of his truck bore the big GP insignia. In emergencies the causeway, which was the only route of entry to the island, would be closed to all civilian traffic. Slayer knew skittish city policemen would be reluctant to admit anybody, even island personnel.

Slayer stopped the truck and handed the policeman his ID.

'I'm Dr George Slayer. I've got emergency clearance.'

The policeman glanced at the card and handed it back.

'Speed limit on these entrance ramps is fifteen miles an hour,' he said. 'See the signs? I suppose you've got a causeway pass?'

Slayer was appalled. The city was not even under alert. The police didn't even know about the island sirens. Car 38 of the Metairie Police was at the causeway because the Metairie Station House had received a complaint that nobody was manning the entrance gates. The toll booth operator had mysteriously disappeared.

Something must have gone wrong with the remote alarm relay circuits, Slayer thought. Chalk up another point for his theory and drive one more nail into the steel dome's coffin.

Slayer was suddenly scared. The policeman asked if he was okay.

6

DOME
Lawrence Huff

NEW ENGLISH LIBRARY/TIMES MIRROR

First published in the USA in 1979 by Pocket Books

© 1979 by Lawrence Huff

First NEL Paperback Edition May 1980

NEL Books are published by
New English Library from
Barnard's Inn, Holborn,
London EC1N 2JR.
Made and printed in Great Britain by
William Collins Sons & Co Ltd
Glasgow.

45004781 4

'Are you sure you haven't heard any sirens?' Slayer asked.

'Turn your engine off and listen for yourself,' the policeman said, impatiently.

Slayer did.

Either the sirens had stopped or the wind was playing tricks with sounds.

A minute later Slayer's truck was speeding over the causeway. The particle counter on the seat had tipped over on its side. The indicator dial, which Slayer could not see, was at the limit of the scale. Then it dropped back into the normal range as the truck left police car 38 and the mystery of the missing gate attendant far behind.

Chapter 2—The Rising Sun

Mayor Dorothy Mathieu heard the sirens from her home on Shore Drive.

The evening weather was unseasonably cool and lakefront New Orleanians were sleeping with air conditioners off and windows open.

She had been lying awake since early dawn unable to take advantage of the one morning she could sleep till nine. She tuned out the light snoring of her husband, Al, listening attentively for the lake sounds she loved. Most of the upper-middle-class residents of Shore Drive owned yachts or elaborate and brightly coloured sailing vessels. They made the lake their playground come Saturday and Sunday. Her attachment to the lake was far less extravagant. She liked the taste of the stiff salt breeze and loved the early morning feeding cries of gulls and the lapping sounds of waves against the concrete steps of the seawall.

She was her father's daughter in this respect. Her father, *the* Mayor. The shrewd, cold, and magnificently strong public figure whose name was synonymous with the highest office of the city. At times her recollections of him were so vivid it was as if he were present in the house.

The six o'clock Angelus bell rang out from St Francis Cabrini and she felt a sense of foreboding in the deep tones. She got up, glancing only once at a dark folder on her desk, and went to the bathroom to wash her face and, hopefully, banish ghosts. The mayor was a good-looking, strong-featured woman with silvery-black hair and an excellent figure. In the mirror her eyes looked tired, and she told herself that after the Fourth she would take her own vacation.

Al was still asleep when she returned to the bedroom. A band of sunlight fell across his tanned face and tousselled brown hair. What were the dreams of philosophy professors, she wondered, that they could sleep smiling like innocents?

She went to the window and pulled open the curtains. It was almost a habit now, watching out of this window as the steel dome took on the colours of dawn, running from blue to grey to blinding gold, becoming a second sun looming out of the lake. Dallas and Atlanta had nothing like it and would not for years to come – an eight-million-kilowatt super reactor that could generate enough electricity to heat and cool the whole state of Louisiana.

Nuclear energy was in the cards for southern cities. Dallas, Atlanta, Houston, even Birmingham were taking bids from Westinghouse, General Electric, and General Power. In the not too distant future a giant nuclear power grid would run from Texas to the Carolinas, providing almost limitless energy at a fraction of its present cost. And any city that did not become a part of the nuclear energy picture would sink to a second-class level.

Her vision of the future had always been so clear. Why was she plagued with uncertainties now?

She closed the curtains and turned from the window with a chill. Her fingertips touched the bottom edge of the Slayer Report as she rested her hands on her desk for a moment. Perhaps if she got her mind on what to wear for ten o'clock Mass . . .

She went to the bedroom closet, shuffled through her clothes, settled on the blue chiffon with long sleeves. When she couldn't stand it any longer, she marched to her desk and snatched up the folder.

'A study of the Hazards to the Mississippi Basin of General Power's Type 8 Sodium Cooled Fast Breeder Reactor,' by George Slayer, Ph.D, Nuclear Ecologist.

There was nothing in the report that she hadn't heard a dozen times before. There were always doom prophets. Why, then, was she obsessed with this report, weighing the arguments, examining mathematical figures and formulae she could not hope to understand? Why was she conjuring up the accusing ghost voice of her father: 'Dottie, Dottie, what have you done to my city?'

Slayer. She couldn't place the name. She paced back and forth across the room, reading the report through for the fifth time. Had Slayer's services been employed by Public Service of the Sewerage and Water Board she would have known about him right off. A 'nuclear ecologist'? He might be with the Federal Government or even General Power.

The report was dated 15 June, more than two weeks ago. Yet she had gotten her hands on it less than twenty-four hours ago. And even then it occurred quite by accident.

The report had been buried in a stack of papers destined for the file room at City Hall. Shirley, her secretary, in going through the papers looking for a memorandum she had mislaid, came upon an uninitialled folder marked 'Office of the Mayor.'

Dottie Mathieu had her father's sixth sense when it came to smelling political rats. Though, on the surface of things, the contents seemed innocuous, she could not shake the feeling that someone had deliberately misdirected this report. The contents had been subjected to intense scrutiny. Whole passages were underlined. A section of mathematical formulae was bracketed and marked 'ATTENTION.' And the word *incredible* was pencilled in the margin in what seemed to her a different hand. What in the report was so special that

9

someone had tried to sneak it by her office?

Should she inaugurate an investigation now, with the Fourth so close? And even if this report warranted it, did she have enough clout to bring the physical and spiritual energies of a colossal seven-year project to a halt two days before its completion?

She knew the answer. Only an act of God could stop the plant from going to full power on schedule. Why, then, was she even thinking like this?

Just how long she had been hearing the faint waves of sound emanating from the centre of the lake, she could not say. Perhaps her mind was reluctant to accept the sudden proclamation of the sirens that some of her most dreaded fears had come to pass.

'Al,' she said. 'Al, wake up.' Her husband turned on his side and growled. 'Al? Can you hear it, Al?' She gave him another shake, then hurried across the hall and down the stairs to the front door. As the door slammed shut behind her she realized suddenly she was still dressed in the see-through negligee. In the bright morning light she appeared absolutely naked, but her embarrassment scarcely slowed her.

'Dottie?'

She turned and looked up at Al, who frowned disapprovingly from the bedroom window.

'It's the sirens!' she cried out. 'There's been some kind of accident!'

The electricity was off but the phones were working.

Dottie Mathieu covered the phone receiver with her hand and told her husband not to bother with the portable radio. 'Fourteen hundred is the emergency frequency,' she said, 'but you won't find anybody broadcasting. All anybody knows is that the electricity's off.'

The sergeant on the phone couldn't explain why the department had not been alerted. That was supposed to happen automatically by battery-powered electric relay.

Any accident on the island that tripped the radiation-warning sirens should have also tripped an alarm downtown. Had that alarm been tripped, the mayor would have been notified at once. She would then have hotlined the steel dome for verification and, if the accident was bad enough, give the order to sound the alarms city wide.

She ordered the sergeant to alert the chief of police. Then she pushed the island hotline button on her phone.

Nobody answered.

She scribbled a name and number on a piece of paper and passed it to her husband. 'Use the house phone in the kitchen.' The hotline continued to ring.

When Al hollered back that nobody was home, she gave him another name and number to call with the same result.

'Damn!' she said.

She traded phones with her husband and called each member of her Nuclear Power Advisory Board. Dyle, Harris, LaRose, Palmer: not a single one was home. She did speak with Mrs LaRose, who said her husband had been gone since yesterday afternoon.

'Gone where? The steel dome? Thank you, Mrs LaRose.'

When she came back to the study, Al shook his head and passed her the hotline receiver.

'I don't understand why they're not answering this damn thing,' Al said. 'It's absolute criminal negligence.'

'I'm going out there,' she answered. She was pensive, but not at all panic-stricken. 'Hotline the police department while I get dressed. Tell them I want a helicopter here in fifteen minutes.'

Much to her embarrassment, Al kissed his wife and squeezed her hand before she climbed into the helicopter.

'Stand by the phone!' she shouted officiously above the din of the rotor blades. 'I'll call.'

And then she was gone.

After the noise died down Al started walking back towards the house. Then he stopped suddenly and turned

11

towards the lake. He was overcome with a sense of relief. Dottie couldn't know it yet because of the noise, but they had stopped. The sirens had stopped. All he could hear were the cries of gulls and the beating of waves against the sea-wall.

Chapter 3—The Hang-Glider

The empty causeway that led straight to the island, the island foyer security posts, parking lots, and administration buildings, even the gleaming dome itself, like something out of the twenty-first century – they were all the picture of early Sunday morning normality.

And the sirens had stopped; he was sure of that. Those big kilowatt blasters could rattle and shake the island and its entrance bridge down to their underwater foundations. Even a deaf man couldn't ignore what was happening.

Slayer relaxed his foot and the truck slowed. His heart had stopped pounding so hard and his nervous system was beginning to unwind. He noticed for the first time the undisturbed feeding antics of the ever-present gulls.

Everything *looked* normal.

Even Earl Parker, the security guard at Post One and a friend, greeted Slayer with his usual large smile.

Slayer asked about the sirens.

Parker held out his hands. 'I still got the shakes,' he said. 'When those mothers went off I thought it was the end of the world.' He shook his big Afro. 'Shouldn't have gone fishing, Doc. You missed all the excitement.'

Parker didn't know what had made the sirens go off. But there was a security red alert in sector six still in effect, though the official word was that the island was in no danger from radiation.

Security had to be extremely tight on the island because of the presence of large quantities of plutonium, the most dangerous element on the planet. Since the early Seventies authorities had feared that terrorists or organized crime might try to gain possession of the substance. One microscopic dust particle entering the human body meant irrevocable and agonizing death. Twenty pounds could make a bomb that could blow away a city.

Beside the eight tons of plutonium which comprised the reactor's fuel core, Slayer estimated there were at least two tons more in the breeding chambers and another several hundred pounds undergoing processing in the labs. Well over ten tons in all on the island. But never, except during times of shipping, was any plutonium allowed beyond the protective cover of the steel dome or in sector six, where the heat exchangers for the giant dynamos were located. If something in sector six had tripped the radiation alarms it couldn't be plutonium. Therefore it couldn't be that serious after all, despite the security red alert. Could it? The sirens had been shut down; nobody was in radiation shelters; and the inimitable Dan Mason was gliding over the dome on his red, white, and blue hang-glider.

Still . . .

Slayer drove his truck around the dome and took the sector-six throughway and met up with a barricade and two security guards.

They wouldn't let him through.

He showed them his emergency clearance and one guard checked it against a roster. The guard handed Slayer back his ID and smiled.

They still wouldn't let him through the barricade. The guards were cordial but firm, assuring him there was no island emergency. Slayer found the episode very odd.

The guards watched passively while Slayer scanned the area with his Geiger counter. Nothing. Before leaving Slayer aimed the device in their direction and frowned.

The hang-glider swung out over the lake gaining incredible speed at the sacrifice of altitude. Then it shot back in towards the dome. Slayer shielded his eyes from the brilliant reflections bouncing off the dome's steel facets to watch the kite.

His friend and colleague, Dan Mason, had been an expert hang-glidist since the age of seventeen. It was said he had begun his aerobatic career from atop the beach cliffs in San Diego while studying for his degree in nuclear metallurgy on the side.

Slayer could not imagine what Dan was doing hang-gliding when everyone had been alerted by the sirens. He figured there had to be a reason besides sheer impulse.

Over the dome the kite slowed and started another spiralling climb, caught in an up-draught of warm air. Slayer sat down on a piling at the island's dock and watched his friend execute the aerodynamic manoeuvres with total precision.

Four months ago when Slayer had first come to the island and become friendly with Mason, Mason had tried to get him to go up. Mason was then using a reel and tow cable from a speedboat. It was a straight-forward proposition. You would take off on skis. Once aloft you could gain altitude by reeling out the cable. When you were ready to glide, you just let go.

Slayer had demurred that first weekend. On the following Monday he made a special trip to the main public library in New Orleans to commence an intense study of the art and science of hang-gliding. He got out half a dozen books and sneaked them back to his meagre island living quarters. There for the remainder of the week he schooled himself on the do's and don't's of gliding mania. By Sunday morning he was a book expert. He could watch Dan aloft and predict his body movements three steps in advance. But in the end he agreed to go up himself only because he didn't want Dan to know how terrified of heights he was.

He took off with eyes shut and body trembling. Coming down, he lost a ski. He ended up with a busted kite, a sprained ankle, an extremely sore belly, and a seriously injured sense of pride.

Slayer watched now as Mason brought the glider down close to the water's surface. It braked on the air and came almost to a complete stop before Mason's feet touched the water only two yards from the boat.

Back at the dock Slayer gave his friend a hand hoisting the kite from the boat into the special hangar Mason had built for it above the pilings.

'Who's your new friend?' Slayer said so the driver of the boat could not hear. 'Nice looking, but not my type.'

'Very funny,' Mason said.

This morning Mason's boat driver was not his usual bikini-clad week-end companion. He was six feet tall, well over two hundred pounds, with predatory features, and he had a Jolly Roger tattoo on his right bicep. The Jolly Roger man didn't say a word. He only smiled.

'Lombardy sent him over,' Mason said. 'Kathy has a cold. I wasn't even going up this morning. I think he's from maintenance.'

Slayer's mind was racing. 'Lombardy sent him over?'

'He's very good with a boat, though he's a little retarded.' Mason whispered the aside.

Slayer was surprised to learn how little his friend actually knew about the sirens or the cause of the red alert in sector six. Mason, a top-rate nuclear metallurgist, and an authority in the field, would be an asset in any kind of island emergency.

'After the sirens were shut down,' Mason said, 'I went over to sector six. They gave me the same story they gave you. No emergency. There were security guards, technicians, and high personnel from Lombardy's staff running around like decapitated chickens. Somebody should have told *them* there was no emergency.'

Lombardy himself, Mason said, had accosted him at the sector-six barricade.

'He told me if I really wanted to help I should go hang-gliding. Seeing me up there, he said, would reassure people that everything was okay.'

'When you went to sector six,' Slayer said, 'did they check your name against a roster?'

'Yes,' Mason looked his friend in the eye. 'What are you

saying? That maybe you and I are on some kind of a blacklist?'

Maybe things were really okay on the island and maybe they weren't. But after talking with his friend, Slayer made up his mind to find out exactly what had triggered off the radiation alarms.

There was no doubt of an emergency in sector six. And if it was serious enough, then Lombardy should have used Dan Mason.

Chapter 4—Slayer

When he was a young boy, he had overheard his Mescalero uncle and aunt discussing his father, who had always been an enigma. Slayer had been surprised and hurt to learn that his father had been married before, to a white woman, as different from his own mother as night from day. This other woman was still alive. And Slayer wondered if she was the reason for his father's mysterious absences from the reservation for lengthy periods of time.

His father was a quiet, sober, and fear-inspiring man. When he had gotten up enough courage, he asked his father where he went on these secretive outings and why he felt compelled to make them.

His father had answered him with a riddle.

'Why does the desert lizard travel back and forth between sun and shade?' he had said. 'To keep the heat in his body at a temperature he can tolerate.'

His father alluded to the white blood in his veins. The outings were excursions back into the world of the white man, the world of his other self. Part white, too, Slayer had come, in time, to understand the meaning of the riddle and to experience the same internal forces which had driven his

16

father from the cool of the desert to the heat of the white man's world and back again to the desert.

Slayer improvised his own escapes.

He was discovered at an early age to be mathematically precocious, so that even at home in the reservation's school for Indian youngsters his sojourn in the land of the whites began. He was schooled intensively in the foundations of science and mathematics by an exceptional teacher for the government-run schools for the North American Red Man. Between 8 a.m. and 3 p.m. he surpassed the expectations of all his teachers. But after hours the side of him that was Indian found solace in long walks in the desert beyond the perimeter of the reservation. On rare occasions, after a heavy rain, seeds lying dormant in the desert sands during months of drought awakened, sharing the rare and precious moisture in the normally barren soil.

After the death of his father and his own voluntary incarceration in the best of eastern white schools, he sought escape in drugs, and read avidly about the drug-induced spiritual heights of his ancestors penned second-hand by sycophant academics bleeding fame and fortune from a dying race. In graduate school in Boston he began to cultivate friendships, realizing their importance in a lonely world. By the second week after his arrival at the steel dome, he had already found the old Cajun fisherman, LaBourgeois, whose Acadian background seemed foreign to the mainstream of white America. The purpose of his week-end fishing expeditions was as much to cultivate that friendship as to check Lake Pontchartrain for radiation poisoning with the Geiger counter.

Then there was Dan Mason.

Mason's friendship was a new height in the irony of human affairs. By every outward sign Mason was an upper-middle-class, spoiled-rotten, completely self-centred, arrogant California sun and beach bum. He was white society. Yet it was through this friendship that Slayer found release for his brooding spirit.

17

Mason was the only person on the island without prejudice. Or perhaps the converse was closer to the truth: Mason was prejudiced against the whole of humanity, thereby treating every race and nationality, including his own, with equal disdain. He was a modern-day gladiator, a man without fear, a man of action He was all those things Slayer was not. And he was the only human being who had ever gotten Slayer to face the spectre of his father.

When Slayer had first completed through eloquent equations his thesis on the instabililty of the super reactor, he brought the news to Mason. Mason was beside himself with a perverse joyfulness. His eyes sparkled like Christmas tree ornaments and he whistled happily under his breath.

'Wow!' he said. 'George, this is really hot stuff! What did Lombardy and Nichols have to say?'

'They haven't seen it yet.'

'You mean I'm the first? Why, George, I'm touched. Come on. We've got to get this stuff to them right away. I can't wait to see the shit hit the fan.'

Later, when the shit did hit the fan, they knew they were in for foul weather. Nobody else on the island would take their side, and Mason asked him why he had chosen the thankless vocation of gadfly. Slayer had shrugged and made a general remark about how somebody had to referee the ball-game of twentieth-century scientific hegemony.

'Yeah, sure,' Mason said with a yawn. And he added, 'How noble.' Then he mumbled under his breath, 'The more I see of people, the more I like dogs.'

Slayer asked him why the sudden knife in the back.

'Listen, pal,' Mason said, 'lofty motives are a crock. People do things out of need or pain, just like any other animal. I'm in this dog fight up to my ears and I mean to stick by you. Not out of some noble need to serve my fellow man. I have to have the excitement to make me feel I'm alive. Now, what's your poison? This theory you've concocted is heavy stuff. The mathematics is something right out of this world. Something like this doesn't float into your

18

head from on high. I see pain and revenge and hate and a lifetime of all the good old stuff that makes us rotten critters crawl. Let's have it. What's the real story? Why is George Slayer so gung-ho, ape-shit, dead-set angry over the whole super reactor programme?'

Mason had touched the nerve.

Slayer was eleven years old when his father had died, and there came into his possession along with other items of scant value which were his father's legacy, a cloth binder of looseleaf pages. The pages were yellow with age and the edges were frayed from a lifetime of handling. It was a diary of sorts, an intermittent autobiography of a soul in torment. And they began with assertion: 'Alamogordo, 6 August 1945.'

As he read on there was enkindled in his soul the hurt and resentment and hatred for the lavish technology of the white man that had ushered in the start of the atomic age and ultimately driven his father to hurl himself from a tenth-storey window of a downtown Albuquerque hotel.

Mason could scarcely have guessed that day of his observation on human pain and need how deep Slayer's feelings ran.

Slayer's father had been a youth of seventeen when the Trinity Project was conceived. His own white father abandoned the family and he had journeyed with his Indian mother from Santa Fe across the Captain Mountains to the Mescalero desert reservation near White Tail. His lifelong habit of drifting back and forth between the two cultures was already well established.

It was a time of war. And the Indian nations across the country were shackled in poverty. Thus, it seemed a godsend when people from the government came to the reservation to announce there would be work and good pay at White Sands for any young brave who didn't mind long hours of hard work. His father became a labourer, mixing concrete and pouring it into wooden forms at the bottom of large pits gouged from the desert floor by steam shovels. These were

19

the foundations for bunkers from which the white man would later observe with cool eyes the scorching blast of the earth's first atomic bomb.

Slayer's father was quick to learn and because he was half white he came to be trusted. They sent him to technical school in Alamogordo and in six short months he became a technician of sorts, operating the metallic hands which fondled a substance that was said to be more precious than gold.

There was talk that the United States was on the verge of a great discovery, an invention that would change the course of history, banishing from the face of the earth poverty, the age-old pestilence of mankind. For, it was said, there was great power in the very stones and someone had devised a means of setting it free.

The day it happened his father had taken ill from a kidney infection and was sent to the White Sands infirmary for tests. He was asleep when the earth quaked and the sky caught on fire. He lay in his bed shaking with fear, for surely a great spirit had devastated the land and the end of the world was near. He did not for a moment relate his work of the last several months with the enormous event.

Only much later would he learn about the bomb from a layout in *Life* Magazine and behold the destruction of Nagasaki and read Professor Oppenheimer's words of self-reproach: 'Behold, I am become Death, the Shatterer of Worlds.' He would vomit and vomit. He would never be the same.

Mason was right about hurt and revenge. Slayer's purpose in exposing the insanity of nuclear fission was to vindicate the suicide of a man who believed he was betrayed into helping to give birth to the Shatterer of Worlds.

Chapter 5—Test Run

In and out among the dynamos white-hooded figures moved slowly and silently, searching into every nook and cranny with Geiger counters. In the cramped sublevel of sector six technicians worked with sound analysers pinging metal conduit for signs of structural fatigue.

Simon Lombardy co-ordinated the search for stray radiation in sector six by short-range walkie-talkie. He and three other high-ranking General Power officials stood motionless near the north wall of the turbo-generator plant, watching. A team of electrical engineers dismantled and ran circuit checks on the alarm panels which had instructed the radiation sirens to sound off.

The three officials standing with Lombardy began to relax. The search for radiation in sector six was almost completed and the results were negative. One official began to tell the others in a nonchalant manner about a false alarm at a Westinghouse installation back in '76, and then made a disparaging remark about George Slayer. Lombardy, who had remained granite-faced, shut him up. Of the four GP officials present, Lombardy was the highest ranking and the only one with intensive scientific training. To him there was no such thing as a false alarm. The sirens had gone off for a reason. Either radiation had been released somehow or there was a faulty circuit in the alarm panel. Either event could foreshadow disaster. And if all their efforts here this morning in sector six yielded no results, it simply meant they would have to intensify their efforts.

In the radar tower at the island's heliport, Assistant Chief of Security Wally Englebrecht spotted the bogey through his binoculars and ordered the air-traffic controller to break radio silence. The pilot of the approaching aircraft was requesting landing instructions.

'ETA?' Englebrecht asked the controller.

'Two minutes, sir.'

'Very well. Have him circle for another ten before landing.'

'Should I give him a reason for the delay?'

Englebrecht did not answer. He strolled out of the tower room to the observation deck, glanced around to make sure he was alone, then pressed the call button on his walkie-talkie.

'Mr Lombardy? Englebrecht at the radar tower. We've got company.'

Lombardy's sigh came through clearly.

'A police chopper?' Lombardy said.

'Yes, sir.'

'Very well.' Again Lombardy sighed. 'I'll be tied up here for another thirty minutes. Maybe more. Extend my regrets to the mayor.'

As she backed out of the helicopter's hatchway, the mayor instructed her pilot to radio the chief of police that the sirens had stopped and that no island emergency was presently in effect.

'But tell him to stand by just in case,' she added.

'Wait here for you?' the pilot queried.

'Lord, no! I might be all morning. And you're not paid by the city to be my personal chauffeur. I'll hitch a ride back with somebody.'

Englebrecht watched the mayor wave the helicopter off and then turn to squint in his direction. He straightened and started walking toward her with quick, decisive steps.

'Englebrecht, isn't it?' she said. 'Security?'

'Assistant Chief,' Englebrecht said. 'Chief Warner is, unfortunately, detained for the moment.'

'And Lombardy?'

'He's asked me to take you to the steel dome. He'll join us as soon as he can.'

'I guess he didn't count on this breeze,' the mayor said.

Englebrecht regarded her quizzically.

22

'Carries sound,' she added.

Englebrecht, who was a native New Orleanian and who had once studied for the priesthood, regarded feminine authority as blasphemous. He did not like Mayor Mathieu and her easy way of snubbing male associates. And he considered her use of her maiden name in the election a political gimmick for capitalizing on her father's reputation. For him, the election of a woman to office merely represented the general perversion of the times.

The steel dome was packed with island personnel on all six tiers. Englebrecht escorted the mayor past groups of busy technicians to the escalators leading to the control deck. They were greeted there by a GP official, one of Lombardy's subordinates, and directed to a soundproof office, encased on all sides by glass. Seated inside were the four grim-faced members of the mayor's Nuclear Power Advisory Board. Englebrecht opened the door for her and stepped aside.

'Gentlemen,' she said with a large smile. In her arms, like a shield for combat, she carried the folder containing Slayer's report.

LaRose appointed himself spokesman since the mayor was predisposed to listen to Frenchmen. 'Technically, you could call it a conspiracy since there were three or more of us involved. But we weren't trying to keep important information from you. We just didn't want to burden you with this till we were sure we had something. Hell, we're still not sure this Dr Slayer isn't some kind of a crackpot. The best mathematical minds here have been going over his equations and they think it all comes down to this: if the reactor does not fail in some important respect within the first seventy hours of full-powered operation, then Slayer's theory is probably hogwash. Nobody believes there's the remotest chance that Slayer could be right. This test run is merely precautionary. We're more than halfway through the seventy-hour time period now and nothing's really happened. The sirens you heard were a false alarm. More than likely a short circuit. Lombardy is checking into that possibility at this very moment. Nothing's going to happen. Take my word for it. This test run will be over with before the Fourth. You'll still get to push that switch for Louisiana Power and Light and nobody will ever know the difference.'

Dyle suggested they get a spokesman who was on top of this test run from General Power to explain their side of it to the mayor in detail. LaRose went out to talk to the GP official who had greeted the mayor at the top of the escalator. Mayor Mathieu got up and walked to the glass panel to watch everything that was happening very closely.

The GP official placed an arm around LaRose's shoulder. He appeared to think things were over and led LaRose to a group of scientists congregated around a bank of computer panels. The group of scientists parted for them, and Mayor Mathieu could see Dr Dennis Nichols, GP's top nuclear physicist, seated before a console screen which was flashing data. Dr Nichols did not look up as the GP official spoke but shook his head emphatically and gestured towards the data screen. The GP official tried again, and again Dr Nichols shook his head. Seemingly as an afterthought, Nichols turned and addressed a young woman on his right. The woman listened attentively, almost with deference. She nodded and glanced once in the direction of the office, catching the mayor's eye. The little drama ended with LaRose, the GP official, and the young woman commencing a stiff march back to the glass office as Mayor Mathieu turned away to mask an over-interest which some might interpret as the first stirrings of alarm.

Mary Wolford, Ph.D, assistant to Professor Nichols, explained candidly and coolly to the mayor her understanding of the Slayer equations.

'Slayer's mathematics are rigorous. Absolutely foolproof. We've already established that on the computer. What we don't know and are trying to establish by this test is how well his equations fit the physical conditions and characteristics of the Sodium Cooled Type Eight. If they fit we're in serious trouble. They call for a better than eighty per cent chance of a complete systems failure. Think of it like this.

24

Everything that happens – and that includes accidents – happens in clusters. The laws of chance are against things running smoothly for long periods of time. That's why you have runs of good and bad luck, ups and downs, days when everything goes right and those other kinds of days. The laws of chance apply to machines, too. We try to get around them by building highly sophisticated back-up systems to keep the machines running smoothly. But those back-up systems are subject to the same laws of chance, so we build back-up systems for the back-up systems. It would be okay if you could keep doing that, but you can't – if Slayer is right. You reach a point of sophistication when your back-up systems accumulate enough risk as a group to actually make the back-up systems themselves hazardous. The time comes when enough minor things happening in clusters in a super-sophisticated machine constitute the makings of a colossal disaster. In essence, what Slayer is saying is that we've got a machine here that is so complex it must, by the laws of probability, at some point become unstable. I must add – but I'm sure you know this already – that my colleagues here, the vast majority of them, think that Slayer is wrong.'

Mayor Mathieu understood, even then, what only the best of them knew: that Slayer had posed them an impossible problem, one that could not be tackled by the watchful eye of a safety inspector or the whole board of NRC officials. Its solution lay not in conscientious building designs, nor in the requisition of proper materials or quality labour. The problem resided in the basic fabric of physical law. Even this test run was a sham. What could it prove? Merely a seventy-hour period of grace – if it got that far. A child's game to pacify second-calibre minds.

They could only hope, not prove, that Slayer was wrong.

Slayer's file which the GP official brought up from personnel was enlightening and a little reassuring. The mayor read through it while Dyle, LaRose, and the two other members of her Advisory Board debated with Dr Wolford.

Slayer, a graduate of Johns Hopkins and MIT, had

excelled in theoretical mathematics but had little training in nuclear engineering or any of the applied sciences except for a minor in ecology. He was three-fourths American Indian, Apache, and had spent his childhood on a reservation in New Mexico. Both his parents were deceased. He had been a student activist as an undergraduate at Johns Hopkins, a leftist, and was very outspoken on problems of ecology and Third World politics. A teacher said of him in a recommendation letter that he tended to get emotionally involved in scientific problems. Attached was a flippant response note Slayer had written thanking the teacher for the compliment. He's young, the mayor thought. And proud. She concluded from the photograph it was a face that few people would take seriously, even with age. It was too pretty and vulnerable and haunting. There was something accusing in the eyes that made you feel uneasy, guilty. People would not tolerate that. Young and inexperienced, the mayor had never wagered on those qualities before. Why should she now?

Later, Wolford, who was herself very young with little more experience than Slayer, would disrupt these temporary feelings of security with an offhand remark.

'Slayer is only twenty-four,' she would say, 'hardly even a mature adult by today's standards. Yet, Einstein, Bohr, Helsenberg, all the big physical theorists had done some of their most important work before the age of twenty-five. Makes you kind of wonder, doesn't it?'

Professor Nichols queried the computer banks and shuffled calculations around on his data display screen. Half the scientific community on the island stood around him as if they were watching a championship chess tournament. He tossed weak smiles at his colleagues and wiped beads of perspiration from his brow. The flashing lights were not that hot.

What was Wolford saying in there? Was she for him or against him? If she were here at his side right now seeing just what he was doing with the computer and the answers he was getting back, her eyes would be out on sticks. She liked a good horror story. And he was concocting one with the help of the computer and Slayer's equation. He hadn't taken that man seriously enough.

He had, of course, realized, ever since he first read over Slayer's equations, that the risk factor was a function of kilowatt size, a geometrical function, which became a colossal threat beyond the five-million-kilowatt range. And with the new, larger machines, it was too terrifying a concept.

Now he had worked out a curve for Slayer's equations. And he was asking the computer if the risk factor for the smaller, older, machines lay precisely on that curve, where it should lie if Slayer was even remotely correct in his basic assumptions.

Too bad he had sent Wolford away. He would have liked to make her pee in her pants with all her colleagues watching. He would not say a single word. He would just point to the figures on the display screen.

Pee in your pants, Mary Wolford.

That fool Ellison was down the hall making noises, trying to draw attention to the normality of the reactor's condition. Ellison was doing what Nichols himself should now be doing. Patting backs, smiling cheerfully. 'Those sirens this morning were just a false alarm.' 'These figures on the screen? They mean nothing at all. I'm just playing a little game with the computer.'

How did it all get turned around?

Nichols left Ellison in charge, with Wolford still talking to the mayor, and his moron colleagues happily oblivious. He walked out of the steel dome and paused to breathe in the crisp, salty lake air. Such a beautiful morning!

Alone, at his modest island residence, sitting at his desk in the little study, he remembered how it was. The hurrahs, the shouts of praise and congratulations. He recalled his own boyish sense of awe and wonderment when it came his turn to shake Professor Fermi's hand. The great god Fermi! Someone had passed champagne around in paper cups they lifted up like chalices. 'Gentlemen,' Fermi had said, beaming at that first pile of graphite bricks beneath the bleachers, 'I

27

give to you the future!'

Nichols opened the bottom drawer of his desk and extracted his own bottle of champagne, unchilled, as near a copy to the original as he had been able to get. Only Wolford was in on his little fantasy and knew what he had planned for the Fourth of July. *Had* planned. How had things gotten so turned around?

He took the bottle by the neck and smashed it into a hundred pieces against the leg of his chair while saying, aloud, amid unexpected tears, 'Gentlemen . . . I . . . give . . . you . . . the future . . . '

Chapter 6—Fire Water

There was something wrong with his skin. It couldn't stand to be touched, as if it were sunburned, but there was no redness. It never occurred to him to tell the others, for it seemed the least of his worries.

What was important now was to crouch low in the tall grass weeds so the cops could not spot them from the beach and to figure out what they were going to tell their parents.

He could run away from home and get it over with. They would never forgive him for this, ever. And his little brother would cry and scream and play it up big just to make his parents come down on him harder.

It was all he could do to keep Mikey's face shut now so the cops wouldn't hear.

'My boat! My boat! A monster ate my new boat!'

'Shut up, Mikey, or I'll smack you one. It wasn't no monster.'

'Pete, what happened to the man?' There were tears in Wayne's eyes. 'Did he drown, Pete? Pete, maybe we should tell the cops.'

Wayne was their neighbour and a schoolmate. Pete had seen him cry before when the other kids made fun of him.

He was tall and klutzy and never got picked for softball. Pete put up with him because nobody else would.

'Did you see him drown?' Pete said.

Wayne hesitated.

'Well, I didn't see him drown, either,' Pete added. 'And I was right there.' He stuck his chin out stubbornly.

Actually, he hadn't seen very much at all. After the explosion that wrecked Mikey's sailboat, he shut his eyes and kept them shut.

He remembered suddenly being in the water, feeling its strange warmness. Hadn't morning lake water always been cold? He knew he couldn't touch bottom there and his head was numb and dizzy. Don't swim for it, he had told himself. Just hold on to that busted piece of hull. Mikey and Wayne were screaming bloody murder from the shore and that's when he had opened his eyes and first seen the man.

The man was swimming for him from the direction of the causeway, treading water like a speedboat. What was taking him so long? When the man reached him he was coughing and out of breath. He was fat and old and not in shape, but Pete hugged him like he was a big Teddy bear.

'Just keep your hold on that piece of boat, kid,' the man had gasped. 'I'm going to push you in to shore.'

There was another explosion. This time Pete saw it start down shore beyond the swimming beaches. Something whipped out toward them at fantastic speed, an underwater cannonball making clouds of steam which hissed and poured from the surface. The water turned hot and Pete had to yell out. He tried to pull himself higher up on the busted hull. A thin jet of red fluid swept by just beneath the surface. It caught the man across his upper right shoulder. Pete heard him moan. And just before he closed his eyes for the last time he saw something long and white like raw bone. He did not open his eyes again till his feet touched bottom and he knew he was close enough to scramble for the shore. He did not see the man again at all.

The police were staying too long and already they had found pieces of Mikey's sailboat.

'Pete, I think we should give ourselves up,' Wayne said. 'You don't look so good, Pete.'

'You crazy or something, Wayne? You want to get sent to Milne's home for orphan boys and juvenile delinquents! Keep your hand over Mikey's mouth so he can't holler out.'

Pete suddenly threw up all over Mikey, who began to scream and kick. Nobody was more surprised than Pete. The fluid from his mouth was thick and laced with red. He got dizzy and his vision blurred.

Chapter 7—Impersonation

'What do you make of it?' Slayer said.

'There's still something very wrong,' Mason answered. 'I know that guy they let through the barricade.' Mason took the binoculars from his eyes. 'Myeburger. Harve Myeburger.'

'The radiation specialist?' Slayer said.

Mason nodded. 'The one and the same. He keeps an apartment in New Orleans East. I bet they flew him over by helicopter. One came in this morning not long after they got the sirens turned off and the electricity back on.'

'What time is it now?' Slayer said.

'Ten to.'

'We better get going.'

They caught Parker just as he was getting off his shift at Post One. They waited in the front parking lot in Slayer's truck till Parker got close to the Security Building walkway. Then Slayer gunned the truck out from the parking space and slid to a stop in front of Parker, backing him up a few steps.

'If I was a regular cop, I'd give you a ticket' Parker snapped.

'Hop in,' said Mason. 'We want to talk.'

'Can't this wait? I'd like to get out of uniform, get off this damn island, go home, and go to bed.'

Inside the cab they told Parker their plan.

'Have you guys lost your marbles?' Parker said. His eyes were half-dollars.

'You still have your key to the ID room, don't you?' Slayer said.

'Yes, but . . .'

Parker was hard-headed, adamant about the role he was supposed to play in their scheme; and in the end they were forced to compromise with him.

'You can borrow the key,' Parker said, 'and the uniform – but only after I'm safely out of it and on my way home. Slayer, you're just about my size, but there's something about your complexion that just ain't right. That's as much as I'll do for you. As it is, I'm going to start looking through the classified pages of the *Times Picayune* when I get home.'

'We won't get caught and you won't lose your job, Earl.'

'Yesh,' Parker said. He fidgeted for a minute. 'Well,' he said finally, 'don't worry about it. Those crackers don't even know who I am. You probably will get away with it. And I hope you find out what's going on. Something sure is.'

The Security locker room was deserted. Slayer buttoned up the front of Parker's jacket, straightened the tie, and placed the wide-brimmed hat on his head. It was too big and it slipped down over his eyebrows. He ruffled his hair to create more tension on the inside rim and tried again.

'How do I look?'

Mason was trying to suppress a grin.

'A Smokey, right? I wish Parker would have played his own part.'

'You look just great,' Mason said. 'You look just like a cop – uh, security guard. You sure you're not?'

'You know they have to pass inspection in this thing every morning?' Slayer said. 'Look at the shine Parker has on these boots.'

'Warner and Englebrecht fancy themselves regular little army generals,' Mason said.

Slayer opened the door to the ID room with Parker's key and stuck his head inside. It was dark. He went in and turned on the lights. Mason followed.

'Place your feet on the markers, sir,' Slayer said, 'and look at the red dot.'

He snapped Mason's picture with the Polariod just the way he had seen Parker do it, and while the picture was developing he typed out information on a blank ID card which he had gotten from the shelf under the counter.

He made Mason a supervisor in operations, Lombardy's staff, and gave him Blue Tag clearance.

'What do you want to be called?' Slayer said.

'Evel Knievel.'

'W . . . C . . . Parker,' Slayer said aloud, typing in the name.

He snatched the card out of the typewriter, placed it on the counter, and peeled Mason's picture. 'Umm,' he said.

'Let me see,' said Mason. 'What do you mean, "Umm"? Nobody takes good pictures for ID's.'

Slayer trimmed the photograph, stuck the picture on the ID card, and placed it in the laminator.

When it came out he gave the ID to Mason, who pinned it on his shirt pocket.

'You should have a more weasel-like expression,' Slayer said. 'That's better.'

'Let's take a Security Go-Cart.' Mason practised his new scowl.

Chapter 8—The Scientific Establishment

After the conference with her Advisory Board, the mayor asked Wolford to join her in the staff lounge on a lower tier of the dome. There was a pay phone there which bypassed the island switchboard. The mayor dialled her home number. Wolford waited at a discreet distance.

'Hello, Al? I've decided to hang around the island for a while. I'll be home to pick up some clothes later this morn-

32

ing. Would you run an errand for me? Leave a key in the flowerpot on the porch. I didn't bring mine. Yes, the sirens stopped right after I left. They think it was a false alarm. In the top drawer of my desk you'll find a Xeroxed copy of a report: "Hazards to the Mississippi Basin . . ." by George Slayer. I want you to get that copy to the head of the mathematics department at Tulane. Oh, he isn't? Then who is the best mathematician in the city? Donahue at Loyola, a priest? That's even better. Swear him to secrecy. I want his opinion of the contents, that's all. Get back to me as soon as you can, but don't call. Can you come out to the island this afternoon? Okay, see you then. And, Al, don't forget to leave the key.'

She hung up and led Wolford to the coffee maker. 'How do you like it?'

'Black.'

There was an entrance passageway from the lounge to an outside veranda with deck chairs. From there you could oversee much of the island complex and on clear days there was a view of the city's skyline. The International Trade Mart, the Marriott, and the Shell Building towered over the others and blended into the grey cloud of pollution which hung perpetually over the city.

The mayor shook her head.

'Downtown New Orleans is only thirty-two miles away,' she said. 'Thirty-two miles. Some members of the city council wanted the reactor built downriver, as far away as Grand Isle.'

'Why didn't you?' Wolford said.

'Your company, General Power, was against it.'

'Yes. I've heard all the arguments.'

'And there are a lot of country people down there,' the mayor continued, 'old, ignorant Frenchmen who couldn't be convinced about how safe it was.' She smiled ruefully. 'Wolford, you believe in our principles of government, don't you? That the people and their representatives should have the final say? I mean, you don't believe in military or industrial supremacy, do you?'

'Or supremacy of the scienific establishment?' Wolford said.

'Precisely.'

Mary Wolford turned to stare out over the lake.

'I have to stand up for Lombardy in this matter,' she said flatly. 'I know the kind of reputation he has, that he's iron-willed and iron-fisted. Members of his own staff call him the little dictator. He's all those things. But if it weren't for Lombardy, Slayer's report would have been squelched by his own peers and there wouldn't have been a test run at all. Lombardy may be a lot of things, and I know he did every-thing to keep you out of it. He turned off the city warning system and he subverted members of your Adivsory Board. But despite it all, he's intellectually honest. He wants to know whether Slayer is right or wrong. And, frankly, that's something the scientist establishment must decide, not the people's representatives.' She was struck by the harshness of her own words and softened her tone. 'And now that you understand the way I feel about Lombardy, I'll tell you anything you want to know because I think there's a very good chance that Slayer might be right about this reactor and I am a member of that scientific establishment. What I'm saying is yes, I do believe the people should have the last say, and I'm gladly passing the buck along to you.' She looked into Mayor Mathieu's large brown eyes. 'Do you think you can stand the heat as well as Lombardy?'

'Wolford, I appreciate your candour. Will you take me to see sector six?'

'You want me to repeat all this in front of Simon?'

'Lord, no! Well, you don't have any hard-core proof that Slayer is right, do you? I need a reputable scientist in my corner if I'm going to butt heads with the powers that be, not somebody whose sanity is as questionable as Slayer's. The time may come when I'll have to put you on the witness stand. Let's just hope we've got a few trump cards by then.'

Before they left the veranda, Mayor Mathieu grabbed Wolford by the wrist.

'One more thing,' she said. 'I've got a gut-feeling the

question of the reactor's safety isn't going to be resolved short of some kind of nuclear catastrophe. I want your honest opinion about something. If it comes to a showdown with GP, will Lombardy stand with us?'

'Without incontrovertible proof that Slayer's thesis is correct?'

'That's what I mean.'

'I don't see how he'd be able to do that.'

Chapter 9—Wolford

Wolford knew she shouldn't have shot her mouth off that way about Simon. She shouldn't even have expressed her opinion so freely about Slayer, though Professor Nichols had appointed her a sort of unofficial spokesman. At any rate, her place now was in the dome, on the top tier with Nichols and the other members of the science staff. She had no business accepting the mayor's invitation to accompany her to sector six. What possible reason could she have to suddenly ally herself with a politician?

Politicians! It was politicians that had gotten her into trouble, almost ending her career in science before it had begun.

It would be three years ago next October. Wolford was a first year graduate student at Stanford trying to hit upon a term-paper idea for her class with the eminent Dr Harold Newton Ashley. Ashley was internationally famous as a nuclear scientist with a social consciousness. His pet thesis was the immorality of plutonium proliferation. Every nuclear reactor, not just the fast breeders, makes plutonium as a waste by-product. American reactor manufacturers, by selling their technology to foreign governments who had neither the money nor the inclination to keep this dangerous element from falling into the wrong hands, could be providing terrorists and international gangsters with the ultimate weapons of terror. Wolford's term-paper was a spin-off of this idea. There was a cornucopia of unclassified data in university and public libraries on the atomic bomb. She wanted to see whether a mere graduate student, using this information of public domain, could successfully construct a device with enough explosive tonnage to hold a city for ransom. In her paper she illustrated ten different ways such a device could be built.

'Wolford, it's frightening,' Ashley had said after his first reading of the report. 'Except for the plutonium, there isn't a single item in your illustrations that couldn't be obtained from a hardware store or chemical laboratory.'

Ashley had sent her paper to five colleagues in the field of nuclear detonation for their evaluation. Each replied they were shocked and horrified. They concurred that Wolford's devices could indeed effect instantaneous plutonium chain reactions.

Then something terrifying happened. Ashley contacted his publisher and the next day a horde of federal investigators descended on Stanford.

Wolford's research was confiscated and classified. Ashley was ordered to report to a Senate investigating committee, Wolford was taken to the FBI office in San Jose for interrogation. The FBI treated her as if she were a left-wing political activist who had traitorously leaked information vital to the nation's security. She was even lectured over the phone by the senior senator from California. She tried explaining that her actions had not been politically motivated, that all she had wanted was an A for the course, and that none of the information she had used was classified. The senior senator said *she* was the one who was about to put a dangerous weapon in the hands of terrorists, proving he had missed entirely the point of her report. Then he intimated that her judgement on matters of state security was typically feminine and that she should keep her nose henceforth out of politics.

Wolford, though furious, was cowed. Her boyfriend at the time a graduate student in English and a Trotskyite, who sported a full red beard and drank like an Irish poet, wanted her to make a full disclosure of the incident in an underground rag which he was affiliated with. He assured her other papers would pick the story up and within a month she'd be a national celebrity. He promised her she'd probably make one of the major TV network news magazines.

But Wolford wanted the incident closed, finished. She certainly didn't want publicity. And she kept putting him off. Inevitably, as was his way, he came to confuse the issue with her reluctance to have sex. He'd decided to leave her.

'I'm splitting for good. But before I leave I'm going to have my say. Your body's got it together, but your head's back in Ogden under a bushel basket. Forget about your parents' expectations, your straight upbringing. Their daughter . . . the nuclear scientist . . . a credit to God and country . . . I say shit to that. If you want to fuck, fuck. If you want to tell those bastards from Washington to go screw themselves, then do it! From day one you've used my reputation as a womanizer to hide from your peers the secret of your intact hymen. That's been your thinking, hasn't it? What you need is to be humanized. Quit thinking of yourself as a goddamn institution.'

Randy's comments on her parents were unconscionable. His criticism of how she had used their relationship as a cover for her virginal status were totally unfounded.

Yet, as she was to learn in time, his words had had a prophetic ring.

Almost three years had passed and she was still a virgin. From time to time her mother would write her letters about eligible young men back in Ogden and tell her not to worry. But she had begun to wonder whether any mortal man could live up to her expectations, and then she began to wonder where she had gotten such lofty expectations from in the first place. On such occasions she would envision Randy's laughing face – mocking her.

Because she was pretty, and for no other reason, many of the important men on the island had taken her into their confidence, disclosing the inside workings of company politics along with some of their most private and personal ambitions and schemes.

Nichols, for example, had that damn bottle of champagne and a plan to re-enact an event out of his past down to the last detail. Except that she was young and pleasing to his appreciative eye, why else had she been made privy to his elaborate preparations? Others used more direct approaches and she now feared that her advancement at GP might be retarded by her continuing refusals to hop into bed.

Simon Lombardy had been her salvation.

Simon had taken a shine to her from the first day of her arrival on the island. Over the coming months they developed a close personal friendship which, to her great joy and relief, remained at a strictly platonic level. In time, however, rumours began that there was hot fire between GP's island chieftain and a certain female physicist who was almost young enough to be his daughter. She did nothing to stop the rumours. And almost right away unwanted flirtations and sexual advances from high island personnel began to decline. It was understood it was company suicide to tamper with Lombardy's own personal merchandise.

Final vindication for her strategy had come on the day of the company picnic last May. They were all on their way to Fountain Blue Park in Mandeville. She was driving a station wagon with seven other women her age from the island, all single and knowledgeable. A mile or so before they got to the park they passed a big billboard which asked: 'WHAT ARE YOU SAVING IT FOR?' They all giggled and winked and basked her in the warmth of their acceptance.

But while Lombardy's fatherly interest made her social life on the island less taxing, the needs of her body were making themselves evident. She felt herself being consumed by a hunger resulting from her years of abstinence. These needs were made more manifest by the arrival of George Slayer.

She knew about Lombardy's interest in Slayer long before anyone else, even before Nichols.

'How do you think the science staff here would react to

some Apache Indian culture?' Lombardy had asked her.

At first she hadn't gotten his meaning. Then the light came on and she whistled.

'Has George Slayer applied for a job here? With GP?'

'Why not?' he said. 'GP had the prototype Super Reactor – the reactor of the future. What nuclear physicist wouldn't give his eye teeth to get on here?'

'But George Slayer is against the whole Super Reactor programme.'

'How many of his articles have you read?'

'He's only published four – to date.'

'Wolford, you're a conscientious scientist. I don't think anybody else on this island has even heard of George Slayer.'

'That can't be,' she had said. 'There was a write-up on Slayer in the last *Physics Quarterly*. He has a lot of disturbing things to say.'

'Wolford, there's a conspiracy of unanimity among the scientists on this island. Professor Nichols has become something of a legend, and the other scientists view him with awe. That's not very healthy.'

'You think there's something wrong with the Super Reactor?'

'I think it's wrong to be so over-confident. Well, hell, you said it yourself. Slayer is disturbing. How many people on this island are the least bit disturbed?'

'Two?' she said.

'Slayer hasn't applied for a position here. But I bet he'd snap at the chance. I'm going to pull some strings and get GP to make him an offer. I've seen the writing on the wall. What this place needs is a fresh point of view.'

Right before Slayer's arrival, Lombardy had confided in her again.

'I've managed so far to keep my name dissociated from Slayer's. I don't want him or anybody else on the island to know I got him this job. If some of the scientists here knew that, I'm afraid they would become too surreptitious even for me. I prefer to know what's going on in everybody's head. If I don't, I might make some bad decisions. I also wanted to mention that a lot of people here know that you and I are good friends.' It was the only time she had ever seen him blush. 'There has even been some petty talk.'

He was finding it hard to complete his line of thought. But she was way ahead of him.

'Would you prefer it,' she said, 'If I didn't become too friendly with Slayer myself?'

'You know I hate to interfere with your personal life.'

'But you think someone might connect the two of you through me.'

'It's a possibility.'

'I'll be very aloof.'

At the time it was an easy enough promise to make, since it went along with her strategy not to complicate her life. But then she met Slayer, the most disturbingly attractive man she had ever seen. And each week her promise became harder and harder to keep. There was a fire inside her. Everything about Slayer excited her, and she had never felt that way before about anyone.

She tried once to write to her mother about Slayer. She praised his style of thinking, his clarity of mind, and his great courage. It was not easy for a dissenter to gain acceptance on the island, especially if the dissenter was an . . . Astonishingly, she could not bring herself to write the word. Indian. It was something her mother would not want to hear. She had cried then and torn the letter to shreds. A vision of Randy's prophetic words haunted her. 'I am not a racist!' she shouted. 'And Slayer is not forbidden fruit!'

But she kept her promise to Simon. She seldom spoke to Slayer, or defended him to his peers, or spoke out against the harsh and unfair criticism against him. Throughout Slayer's ordeal on the island she had remained proper, aloof, and silent.

And all the while she was a smouldering bed of hot coals.

Chapter 10—Sector Six

Slayer didn't see Englebrecht stepping out from the kerb with his arm raised till it was too late. Then he was committed to stop. How could a security vehicle bypass the assistant chief?

'Do you know who that is?' Slayer said between gritted teeth.

'Just don't lose your cool,' Mason answered.

Englebrecht led two women into the street and squinted at Slayer's name tag.

'Parker,' he said, 'I want you to drop us off at sector six.'

'That's where we're headed,' Mason said before Slayer had time to answer. 'I'm Parker, Lombardy's staff.'

'Glad to meet you, Parker,' Englebrecht said. 'This is Mayor Mathieu and Dr Wolford, from Professor Nichols's staff.'

Wolford and Mason turned pale.

'Uh, hello,' Wolford said, playing along. Mayor Mathieu eyed Wolford and said nothing.

They passed through the barricade with no trouble. Englebrecht, Wolford, and the mayor got off at the entrance to the turbo-generator building. Before leaving the vehicle, Englebrecht leaned in Slayer's direction and whispered.

'What did he say?' Mason wanted to know.

Slayer shook his head. 'He said, "Parker, get a haircut."'

They rode around sector six for a while, confirming what they already knew: that the trouble was in the turbo-generator building.

'We'll have to go back there,' Mason said.

'Wolford recognized us.'

'But will she tell?'

Slayer turned the vehicle around. 'I'm not sure,' he said,

'but I think the mayor recognized me, too, though we've never met.'

'Paranoia.'

'No, really, I think she did. She gave Wolford a look. I saw them in the mirror.'

'I don't think we should back out now.'

The turbo-generator plant was a low-lying and apparently endless building. Stretching far into the distance were files upon files of stainless-steel machinery which hummed and bristled with power. Slayer's scalp tingled and the hair on his arms stood on edge from sheer proximity of such enormous quantities of electrical energy.

Beneath floor level giant heat exchangers transformed heat drawn off from the reactor into super-steam, shaking the entire complex in the process.

Slayer nudged Dan Mason, glancing up to the second-floor level, where Lombardy, Wolford, and the mayor were congregated with several others at the railing's edge.

'Brass-ball it,' Mason said.

A team of men with radiation detectors were taking five. Mason walked right up to them so they could see his fake ID. 'No luck?' he asked. And when they shook their heads he looked at his watch and ordered them back to work.

He then turned to Slayer and led him to a spot where they could not be seen from the second-floor level. 'George, old pal,' he said, 'this is just no good. You're as nervous as a long-tailed cat in a room full of rocking chairs. And that uniform is drawing everybody's attention. I'll stay and find out what I can. You hightail it out of here and get lost in that crowd of security people they've got posted outside. I'll look for you there later.'

Slayer felt a hundred eyes on him as he worked his way, leisurely, he hoped, back towards the entrance of the building. He didn't respond the first time a voice called, 'Parker!' from behind. The second time the voice called out, he almost jumped a foot off the ground.

'Glad I caught you, Parker,' the mayor said. She was almost out of breath. 'Can you drive Wolford and me back

42

to the steel dome?'

When they got outside, the mayor addressed him by his right name.

'Damnit, Slayer, you had Wolford here scared to death. And me, too. Suppose you'd gotten caught? Do you think Lombardy would still go through with this test run?'

'So that's what's going on,' Slayer said. 'I thought those generators were making an awful lot of electricity.' Suddenly he stopped in his tracks. 'But that means they're running the reactor at full power!'

'Yes, of course they are,' the mayor said. She observed his stricken expression. 'Good God, you really do expect the damn thing to blow up!'

Chapter 11—Pact

The mayor pressed Slayer into service to drive her home. Mary Wolford went along for the ride.

After he had shed his security-guard identity, Slayer met the two women in the front parking lot and guided them to his truck. He stowed his Geiger counter and binoculars under the seat and scooped up the bubble-gum wrappers he had deposited on top of the dash, trying to hide the wrappers and his embarrassment. Wolford sat in the middle and acted as general referee and interpreter in the conversation that ensued.

They went back over Slayer's ideas about the reactor at the mayor's insistence – not because she expected an instant, in-depth understanding of nuclear power, but because the mayor knew how to get to people, and she wanted to see more of the inner man. How did he respond to bull-headed opposition? Would he balk pressure or be intimidated by loud-mouthed filibustering? Could she rely on him to present his views clearly and logically in the upcoming crisis? That was the bottom line, and she knew it.

43

Because that was her plan of action. She wasn't going to push that switch for Louisiana Power and Light on the Fourth and commit New Orleans to a twenty-five-year lease of the giant reactor from General Power. She planned to throw everything out in the open and rely on a public forum to get at the truth. Hang the money the city, state, and federal governments had already shelled out. Hang the opposition and hang her own political future. Hang even the good reputation of the Mathieu name. She'd be damned if she was going to let an eight-million-kilowatt nuclear time-bomb set up house in her own backyard.

'Slayer,' she said, 'give me a piece of that gum. I always liked the damn stuff, but I've been reluctant to show my frivolous side for thirty years. I never knew of anything better to hold people together through thick and thin than the knowledge they share a secret vice in common.'

Chapter 12—Lost and Found

Traffic was backed up on the causeway though it was still early Sunday morning. Car 38 was still at the New Orleans exit. But now there were two more cars and a police emergency vehicle. Slayer remembered there was a man missing; and a thought at the back of his head made him suddenly uneasy.

'They had trouble here earlier this morning,' Slayer said. 'Mind if we stop?'

The police wanted Slayer to keep going, but one of them recognized Mayor Mathieu and suddenly they were laying out the whole story.

'We found the boys over that sand hill,' one of the police-men said, 'back up there in the tall grass. They're pretty frightened and one of them is sick.' The policemen then relayed the information they'd gotten from the other two boys. 'Incoherent and damn weird. But both their stories match, and we have no reason to think they're lying. If Webre drowned – that's the name of the tollbooth attendant who was on duty at the time, Sam Webre – we have a good chance of finding his body this morning and clearing all this up. Tide's out and there's little wave activity. We've got three boats out looking, and the Coast Guard is on its way over from the point at West End. One other thing: the kids said they heard an explosion. And that had us puzzled.' The policeman reached into his pocket and withdrew a clump of shredded paper with powder burns. 'We found lots of this stuff down the beach. Firecracker fragments. Some kids must have been celebrating the Fourth a little early.'

The two boys were sitting in one of the patrol cars with the doors open. The smaller one was crying and kept mentioning his boat between sobs.

The policeman nodded his head. 'We did find pieces of a boat,' he said. 'Something might have smashed it up against the causeway pilings. But, then again, maybe it was somebody else's boat.'

'Where's the third boy?' Slayer said. 'In the first-aid truck?'

Again the policeman nodded. 'He's being treated for shock. I think he'll be okay.'

'Mind if we have a look?'

The boy was on oxygen. Slayer took the boy's hand and applied pressure to his palm. The boy winced.

'Skin's very sensitive,' Slayer said to Wolford.

Slayer then reached for the oxygen mask.

'Hey, what do you think you're doing?'

The paramedic put his arm on Slayer's shoulder.

'I thought you paramedics knew as much as doctors,' Slayer snapped sarcastically.

Mayor Mathieu looked at the paradmedic, who replied sheepishly that he wasn't the paramedic but only an attendant. 'Paramedic Bowers hadn't gotten . . . wasn't on duty yet when we got the call.' He took his hand away from Slayer's shoulder.

Slayer removed the oxygen mask and parted the boy's lips

with his fingers.

'What is it?' the mayor said.

'His gums,' Wolford said, 'they're bleeding.' She felt faint and had to sit down on the edge of the cot. She looked up at Slayer.

'Yes,' Slayer nodded. 'It's radiation poisoning.'

The mayor moved forward and automatically touched the boy's hair, as if to protect him.

'What are you saying, Slayer?' she barked. 'That just isn't possible.'

Slayer told them to wait while he fetched something from his truck. The mayor continued holding the boy's head, whispering to Wolford, 'Slayer's not a medical doctor.'

When he returned he had his Geiger counter with him. He pressed it lightly against the boy's chest and watched the reading on the indicator dial.

'Is the dose fatal?' Wolford asked.

'Can't tell, but he should be in a hospital.'

'Well, that's where he's going!' The mayor gave orders to the police standing by. Then she turned to Slayer. 'I'm getting this boy to a hospital. Stay here and find out what the hell is going on. That boy hasn't been within twenty miles of the reactor.'

The wind had long since died down and the lake was calm, its surface only slightly indented by the police and Coast Guard boats which plodded slowly over the area in lattice courses. Every now and then a diver's head would break surface only to pause, look around, and descend again. They reminded Slayer of sea turtles.

For about an hour Slayer had accompanied one of the boats, taking water samples at various locations and testing them for radiation. He had gotten no unusual readings.

Some of the police boatmen were amused at the way he kept looking over his shoulder in the direction of the steel dome, a tiny hump on the horizon. One of them nudged a companion and said jokingly, 'Maybe he's afraid it's going to blow up!'

He had a question for Wolford and he wished now she hadn't left with the mayor. At his request the police had tried contacting the first-aid truck by radio so he could talk with her, but nobody answered. 'Probably already at the hospital,' the policeman said. Slayer had merely nodded and walked back down to the water's edge. His eyes followed an imaginary path from the shoreline down the beach and across the lake to a section of causeway five miles or so out, and beyond to the steel dome. He kept turning an idea over in his head. It could at least explain some of the things that had happened.

The policeman who had first met them at the exit ramp and who had been at the first-aid truck when Slayer examined the boy joined Slayer on the beach.

'Funny how we haven't been able to find the body,' he said. 'That water's just as smooth as glass and our divers haven't reported any strong currents.'

'There may have been some pretty strong underwater currents earlier this morning,' Slayer said. 'Violent and sudden changes in water temperature can do strange things.'

He didn't have time to go into his meaning. Far down the beach a diver was standing at the waterline and waving excitedly.

Policemen started running. Slayer did, too, and was two-thirds there before he saw the reading on his particle counter.

Whatever the diver had found, he was now holding it up in his hand.

'Put it down!' Slayer shouted.

The diver didn't hear him.

Some of the running policemen did and turned to see Slayer pointing his Geiger counter.

'Jesus Christ, Barney, put it down! Throw it away!' they yelled.

The diver heard his nearer comrades, looked down the beach towards Slayer, saw the Geiger counter aimed at him, stared at the thing in his hand, then jiggled it away in a burst of frantic hand and arm movements.

The thing was a bone. Human bone from the upper arm.

'And it's hotter than a blast furnace,' Slayer said.

They all stood around the thing on the beach in a wide circle. The diver was looking at his hands and weeping quietly.

'You've got to get this man to a hospital,' Slayer said to the policeman in charge. 'He's received a bad dose, and pretty soon those hands will start to blister.'

Two policemen moved the diver towards the cars. The rest continued standing, silently, as if in a stupor.

Slayer moved his eyes from the thing on the beach and out across the lake. The great body of water stood shiny and placid under the rays of the midday sun. It appeared almost benevolent.

Chapter 13—Breakdown

Nobody else saw the computer statements which lent credence to Slayer's hypothesis. Lots of people had been standing around, but they hadn't been following all the steps and had no idea what the computer was saying or to what questions it was responding. And nobody else on his staff was likely to work out the correct curve for Slayer's equation. Maybe Wolford who was something of a genius in her own right, though he would never tell her so; or Slayer himself. But since Slayer hadn't suggested this method of testing his ideas, chances were the method would not occur to him.

Chances!

Perhaps all need not be lost, after all.

Professor Nichols got up from behind his study desk, went to the wall which was bare except for the roller that extended across the top from corner to corner, and rolled down the schematic diagram of the reactor's anatomy.

The sodium-cooled fast breeder was the culmination of almost forty years of untiring research. Thousands of the best minds science had to offer had spent themselves during those forty years to make this scientific marvel a reality. Fission: controlled in such a way that every pound of atomic fuel consumed made one and a half pounds more. It was mankind's most pressing fantasy to emulate the creator: to make something from nothing, to bring more from less. Had God performed an act any more marvellous by reaching into the primordial stuff and fashioning a creature after his own image?

Nichols pounded his fist against the wall. Slayer! You villain! You slayer of dreams!

What, after all, were the weapons Slayer wielded against the future of humanity?

Calmer after his sudden explosion, Nichols backed away from the wall and rested against the leading edge of his desk.

Suppose he were to say simply, once and for all, that Slayer was wrong? He had the clout to do that. He was GP's number-one nuclear physicist, esteemed by his peers and colleagues – dare he say revered? – while Slayer . . . who was Slayer, really? A nobody, a boy, a trickster. That was his reputation. Everyone on the island had heard about his childish avocation. His weekend 'fishing trips,' parading himself as a 'nuclear ecologist,' while all the time he had been hired by GP as a theoretical physicist, assigned to his, Nichols's, own staff, to learn . . . yes, to learn! That's what he was here to do. He had the makings of a first-class scientist. But he was not there yet. Not by a long shot!

Nichols clenched his hands till the fingers turned white. He breathed in deeply. Once. Twice. That was better. Much, much better. He felt his muscles relaxing once again. Why should he feel anger for this boy?

It would not do for him to show anger. Where there's smoke, there's fire. People might suspect. He must undermine Slayer with subtle smiles of dismissal. He must find small ways of denying Slayer parity with the other members of his staff. He must praise Slayer's efforts, his *attempted* contributions; he must learn how to plant doubt in the minds of Slayer's peers.

What was Slayer's career against the benefits to be derived

49

from the success of the breeder reactor? Did he not owe Fermi and those countless others one sacrificial lamb?

What did Slayer's equations prove, really? Would the reactor fail merely because Slayer said it would? Could one man be right and so many wrong?

The breeder offered mankind the access to vast sources of energy and perhaps ultimate liberation from the accursed toil of existence: the time when man would finally be able to harness the power of the sun in fusion reactors whose fuel would be the most common substance on the planet. These breeders could now provide the surplus energy needed to advance technology to that stage.

Slayer's was a near-sighted vision. He could not see the consequences of his accusations. Certainly Slayer was not a pernicious being . . .

A person with Slayer's intellectual skills, with logic and rhetoric at his command: What might he not accomplish?

Look what he had done already. After only four months! What kind of a man could undermine the work of generations in four months? Yet, clearly, Slayer was not pernicious.

People did have destinies. Some for good. And others . . .

Slayer's features were so innocent. His whole comportment inspired paternal affection from his elders. Yet he could somehow be disarming, as disarming as a woman. He could readily manipulate.

But was he pernicious?

What kind of a man could undermine the work of generations? Was there something more here than met the eye? Something malevolent at work?

He must tread very very lightly, must not be obtrusive in his campaign to lay bare Slayer's true nature. If Slayer was clever, he must be more so. By degrees he would reveal Slayer for what he was.

But what had he done with his notes! The pages containing all his figuring? The key steps for working out the curve for Slayer's equation? Dear God! He had had them on the desk at the computer console. He had used them to feed information to the computer. When he had gotten the answers back he had crumpled them up and . . . did what? What had he done with those notes? Oh, God! He had tossed them into the waste basket right there on the floor next to the desk! With all his colleagues standing around! How could he have been so stupid!

Anyone could retrieve those notes, follow his steps, work out the curve, learn what he had learned.

Then, where would he be?

All his plans would be undermined, and Slayer would win. Humanity would lose.

Aicklen. Bill Aicklen. Wasn't he a friend of Slayer's? And hadn't he been standing by the computer? How much had he seen? Aicklen was a keen observer. He was known for that. Nichols himself had gotten him hired for his astute powers of perception. Aicklen must have seen the notes, watched him throw them away. What scientist worth his salt would not succumb to curiosity?

What time was it now? How long had it been since he left the steel dome? Would Aicklen have had time to decipher those notes? Programme the computer?

He had to get back there. Stop Aicklen. Stop Aicklen from finding out. Stop Slayer.

Chapter 14—Diagnosis

Dan Mason's fake ID allowed him free movement in the turbo-generator plant and placed him above suspicion from the men in the radiation search parties. They talked freely and began expressing doubt about the validity of the radiation alarm. There was no radiation leak on the premises at all. The fault had to lie in a radiation alarm system itself. A faulty circuit. It had to be.

The answer indeed had to lie in the radiation alarm system, but was it a fault? Mason was churning an idea over and over in his head. He kept looking up at Lombardy's party on the mezzanine. He wanted to know how the electrical engineers were making out. If they couldn't find a bad circuit . . .

There were coffee, Coke, and candy machines in an alcove beneath the mezzanine. Mason hung around and it paid off. One of the electrical engieers descended, after a time, with orders for Coke and candy. Up on the mezzanine they were taking a break.

Mason buttonholed the engineer.

'You guys find the trouble yet?' Mason said. He turned so the electrician could readily see his ID.

'You kidding?' the electrician said. 'We've gone over those panels for your boss three times already.'

'Well, there's nothing wrong down here,' Mason said. 'And something made those alarms sound off.'

Before leaving, the electrician looked again at Mason's ID and shook his head. The meaning of the gesture was unmistakable. 'Another Lombardy,' it said.

Mason drank a Coke. He felt he had the answer to the mystery. But how could he get it across to Lombardy? Could they all be so blind to the obvious? If he was right, damage may have already been done to the reactor. They might be in danger at this very moment.

Mason finished his Coke and placed the empty in the bottle rack. And still he lingered. There was definitely something very exciting about sitting on a powder keg.

Then he headed for the stairs to the mezzanine. He traded his proper ID for the fake one which he discarded over the banister. When he reached Lombardy's party he pushed his way through to the centre.

Lombardy, who was on the phone, looked up at him in surprise.

'Mr Lombardy,' Mason said in a level voice, 'I believe I know what made the sirens go off.'

Lombardy had been in contact with the dome by telephone twice. The first time *he* had initiated the call. He had wanted to speak to Professor Nichols. He had wanted Nichols to run another complete check on all the data the computer had concerning the present condition of the reactor's core. He had been surprised to learn Nichols wasn't there. This was no time for the chief physicist on the island to leave his post. Lombardy had expressed annoyance and told Ellison, GP's number-two man on the science staff, to run the check. Then, because he was distracted by a host of other problems, he thought no more about it. For all he knew, Nichols was in the john.

Now the dome was calling him. They had a problem. It was Nichols. He was wandering around the dome emptying trash-cans on the floor. GP's number-one physicist had flipped his lid.

Lombardy hung up the phone and stared at Mason.

'You,' he said, 'come with me. The rest of you get back to work. I'm not satisfied with your results.'

'Listen to what I'm telling you,' Nichols said. He emptied another trashcan and examined its contents. The scientists and technicians in the upper tier of the steel dome backed off, giving him a wide berth. 'Zeno proved mathematically that motion is impossible. But see, I move. Do the senses lie?' Nichols grabbed up a crumpled sheet of paper from a pile of trash. He paused to examine it carefully only to discard it a moment later. 'They didn't know about converging series,' he continued. 'So, of course, Achilles can never catch the tortoise. Only he can. He can!' Nichols ran his hands over the data panels which monitored the chain reaction in the furnace. 'Everything's really okay. Despite what anyone might *say*. Or *prove*. Just read the data panels. The senses don't lie. Listen to what I'm telling you!'

Ellison turned to Lombardy.

'I know what he's trying to say,' Ellison whispered, 'that maybe there's something wrong with the assumptions of statistical analysis as we know it today. That's actually going one step further than Slayer and could vitiate all of Slayer's equations. It's a provocative idea. Hardly the kind a

53

madman would concoct.'

GP's staff psychiatrist, who had been called to the scene, stepped forward.

'Professor Nichols keeps saying, "Listen to what I'm telling you." But he's speaking to us more by his actions than his words. His actions belie his words. What he's saying may be completely reasonable. But his actions . . . what do you suppose he's looking for in the trash? Something he wants to find very desperately. Something he wants *us* to find. Something his conscious mind can no longer cope with. That's what he's telling us, pleading with us to do, in fact; find that something he can no longer cope with on a conscious level. Gentlemen, I suggest *we* start rummaging through the trash. That's what he's really telling us to do.'

'I'll get some men together right away,' Lombardy said.

'I don't think there is any need for that,' the psychiatrist answered. He walked over to the trash-can Nichols had left untouched. 'Nichols has actually made a point of bypassing this particular can, a clue for our benefit. I think we'll find what he has been trying to tell us about right here.' The psychiatrist was lame and walked with a cane. He used it to tip the can over. Then he started rummaging through the contents, moving the cane's tip back and forth in slow sweeps.

Nichols, from the far side of the data panels, watched fascinated.

While the best mathematical minds on the island poured over Nichols's discarded notes, Lombardy assembled an audience of nuclear engineers, physicists, metallurgists, and technicians. They met in the dome's glass office. There Dan Mason repeated to them the bold statement he had made and gave his reasons.

'When a radiation leak occurs in sector six it must be accompanied by a sudden drop in pressure of reactor coolant in the heat-exchanger ducts. That's why there's a circuit in the radiation warning system of sector six that responds to a sudden drop in coolant pressure. It's kind of a back-up circuit in case the main radiation detection circuits fail. I believe the sirens were triggered by that back-up circuit.

'In other words, there was a sudden drop in reactor coolant pressure this morning in sector six without the liberations of radioactivity. That's why the sirens went off and why search parties couldn't find any radiation. I came to this conclusion when I learned that all the circuits in the warning panels of sector six had been checked and okayed by the electrical engineers.

'The sirens this morning weren't lying. A sudden drop in reactor coolant pressure means we've got a leak somewhere in the coolant system, and that implies the liberation of radiation. All we've really established so far is that the leak didn't occur in sector six.'

While Mason spoke. Lombardy activated the large computer monitor screen which could be viewed through the south wall of the glass office.

'What you see is an overview of the island,' Mason said, 'split up and marked into the ten radiation warning zones. At this very moment we have ten teams of electrical engineers running circuit checks on the warning panels in each zone.'

One technician pointed to the screen. 'You just lost a section of the island. Sector eight just winked out.'

'That means the electrical engineers in sector eight have completed their check of the panel circuits and found everything okay. What we're hoping to find is a circuit malfunction in one of the ten sectors which could be masking the radiation leak.'

After ten minutes three more sectors winked out. Lombardy, who was sitting at the desk in the glass office, pushed a button on the desk console which winked out sector six. 'No sense keeping that lit up,' he said. There was nervous tension in his voice, betraying what all of them felt.

There were five sections left. Then, suddenly, four.

The phone rang on Lombardy's desk.

Lombardy just listened. His eyes met Mason's once and held. They seemed to confirm Mason's thoughts. And fears.

When Lombardy hung up, he stood and deactivated the large monitor screen, winking out all sectors.

'Gentlemen,' he said, 'I've just gotten word from the Coast Guard. We have a liquid sodium leak with high radiation readings from somewhere along the Kenner pipeline. And . . .' – his face was ashen – '. . . there's been a death. A causeway worker. A ticket-taker. His body was demolished by a water-sodium explosion. The Type Eight is now officially a man-killer.'

Chapter 15—The Kenner Pipeline

The Coast Guard boat stood off the Metairie shoreline in deep water beyond the swimming beaches. They were using metal detectors lowered to within a foot of the lake bottom to locate the exact position of the pipeline. It was buried deep in thick insulation and non-corrosive outer plates. Detection, even with the Coast Guards's sensitive instruments, was difficult.

The commander of the boat came back on deck. Slayer was aft, taking water samples.

'I've contacted the steel dome,' the commander said. 'Told them everything you told me. A sodium-water explosion. How powerful an explosion is that?'

'Powerful enough to knock this boat out of the water,' Slayer said.

'Are we in danger, then, just sitting here?'

'A great deal of danger.'

The commander whistled a little tune. 'We still haven't located the damn thing,' he said, 'but it can't be very far away.' He nodded toward Slayer's Geiger counter. 'Got any readings on that thing yet?'

Slayer shook his head.

'Oh, yeah,' the commander said, 'your people are flying

over a container for that bone you found. I told them it was hot.'

Slayer nodded.

He was only half-listening to the Coast Guard commander. His mind was turning furiously, trying to get an angle on what really happened here this morning, and on what was going to happen.

There were a lot of inconsistencies.

If there was a leak in the hot sodium pipeline – and there had to have been to explain that radioactive bone and the explosion the kids heard – why had it stopped? Why wasn't there a continuous series of explosions, ripping the pipeline right out of its underwater bed?

And if there had been a leakage, why hadn't they noticed a drop in sodium pressure at the big desalination plant in Kenner? Today was Sunday. And that might explain why no human eye had witnessed the drop in pressure; but there were automatic alarms there, just like on the island.

He realized, suddenly, he had the answer to the sirens in sector six – a drop in liquid sodium pressure detected by some back-up warning system. He felt inclined to radio the steel dome, then realized they would have come to it themselves once they had received word of the pipeline leak.

'Commander Higgins,' Slayer said, 'are there any extra tanks, a set I could use, on board?'

'Ever use tanks before?' the commander said.

'No.'

'Then my answer is no, too.'

'Couldn't one of your divers go with me, in case I do get into trouble, which I won't?'

'Why can't you just tell one of our divers what you're looking for?'

'Because,' Slayer said, 'I'm not sure what I am looking for. I have to have a look around down there for myself.'

Commander Higgins thought it over, then nodded. 'Okay. But you're going to get a little course on aqualung procedure before you go over the side.'

While they were fitting Slayer up, a low-flying helicopter from the direction of the dome set down at the shoreline. Slayer could just make out who the figures were that disembarked.

'Do me a favour,' Slayer said to Higgins. 'One of those men is a friend of mine. Dan Mason. Could you send somebody over there and get him to stick around for a while?'

'Want us to bring him aboard?'

'No. Have him stay on shore.'

Slayer had enclosed his Geiger counter in a waterproof camera case with a glass aperture which the Coast Guard divers used for underwater photography. He had stuffed wads of paper towels from the boat's head into the case to hold the counter in position with the indicator dial beneath the glass aperture. Now, underwater, he could read the Geiger counter if he held the glass aperture close enough to his face mask.

His diver companion followed him down to the bottom of the lake and he began taking readings with the counter. There was an abundance of sea life in the vicinity: a school of minnows hounded by a number of hungry bass; miniature squid zipping by like little darts, leaving black ink tracers; and on the bottom of the lake, cockeyed flounder looking skyward, and shrimp by the hundreds. The slit stretched smooth and undisturbed in all directions, grey and placid like a mirror image of the surface. Could he be wrong about the pipeline?

The needle on the Geiger counter ambled calmly in the lower range as it registered the background radiation of the planet. Now and again it jumped as a cosmic-ray particle punctured the surface of the lake above Slayer's head. The first few times that happened, Slayer's heart skipped a beat, though he was perfectly acquainted with the effects of cosmic rays on the innards of a particle counter.

Just to make sure everything was as it should be, Slayer motioned for his diver companion to come forward. He did and Slayer grabbed his arm. Slayer then pushed the Geiger counter against the diver's wrist. The needle moved up a few levels as it counted emissions from the radium-based paint on the luminous hands of the diver's wrist-watch.

When Slayer let go, the diver signalled him to surface.

There heads bobbed up and down on the water like corks. The diver had his face mask pushed up on his forehead and water dripped profusely from his chin. 'What do you think?' the diver said. 'Everything down there looks pretty normal to me. Did we run into any radioactivity?'

'Just your watch,' Slayer said.

'My what?'

'No radioactivity,' Slayer said.

The diver seemed relieved. 'How you like being underwater?' he said. 'The skipper says it's your first time. It's another world down there, ain't it?'

'I've been down before,' Slayer said. 'Skin-diving. It's just that I've never used tanks before.'

'Yeah,' the diver said. 'Takes getting used to. You think maybe they're wrong about that pipeline?'

Slayer didn't answer right away. He looked over his should at the beaches.

'Something happened out here this morning,' he said.

'Maybe it happened farther west,' the diver said.

'No, this is the right spot. I just can't understand why everything looks okay down there.'

'I could have told you that,' the diver said. 'I've been down so many times today I feel waterlogged.'

They stayed up close to the surface till they got nearer the shore, then plunged down to the bottom. Currents had eaten out a steep incline beneath the levee, making that area of the shoreline more characteristic of a deep river embankment. Slayer covered the area but got no unusual readings. Nor could he see signs of damaged pipeline. The slit remained homogeneous; the fish life thrived; there was no evidence of any kind of explosion whatsoever.

The diver had them surface once again. He pointed to his watch.

'Getting into the red,' he said. 'Better start back.'

'How much time?' Slayer said.

'Twenty minutes.'

'Let's look around some more. When it's time we can surface near the beaches and walk ashore.'

As the underwater search continued, Slayer's second thoughts increased. It didn't make any sense at all. There couldn't have been a chemical explosion because there was no broken pipeline. He entertained briefly the diver's opinion that they were at the wrong location. But these were the Coast Guard's co-ordinates for where the pipeline met the shore, confirmed by the co-ordinates on record at the steel dome. Of course, they might both be wrong, containing in common some clerical mistake. But the overriding fact was that the accident had occurred right here and not farther west. Or east, for that matter. A little boy's sailboat had been wrecked by an explosion; a man was dead; and a boy was injured by radiation burns, maybe fatally injured. And it had all happened right here.

If only the boy hadn't been unconscious. He was older than the other two, and had been on the boat that exploded. Perhaps his story would be the key. There had to be some plausible explanation. The busted pipeline had been such a good one, till all this new evidence – or, rather, lack of it. And lack of corroborating evidence was evidence enough against an inconclusive theory.

What the hell had happened?

Down the underwater embankment, fifty feet or so in the wrong direction, something was happening to the sunlight. The diver was signalling again and pointing to his watch. Slayer shook his head and pointed down the embankment. He started swimming hard and gestured for the diver to stay put.

The rays of the sun hit the surface of the water and ricocheted towards the wall of limestone which formed the foundation for the levee. This wall, encrusted with shiny barnicles, caught the rays like a mirror and angled them back out to sea. Except for one spot. That one black hole devouring the sunlight.

Slayer kept his Geiger counter aimed at the spot with one eye on the dial as he approached. But, as before, the readings were entirely normal.

Still Slayer was very cautious when he reached the area. He had to give his eyes time to adjust to the blackness which almost seemed to emanate. A source of negative light, as it were. A blinding flash of nothingness.

The dark cavity resolved itself, finally, into a funnel-like aperture of pointed rocks and jagged sheets of limestone: the abode of a large and aged catfish that confronted Slayer face to face with gaping mouth and mournful eyes.

Slayer, who had perceived its movement deep within the cave, breathed a sigh of relief that manifested itself in a shower of dancing air bubbles which sped towards the surface. He turned and signalled to the diver that everything was okay.

And everything really was okay, wasn't it? Slayer thought. For this cavity, this excavation, made by man and machine, no doubt, marked the site where large volumes of earth had been moved aside to make room for the Kenner pipeline. Here at last was proof they were at the right spot, and there was no pipeline debris or radiation.

Later, Slayer would remember those pointed rocks and jagged sheets of limestone and wonder how he could have been so stupid.

Chapter 16—Talk

They walked up and down the beach filling each other in.

'We came to the same conclusion about the sirens from totally different data,' Mason said. 'Could both of us be wrong?' He noticed Slayer's eyes mist over. 'Hey, George, about Professor Nichols, it's not your fault.'

'Here come my clothes,' Slayer said. He wiped his eyes. A

Coast Guard dinghy was approaching the beach.

'What are you going to do now?' Mason said. 'Go back to the island?'

Slayer shook his head.

'I'm going to the hospital to see about that little boy.'

'The one that got burned,' Mason said. He walked with his hands in his pockets, looking down at the sand. 'Hell, George, we can't be wrong about that pipeline. It's the only possible source of radioactivity for miles.'

'Maybe we should have them turn the pipeline back on till the damn thing fails completely and burns about two or three hundred people.'

'George, buddy, old pal, you haven't been listening to everything I've been telling you. That pipeline is turned on. Was turned on. And will be turned on. Right after Lombardy got the Coast Guard call, they had a meeting of the minds. I don't think they conferred for more than ten minutes before they rejected the idea of a pipeline leak. They said the absence of continuous water-sodium explosions was compelling evidence against it. And, of course, the sensors monitoring the coolant pressure inside the reactor say everything is A-OK.'

'What are you going to do now?' Slayer said. 'Take that bone back for analysis? I'd like to hear their explanation for that.'

'I'm going over to Kathy's,' Mason said. 'She's the only thing I care about in this whole damn town. I'm going to try to talk her into going up to Jackson to stay with her parents for a while.'

'I wish you could talk the whole town into going up to Jackson.'

'Yeah,' Mason said. He put his arm around Slayer's shoulder. 'When are you going to realize that ninety-nine per cent of the entire human race are mindless idiots and not worth the effort?'

'They're not mindless,' Slayer said. 'They're exploited.'

'Yeah. Okay. I'll tell Kathy you said hi.'

Chapter 17—Conferences

Lombardy waited alone in the glass-enclosed office for the president of General Power to return his call. GP had a WATS line and the steel dome didn't. It was a cheap company policy, and degrading to have to wait for company officials to call back to the WATS. When the bosses were really out of the home office, the secretaries would say their proper names; otherwise, they would say 'the president' is out or 'the vice-president,' and so forth. On this particular call the woman at the other end said, 'The president is out. May I have him return your call?'

Lombardy said, 'Yes,' hung up, and waited.

In this way General Power cheated the telephone company out of thousands of dollars a year.

But there was another reason why GP had established this procedure – at least Lombardy thought so – and that was simply because it was degrading. It made him feel part of a collusion; it made him feel dishonest, undignified, fraudulent. It was ego-crushing. And that was an advantage for the big bosses of General Power on the other end of the line. Emotionally distracted subordinates could be more easily manipulated.

Lombardy had his own trick for dealing with this state of affairs. Whenever he had to call the home office and needed to take an aggressive stand, he would get his blood boiling by conjuring up the image of Ralph 'Pop' Wilson, the ugly, squat, ignorant, inhumane, penny-pinching founder of General Power, Inc.

Wilson had started out as a young man making soap in a tub in the basement of his mother's house in Camden, New Jersey, to supplement the income he got as a welder for Lee's and Sons, a small manufacturer of boilers. Wilson was a man of luck. His soap, made from an old Irish recipe from his mother's side of the family, caught on. With the money he had accumulated after only five years, he bought out Lee's and Sons and had other people welding for him at less pay and longer hours. He made boilers the way he had made soap: cheaply and in large quantities. And his luck ran true.

Twelve years later he was a millionaire with one of the largest boiler-making companies in the country. When the technology of fission reactors came along in the Forties, Wilson was there on the ground floor along with Westinghouse and General Electric. The big tax breaks, loans at little or no interest rates: Washington had launched an all-out campaign to lure private business manufacturers into the commercial use of fission reactors.

Wilson jumped at the bait and almost went bankrupt. He had very few friends in Washington and many enemies. His reputation for second-rateness, with respect to both his products and his character, made the rounds. Favours were not forthcoming. Westinghouse and General Electric got all the green lights. Wilson found himself on a one-way street headed in the wrong direction.

But Wilson had something that would beat out all other competition in the end. He had Dennis Nichols in his company, a Fermi protégé, a genius.

While Wilson's rivals were experimenting with and manufacturing air- and water-cooled slow uranium furnaces, Nichols's brilliant techniques and far-sighted thinking advanced the technology of the breeder reactor beyond anything ever dreamed.

The wind changes; emotions dissipate; Washingtonians come and go; all Wilson had to do was wait. In the meantime he went back to his staple. He manufactured more and bigger boilers than ever before; he amassed another fortune; and he held on to Nichols.

When the Seventies arrived with the energy crunch, the search for more efficient fuels, and the needs for the Super Reactor, Wilson had it all put together. He stepped in with Nichols's plans for the multi-million-kilowatt fast breeder.

And almost overnight General Power was born.

Lombardy had met 'Pop' Wilson for the first and last time on the occasion of the old man's seventieth birthday in Wilson, Nevada.

Lombardy had just come to General Power from Westinghouse and felt singularly privileged to receive a birthday-celebration invitation. As it later turned out, everybody in the company got one. And everybody was expected to accept. Lombardy was working out of New York at the time and had to travel over three thousand miles to be present. His predicament was not the exception.

The entire town of Wilson turned out for the celebration. There was a parade down Main Street, public presentations of expensive gifts from company luminaries, speeches, a huge catered buffet, a fireworks display at the main plant, and a birthday cake in the shape of a boiler that weighed over five hundred pounds.

Throughout the festivities Wilson comported himself like a feudal lord. Lombardy had never seen anything like it before or since.

At the buffet Lombardy was finally introduced. Wilson took his hand limply, conferred with an aide to find out who Lombardy was, said he expected good things, then turned sideways and farted.

Six months later when Wilson died, Lombardy learned about his cancer of the colon. But by that time it didn't matter to Lombardy that Wilson may have not been responsible. A man leaves his mark on the company he founds. Ignorance, abuse of power, intimidation of subordiantes, dishonesty, pettiness, indifference to talent, discrimination; and, in spite of it all, superlative luck: Lombardy came to know and despise Wilson during his first months with General Power, though he never saw or dealt with the man again.

Lombardy chose to regard phone-call procedure to the home office in Nevada as part of the old man's legacy. Doing so fired his anger and hatred and steeled Lombardy for dealing with high company officials who might otherwise bend his will in their direction.

The president of the company whined about it being the weekend of the Fourth. Sunday, yet. Did Lombardy realize how much it was costing, both moneywise and in resentment, to keep the administrative staff on duty in Wilson, not to mention the advisors, technicians, and scientists who were on standby? Why couldn't the seventy-hour test run have been scheduled some time last week?

'Because we didn't have the information we do now,' Lombardy said. Then, refusing to be side-tracked: 'Mr Carlleston, I'm recommending that General Power postpone delivery of the Type Eight till after further testing. There have been some developments. As it stands now, I'm not at all convinced the Type Eight is a safe, realiable machine.'

'We have a contract commitment to deliver on the Fourth,' Carlleston said. 'What do you mean by "developments"? Certainly not that Indian's mathematical gibberish?'

'I'm not talking about Dr Slayer's report,' Lombardy said. 'We've had a breakdown in our warning system. And there's been a death as a result of reported radiation leakage.'

Lombardy explained about the disappearance of Sam Webre and the boy the police had found on the beach.

'We've picked up the arm bone the police found, and I have technicians running tests on it right now.'

'But you don't have corroborating evidence that the pipeline is responsible,' Carlleston said. 'What does Professor Nichols think about all of this?'

Lombardy hesitated.

'Like all of us here, he is reserving judgement.'

'Sand by, Lombardy,' Carlleston said. 'I'll get back to you shortly.'

Carlleston hung up and Lombardy just stared at the receiver before replacing it in the cradle. Then he put his hands flat on the desk and waited.

Twenty minutes later the phone rang again.

'Lombardy here.'

'Yes,' Carlleston said. 'First, you must make it clear to the authorities that accepting the bone for analysis testing is not in any way an admission of culpability by General Power. Second you must emphasize the lack of corroborating evidence that the sodium pipeline was responsible. Third, you must say that General Power has every reason to believe the bone is a plant.'

'A plant?' Lombardy said.

'Listen, Lombardy, the whole future of General Power is at stake here. We've invested everything in the success of the Type Eight. A competitor would find it convenient if suddenly the Type Eight were thought to be unstable.'

'You're suggesting sabotage, then?'

'I'm suggesting the very strong possibility that someone may be trying to discredit us. Lombardy, you have been part of the Type Eight since the start of its construction. You know the quality of the material and workmanship that has gone into it. We've done everything by the book. We've gone beyond the book to ensure success. Our reputation is somewhat less than spotless. In the past we have been known for cutting corners. But you, better than anyone, should know that's not the case here. Someone literally may be trying to plant a skeleton in our closet. Make us look like the old Wilson Boiler Manufacturers of ten years ago.'

Lombardy had not prepared himself for this sudden display of candour.

'I hadn't really considered the possibility of sabotage,' he said.

'Then, start considering it.'

'Have you contacted the NRC yet?'

'Uh . . . no. It's Sunday. But we're working on it.'

'Mr Carlleston, it's imperative that you get a team of NRC inspectors down here to reissue a clean bill of health. Mayor Mathieu was here this morning. She's on top of everything that's been happening. I've got a feeling that if we go ahead with our plans to deliver on the Fourth, she's going to renege on her part of the contract. She may even go public with everything she knows. She's scared and possibly

67

misinformed. She could do more harm than any saboteur.'

'She'd have to be pretty gutsy to do all that,' Carlleston said. 'Her career is at stake.'

'Don't underestimate her.'

'Okay. I'll talk to her myself. I don't know about those NRC inspectors, though. Those people are immovable objects. And it's Sunday.'

'Try,' Lombardy said. 'For God's sake, try.'

Sabotage. Lombardy hung up the phone. Sabotage. He turned the word over in his head, getting the feel of it. Did Carlleston have good reason to suspect sabotage? Or was he just grabbing at straws? One thing, Carlleston wasn't stupid. And he didn't scare easily. GP, like all the big corporations, had spies everywhere. Maybe Carlleston had heard something. If it was corporate sabotage, which competitor was responsible? And would they go so far as to kill a man? Sam Webre could be in on it, could possibly have been paid off to leave the state. But what about the boy? There was nothing fake about radiation burns.

Lombardy buzzed the analysis lab on the intercom.

'Got anything on that bone yet, Harley?'

'We've got some information, yes,' Harley said. 'Let me see. Radioactive carbon, radiocesium, radioiodine, strontium . . .'

'In other words, you're finding traces of substances you'd expect to find in hot coolant from a reactor with problems.'

'Affirmative. We're checking for Zirconium fourteen right now – alloy used in the pipeline and the fuel rods.'

'Zirconium fourteen,' Lombardy said pensively. 'That's a General Power pattern. A well-guarded secret process and formula. None of our competitors has Zirconium fourteen.'

'That's right, chief,' Harley said. 'But so what?'

'So . . . you just keep checking. I want to know the minute you decide one way or the other whether that bone contains traces of Zirconium fourteen. Got it?'

Lombardy punched the button for the public address system, which carried his voice all over the island.

'Code seven-nine,' he said. 'Seven-nine.'

Seven-nine was that day's code for a security standby and possible red alert. Security Chief Warner and Assistant Chief Englebrecht called in as dictated by procedural regulations.

'The glass office,' Lombardy said to both men in turn.

Awaiting their arrival, Lombardy activated the computer monitor screen beyond the south wall. He swivelled gently in his chair in a nervous manner and chewed his lower lip as he viewed maps of the whole Lake Pontchartrain region, including New Orleans, New Orleans East, Matairie, Kenner, and beyond. He posed a question to himself in a hypothetical manner: If I were a saboteur, how would I get the job done?

'Well,' said Englebrecht, 'if I were a saboteur out to cause GP a lot of trouble, I'd do something big, something that would get a lot of publicity. It wouldn't be something here on the island – because, one, the security is damn tight and I might get caught; and, two, GP would have a better chance of covering up anything that might happen on the island.'

'Which brings us back to the sodium pipelines,' Chief Warner said. 'We can't very well cover up a man's death that happened over twenty miles away. And it's very scary to have a radiation leakage right at the outskirts of a densely populated area like Metairie. The news media would crucify us. "Public beaches contaminated by lethal radiation." '

'Okay,' Lombardy said, 'I'll buy that. Now my next question is: Why the Kenner pipeline?'

'That's easy,' Warner said. 'The New Orleans East pipeline goes through the swamps. And swamps don't have the scare value of public beaches when it comes to a radiation leak. And, of course, the Kenner pipeline is right near the causeway, where people are coming and going all the time.'

It all seemed to add up, all right. Just enough evidence planted to make it look like a sodium pipeline leak. There may even have been somebody on the inside, somebody working for GP, or security, or maintenance. Somebody with access to that radiation alarm panel in sector six.

'Is that it, then?' Chief Warner said. 'Are we going to work on the assumption we have a saboteur on board?'

'It's tempting,' Lombardy said. 'I hope to God we're only dealing with a saboteur.'

But the Zirconium fourteen came out positive. Harley called Lombardy on the intercom the minute he was sure.

Lombardy glanced at Englebrecht and then at Warner. He pushed the intercom button.

'Say again, Harley.'

'I said we've got a positive. There are definite traces of Zirconium fourteen in the marrow of that bone.'

Lombardy got up from his desk.

'Well,' he said to his security chiefs, 'if this is the work of a saboteur, do you mind telling me how he got hold of one of the best-kept secrets in the world? Either one of our competitors has done the impossible, or we really do have a genuine, bona-fide liquid sodium leak somewhere along the Kenner pipeline ... with everything that implies. Now, how are we going to find out the truth?'

Chapter 18—Emergency Ward

The boy's full name was Peter Joseph Beiser. He lived in Metairie. His father's name was Joseph Beiser, his mother's name was Margerie, née Earnest. He had one brother, Michael, who was seven. Peter Beiser was twelve.

Their aunt was watching the boys for the weekend, and she had taken pills for a headache and overslept. Joseph Beiser and his wife were in Covington with friends at a clubhouse along the Bogue Falaya. They were expected back Sunday night.

The police had gotten their information from the aunt, who had to be calmed with tranquillisers. The mayor filled in the hospital form herself. Then she told the police to contact the

Highway Patrol since the clubhouse where the Beisers were staying had no telephone.

The hundred things Mayor Mathieu had to do she did by phone, for she refused to leave the hospital till the boy's mother arrived.

Mary Wolford acted as secretary and together they took over the office of the hospital's assistant chief administrator. When one of her phone consultations dragged on, the mayor would send Wolford down to Emergency to ask after the boy. Wolford was impressed by the mayor's energy and stamina, but most of all by her compassion. Somewhere beneath that hard, politician's exterior was a heart.

This knowledge made it all the more difficult for Wolford, because the news she carried back from Emergency was bad news.

The mayor knew at once.

'Hank,' she spoke into the phone, 'let me get back to you on this. No, I don't care what Public Service red tape there is. Listen, Hank, what are you telling me? If you can't do it, who can? Okay. Okay. Do whatever you have to do. But just remember we don't have much time. I want at least three plants reactivated and on standby. That's right. No later than noon tomorrow.'

After she hung up, she said to Wolford, 'I suppose we could get by with just two of the old plants. Maybe even one. What do you think?'

'Well,' Wolford said, trying to mask the emotion in her voice and failing miserably, 'you have to figure one kilowatt of power per resident. Those old electric plants were normally a half-million kilowatts each. You'd have to get people to stop using their air conditioners for a while and to take cold showers, but I think you could get by – for a while. I don't know what the greater New Orleans area people are going to do, though. Are you really going to switch the city's electric power back to the old plants?'

'I just want an alternative in case we have to shut the reactor down for a while. I don't want the city to be without power.' The mayor leaned back in her chair, but she

71

wasn't relaxed. Wolford could tell by her voice. 'A lot of the people don't even know they're getting their power from the dome. The Fourth is the official day for the switchover.'

Wolford nodded her head, as if to say: I know and I'm sorry.

'No, Lombardy was right in that,' the mayor said. 'I'm glad we switched over early. At least we know before the public knows that we've got problems. I'd hate to have to cope with a panic, too.' She became very pensive. 'I just don't want the city to be without ice.'

Wolford swallowed. 'Ice?'

'I remember once my father had to ask the governor to call in the National Guard. It was after a hurricane – Edna, I think it was. The power was off all over the city, and after one day the people began to get very cowed. It was a hundred degrees in the shade. Well, you know how it is in the summer here. It's probably that hot right now. And there wasn't a cold beer, a cold soft drink, a cold glass of water anywhere in the city. Funny how you get used to something like that. The people didn't complain. What good would it have done? But you got to craving it – the way you do a cigarette, or anything addictive. My father arranged for a convoy of trucks to deliver a thousand tons of ice to the city. A thousand tons. It was a token gesture, really. My father was a very compassionate man. Well, we still have old ice houses here. Some are in the Quarter. There's one still near the riverfront on St Thomas Street. Maybe you've seen one? My father set the times and places for the deliveries, most at those ice houses, and got the word spread around. The people came in droves. There were lines at those ice houses as long as thirty blocks, some people said. Just to get a five-pound block of ice. It was okay till the people began to see just how far a thousand tons would go. Then the riots started. There were almost twenty people killed that first morning of the deliveries. Fifteen were kids. My father had to call in the National Guard. No. No, indeed. I'm not going to have that on my hands. They're not going to be without ice this time. Wolford?'

'Yes?'

'The boy's dying?'

'Yes.'

The mayor nodded her head. 'The kids,' she said, 'it's always the kids first.'

Chapter 19—Chances

The mayor's husband waited in the foyer of the priest's residence on the Loyola campus. He thumbed through a *Time* Magazine, glancing at the pictures. Thinking how this priests' foyer was just like a doctor's reception room.

Fr Donahue had left the choice up to him. 'I'll have to use the school's computer on this stuff,' he had said. 'There's a terminal down in our cellar. It may take some time. Want to visit our cellar for a while?'

He preferred the foyer. Perhaps if Fr Donahue had said 'basement.' 'Cellar' was too clerical, suggesting the smell of old cassocks and stale altar wine. And he'd had plenty enough of that over the years with his wife being Catholic and politically prominent. In just this past year he had experienced enough proximity to monsignors and bishops to last him the rest of his life. He had often threatened to broach the subject of his atheism before a gathering of high prelates, but his threats only made Dottie laugh. 'Go ahead,' she would say. 'You won't find a theologian among them. They're all diplomats and politicians like your wife. If you want to draw return fire with your philosophical arguments, you'll have to go where they keep the minds locked away. Try Notre Dame Seminary down on Carrollton Avenue. Or become drinking buddies with a Jesuit.'

He wondered now whether Fr Donahue drank and smiled as he realized he was pondering perhaps the one absolute certitude in all of reality.

He considered the Church a dangerously conservative

institution, perpetuating ideas that stifled the imagination and practices that rent the human heart and subverted human nature. Dottie, a devout Catholic like her ancestry *ad infinitum*, had never been able to accept that side of him. All she ever understood was that he felt uneasy around churches and clerics and despised medieval architecture. It was her stubborn hope and belief that one day he would relent and join the faith.

He, in turn, had never been able to wage his anti-clerical crusade beyond the classroom. New Orleans was a Catholic city where his convictions, publicly flaunted, could irreparably harm his wife's political career. Lately, he had even adopted a live-and-let-live attitude unbecoming to a man of philospohical bent. Let people believe what they want to believe? Was he finally getting old?

Fr Donahue took forty-five minutes to programme Slayer's equations and transformations into the computer. The verdict on their rigor came back almost at once. Valid . . . valid . . . valid . . . valid . . . That took care of the preliminaries. Now to get on to the hard part. What exactly were the equations trying to say? What applications, if any, did they have in the real world? Slayer had his own interpretations of the equations, scary ones at that, in a latter section of the report. But were they correct interpretations? For here in the jump from the rigor of mathematics to the ambiguities of language lay a thousand pitfalls. It was not uncommon in the history of mathematical development for a man to mastermind a work of genius and then completely misinterpret the nature of its application. Was such the case here?

What information did the computer have on the Super Reactor in the steel dome? On reactors in general? On the accepted odds concerning their safety? On the estimated chances of an accident causing extensive damage to life and property?

Fr Dohanue lucked out.

Construction of GP's Super Reactor had kindled the

interest of Loyola graduate students in several fields over the past several years. There was a wealth of data available still in the memory banks of the school's computer as the result of their efforts.

Donahue began his probe with the question foremost in his mind. What odds did the experts give on the safety of the breeder reactor?

The computer presented him with a compilation of quotes spanning a twenty-year period. Experts from nuclear scientists to chairmen of the AEC and NRC were very optimistic about the chances of complete success. The risk of accident was minimal. References were continually made to statistical analysis and comparisons drawn to meteorites striking the earth and other million-to-one chance events. An impressive display of positive thinking.

The references to statistical analysis kept bugging Donahue.

He asked the computer to zero in on that and got a reference to a lad who had graduated from Loyalo three years ago. The computer still had the essential data from his thesis. It summarized the thesis in the lad's own words: 'Statistical analysis, by obtaining particular random samples, predicts the general characteristics of the real event from which the samples were chosen. It is hard to see how statistical analysis can be applied to questions of nuclear reactor safety. The technology of the nuclear reactor is in its infancy; this is especially true of the Super Breeder. How can you take random samples of machines that have not been made yet? When experts speak of the safety of these machines by reference to statistical analysis, I can only conclude they are speaking analogously and with absence of rigor.'

Donahue nodded his head and mumbled, 'I hope I gave you an A for that.'

Slayer had certainly realized this, too, that an appeal to statistical analysis could not be made with absolute mathematical rigor. What his equations did was to describe traditional probability games of chance with many of the assumptions of these game models changed. Changing the assumptions turned the odds around towards favouring the occurrence of a nuclear accident. The question now was whether the assumption changes were warranted. Did the traditional probability game models better describe the physical conditions of the Super Reactor? Or did Slayer's new game models?

Donahue decided to get down to the nitty-gritty and instructed the computer to turn to the question of insurance.

'Sorry, it took longer than I thought,' Fr Donahue said.

Al got up as the priest re-entered the foyer.

'What did you find out?'

Donahue scratched his head. 'Sit down, Dr Jaffe, please.'

The priest handed him back the folder with Slayer's report and paced up and down near the magazine rack before speaking.

'This morning when I was saying Mass the electricity went off. It was a little past six. It stayed off for about a half-hour. Are they having trouble out at the dome? Is that why you are here with this report?'

'I'm here at the mayor's request. She wanted an outsider's opinion. The best she could get. I recommended you.'

'I'm flattered. And your being here has nothing to do with that blackout this morning?'

'I don't know. My wife flew out to the island this morning after the blackout. Then she called me about getting this report to you. *Post hoc ergo propter hoc?*'

'Umm,' Donahue said. 'Do you know what's in that report?'

'Vaguely. All I had was a chance to skim it. And I'm no mathematician. If you could put it all in layman's words together with your evaluation, I'm sure that's all the mayor wants from you.'

'All right,' Donahue said. And he explained about Einstein.

'I know all about Reimannian Geometry,' Al said, 'and how you get it by changing one of Euclid's assumptions.'

'Then you know, too, that it's a more precise description of physical reality than Euclid's geometry, though it appears to go against common sense a little.'

'Yes,' Al said.

'Well,' Donahue said, 'excuse the pun, but I think we have a parallel situation here. Slayer has taken traditional probability models and changed some of their assumptions. And he believes his new models represent a more precise description of physical reality than the old models.'

'And Slayer has used his new models to make a statement about the steel dome?'

Donahue nodded. 'By using certain theorems of transformation, Slayer has been able to show that if his new models do apply, then the odds for and against the possibility of a nuclear accident have been switched around. If Slayer is right, then sitting out in that lake is a nuclear gun aimed at this city and it's cocked and it's got a hair trigger.'

When Al spoke again his voice was strained.

'Fr Donahue, this Slayer . . . he just . . . can't . . . be right.'

'There's no way to tell if he's right or wrong – except the one obvious way, of course. Sit back and wait and see if the gun the experts have been telling us is perfectly safe goes off.'

Fr Donahue strolled back across the room. 'I have something more practical to suggest. And I strongly recommend that the mayor act on it immediately. Have you ever heard of Eagle Mutual?'

Al hesitated.

'The company that insures the steel dome?'

'Insurance company, my eye!' Donahue said. 'It's the government. The federal government. They've picked up the policy on the dome. Know why? No regular insurance company would touch the Super Reactor with a ten-foot pole. Insurance people have a sixth sense about odds. If it were really like the experts have been telling us, insurance companies would snap up that policy. Well, hell, wouldn't you like to insure New York against being struck by a large meteorite?

'Tell the mayor this. Send investigators around to all the

77

large insurance companies to find out why they haven't bid on the steel dome. What do they know that we don't? The mayor should be able to get enough ammunition to start a public investigation on the real safety factor of that thing out there in the lake. The Slayer report by itself isn't enough. It's too theoretical. And people listen to emotions, to their guts. Get the insurance companies to spill their guts to you. Then you'll really have something to fight with.'

Fr Donahue returned to the priests' chapel after his visitor had left. He knelt before the picture of the Woman with the globe in her hand, cradling the child, crushing the serpent with her heel.

'Lord,' he whispered, 'hear the prayer of your foolish servant, that the head of the snake be subdued, and your children be delivered from evil.'

As he spoke the lights in the chapel flickered. And in the moment's darkness the serpent's fangs dripped venom. A thought rattled in his head like a child's chant. 'As the foot strikes, the snake bites.' Over and over, in his head, like a child's chant.

Chapter 20—Blackout

Kathy Raffer shared a very fine apartment with another woman graduate from Tulane. It was on the corner of Dumaine and Royal Street in the heart of the Quarter. Dan Mason had gone back to the island in the chopper carrying the bone just to pick up his car so he could drive in to see Kathy. It was a clear, hot afternoon. And Mason worked up a sweat just driving.

He wondered how his plea for her to leave the city would go over. They had kept the relationship loose and non-committal up till now. He dated other women. She dated other men. At least that was the impression she gave. It had always been in part her desire to keep the relationship free, hadn't it? Why, then, was she the one and only one he felt compelled to warn? Why wasn't he on his way in to see any of the others? Kathy was no dummy. She would be asking herself the same question. Maybe he should fabricate a few saving lies?

What had he told George Slayer back there? That Kathy was the only person he cared about? Did he mean that, really?

What kind of trouble was he in, anyway?

How could he phrase his plea to Kathy to make everything work out okay?

What he needed now was a Cyrano — not one to help him win a lady fair, but to keep her safely at a distance.

He supposed it was her accent. Her figure was marvellous, of course, especially her legs. She had great legs. But he was from California, where figures and looks were all presupposed, as indeed they were here in New Orleans. In both places women splendidly sculptured merely faded into the background. One had to, in some respect, almost possess a flaw. And the closest she came to that was in the twang of her voice.

It had been at Charley Rich's New Year's Eve party. (Had it been that long already?) She was in one room of Charley's huge apartment and he in another. There were so many people it was like Mardi Gras on Canal Street. Charley was a local who had gotten his degree in nucleonics from Tulane, and knew all the pretty local people.

He was a celebrity that night. *Charley's* friend. One of the *island* people. A *nuclear* scientist. They had asked him a thousand boring questions in their New Orleanian tonalities, to which he responded with nods and shakes and monosyllables. He kept hearing that one voice. From somewhere across the void. Irritating. Something to latch on to. Distinctly Southern, yet foreign to the New Orleans Brooklynese. When they were finally introduced, Charley nudged his shoulder and whispered in his ear, 'Jackson, Mississippi.'

79

She didn't pay much attention to him, but she did cock her eyebrow at him, once (pow!,) like a shot from the forest.

The party dragged on and he found himself separated from her. He was on his sixth Tom Collins and he could no longer even hear her voice amid the discord. He hadn't even caught her full name, but he had already come to a decision. He would see her the following week. Charley would supply him with all the vital information. Dear good friend Charley. He joined a circle of joint smokers on the living-room floor and soon found his head, Alice-fashion, bumping the ceiling. Charley could be counted on to put his hands on the best stuff available. At five minutes to midnight couples began pairing off to celebrate the new year more intimately. He began to feel lonely and embarrassed. He couldn't recall why he had agreed to come here alone. He drifted to a corner of the room still feeling out of place. Right before midnight he sneaked into the bathroom.

He was relieving himself when the party horns sounded and sundry voices broke into nostalgic and disjoined choruses of 'Auld Lang Syne.' His mother used to sing that song when he was just a kid. It always made him want to cry. His mother was now a distant relation, a divorcee twice-removed, married to a film producer, a porno-film producer. She wore her hair short and bleached blonde and she dressed like a film producer's wife. He never saw his mother any-more. The goddamn song! He was drowning in a pool of sadness.

The party volume suddenly rose and fell several decibels. Somebody had quickly opened and shut the bathroom door behind him.

'I'll be finished in a second, buddy.'

There was no answer. He zipped up and turned to find her standing with her back to the shut door. Her eyes, which had been levelled at his midsection, quickly met his. They were luminous and without shame.

'I saw you come in here,' she said with only a trace of hesitation. And when he didn't answer, she added, 'It's midnight.' And when he still didn't answer, she came up to him. 'I'm for you,' she said. 'Didn't Charley tell you?'

He shook his head.

'Well, that's Charley.' She put her hands on his waist. 'He asked me to come alone, too. He wanted us to meet. But he got side-tracked. Maybe he was going to leave this up to fate. Charley is a great believer in fate.' She brought her lips up to his. 'Happy New Year.'

They slipped away from the party – but only after she had exchanged a few quiet words with a shy young man who was slightly overweight and slightly bald; and he wondered whether she had been telling the truth about coming alone.

Back at her apartment she did a Patti White number for him, and she did it better than the strip school teacher herself. Then, dressed only in a garter belt and stockings, her long legs the colour of honey, she moved to him and then on top of him, and they went about pleasing each other slowly, taking a long time at it.

Afterwards, they talked.

He found himself telling her things he never told anyone. He talked about his mother, who found her liberation in Clairol hair colouring and hotpants, about his 'philanthropic' father, who ran a bevy of fast-food chain stores, owned more ghetto apartment complexes than he could keep track of, dabbled in politics, and made the quick big bucks when California passed the notorious Proposition thirteen, which his father had in part initially sponsored.

He told her about the time he felt most loved: when, as a boy, he had entered the California motorcross intermedials to capture the slackening attention of his mother, who had always adored fast cars and motorcycles. He had pushed himself and his bike too hard. He flipped over on the side of a hill and came out of it with a compound fracture of his left leg. His mother had fretted and fussed and patted and pampered him for a full month.

She listened well and jokingly asked him where all his lofty ideals were, his talk of mankind's future, and that sort of thing. He had thought to himself: My God, she's no neophyte to the techniques of nuclear physicists. How many

81

men on the island had she known?

It was the first stab of jealously in their relationship, because he had known already it was a relationship.

Now Kathy met him at the door to her apartment. Her eyes were swollen, her voice was a bit more nasal than usual and she had an ice bag to her forehead. She had on a loose-fitting blouse and shorts.

'Dan!' she said, genuinely surprised and pleased. 'Back off! No kisses! Umm. Oh, well. Now you're going to get this, too. Come into the bedroom. That's where I've got myself set up. Nancy's gone for the weekend. She's scared to death of coming down with this.' She led the way. She plopped down on the bed, supine, and crowned her feverish brow with the ice bag. 'How'd the hang-gliding go this morning?' She raised one eyebrow mischievously. 'Find a substitute playmate?'

Mason flicked a droplet of sweat from the tip of his nose.

'Are you keeping it hot in here on purpose?' he said. 'You've got chills too?'

She shook her head and pointed to the hallway.

'I've been fiddling with the thermostat.'

He checked and found it was eighty-eight degrees. He turned the temperature control and heard the circuit clicking. He waited with his hand against an air vent, but there was no onrush of cool air.

'Better call your landlord,' he said. 'The central unit must be out. I'll open some windows.'

He returned to her bedside and stood over her, silently.

'Know something?' he said finally.

'What?' she answered.

'You look just awful.'

She popped him in the gut with a light punch.

He doubled up and fell on the bed next to her, feigning distress.

'Quit beating around the bush,' she said, intending the pun. 'Are you here for a little fooling around, or what? I feel as awful as I look. But you could maybe coax me into feeling better.'

82

'I thought you were worried about my health.'

'Just restrain yourself from kissing me.'

She pulled the blouse over her head. He reached for her with an urgency that surprised him. She was warm, and soft. She was everything right then. In their long kisses, her fingers on him, his lips on her breasts, and their first supple motions together, he wanted to forget the morning. He moved hard, his desire a separate world from his fears and suspicions. He wanted to squeeze her inside him. He wanted her desperately.

They made love with more abandon than on their first drunken night, when she had danced naked and he had needed her like a drug. Then he lay on her, sweating, his head on her chest. She ran her fingers down his back. He felt the fever in her body. She was as warm as the afternoon light, and her touch excited him again. He needed her more than he ever had.

Later, he took her hand in his, playing with her artist's fingers, and said too lovingly, 'How would you like to pay a little visit to your parents up in Jackson?'

She propped herself up, and she stared at him in shock. Fragility, fear, tenderness, confusion, desire – he saw it all in those big brown eyes and realized he had screwed it up, after all. She was misinterpreting. The words sounded all wrong.

He shot out of bed, pacing the room. He couldn't think straight.

When he calmed down he realized she was smiling at him from the bed. 'Be a dear and get me some more ice,' she said. She held up the soggy bag.

He departed from the bedroom with relief. What was going on in that mind of hers? His suspicions about their relationship were correct. She was more deeply involved than she let on, too. In one drawn-out, forlorn look, like a little dog cornered and pleading for . . . kindness (?), she had revealed it all. If he had just come right out and said, 'Kathy, let's get married,' could her answer have been any more direct?

He opened the door of the refrigerator. He withdrew an

ice tray and splashed cold water all over himself and the floor. He uttered an obscenity and shouted, 'Kathy, you used up all the ice.'

'It's the electricty,' she shouted back. 'It's off.'

He noticed the unlighted bulb inside the refrigerator.

He mumbled to himself, 'And that's why the air conditioner isn't working.' Isn't working. He latched on to those words. 'Kathy!' he shouted. 'The electricity isn't working!'

'That's what I said.'

She strolled into the kitchen. Her voice was low and soft and soothing. Her cheeks were red, as if she were blushing. She wore only the loose-fitting blouse.

'Kathy!' And his voice cracked with emotion.

She smiled as if to say she had never seen him this way before and that she was amused.

He grabbed her by the shoulders and sat her down on a kitchen chair.

'We've got to talk,' he said, more calm now. He was forcing the calmness.

She nodded.

'Where's the fuse box?' he said.

She looked at him funny, pointed to the back door.

He started fumbling with the safety latch.

'No, silly,' she said. 'In the cabinet next to the door. Circuit breakers.'

He checked and flipped them all in one sweep.

'It's the dome,' he said. 'The power's off again. The city is in terrible danger.'

And when he had explained the situation to her and what they each must do, anger came into her face and she glared at him for a full ten seconds before softening. 'Dan. Please. Come to Jackson,' she said. 'Don't go back to the island.'

He shook his head. This was why he had come to the island in the first place. He had never needed this job, and he certainly had no illusions about the future of nuclear energy. Fission was a crock, and sooner or later the human race would find it out. He didn't even particularly care about the human race. But that island out there was the most dangerous place on the planet. It was a cage for the wildest and deadliest and most exciting beast ever. He realized that was what her anger was all about. She had just made love to him. She had sensed his excitement. She could see now the eagerness in his eyes.

'You know I can't go to Jackson,' he said.

She was getting a mop to clean up the water from the ice trays.

'You haven't got time for that!' he shouted.

'That island out there,' she said, 'it doesn't frighten me half as much as you do.' But when he asked her to go to Jackson, she promised him she would and kissed him hard.

They were keeping Professor Nichols under sedation in his room with a security guard posted at the door. He hadn't spoken to anybody since the incident in the dome. The island psychiatrist wanted it kept that way. Lombardy didn't. Rational or irrational, Nichols was still the best mind on the island and knew more about the Super Reactor than anybody else, Lombardy needed the help of that mind. But the psychiatrist stood firm. And there was nothing Lombardy could do. At least for the present.

Ellison, GP's number-two man on the science staff, was efficient if not brilliant. And after several hours of working with a team of mathematicians and the computer, he managed to reconstruct from Nichols's notes the curve for the Slayer equations. He didn't realize immediately the significance of this curve, and it was only after continuous questioning of the computer and fishing into its data banks that he was able to guess what Nichols had been up to.

Ellison, then, was engaged in work that would ultimately establish the credibility of Slayer's statements. Lombardy, with nothing better to go on at the moment, revved up his security force for an investigation into the possibility of sabotage.

Security Chief Warner launched this investigation on two fronts. First, he began a thorough sifting-through of all the personnel files. He had the computer look for possible criminal traits, signs of mixed loyalties, connections with the other large reactor manufacturers. Secondly, he established two reconnaissance teams to travel by speedboat up and down the length of the two liquid-sodium pipelines. Their mission was to look for anything 'unusual' and to question anyone – fisherman, boatman – loitering in the vicinity.

Assistant Chief Englebrecht went along with the team assigned to the New Orleans East pipeline, because he liked riding in boats and thought nothing important would come of it. He craved a little relaxation after a trying day. And it was, after all, the Kenner pipeline that was under suspicion.

The efforts of all these men mattered not in the least.

One of the science technicians who was sitting before a series of computer screens and control panels on the upper-most tier of the steel dome had become so mesmerized by the flashing displays and blinking lights that he was half asleep. Before him a computer reconstruction of the plutonium fuel-rod lattice inside the core of the reactor revolved slowly in a 360-degree rotation that repeated itself every sixty seconds. The image was not a true picture of the innards of the reactor, for no camera could survive the tremendous heat. Heat of that magnitude existed nowhere else in the solar system except near the surface of the sun. The image, rather, was a computer composite assembled from data gathered from thousands of heat and neutron sensors placed along the outer skin of the fuel rods at strategic locations. Right now the composite picture displayed an abnormality of which the nodding science technician was oblivious.

The science technician got an elbow in his ribs from a passing buddy.

'Wake up, Matty, for God's sake. You want the old man to catch you like this?'

Who was the 'old man' now? Nichols was out of com-mission. Ellison. Yeah, he was a bastard, too. Matty flashed a peace sign at his passing friend and tried to keep his head balanced on his shoulders. What a long day this was

86

turning out to be!

The abnormality on the display screen was not immediately obvious. The image turned and turned, like a geometric sculpture on a lazy Susan. Matty drummed his fingers, rubbed his eyes, drummed his fingers again, yawned. He looked over his shoulder at the other personnel along the tier. Everybody was tired and gloomy. When were they going to take a break?

He looked back at the display screen. It was blurred. His eyes were bleary. He rubbed them again and propped his heavy head on the palms of his hands. He watched the image turn.

Something about it was different.

Matty blinked several times and stared intently at the screen.

There was something wrong with a section of the base of the lattice structure. Some of the fuel rods there seemed out of proportion to the others. Matty watched, fascinated, as these rods seemed to swell, ever so slightly, before his eyes. He queried the computer and got a number count of the neutrons being liberated at that area. At first he couldn't believe his eyes. Then a whistle escaped his lips a second or so before the lights went out and the sirens blasted. The independent generators kicked on and the dome was bathed in that eerie yellow back-up light.

It was this morning all over again.

People held their hands to their ears; some made false starts from their chairs; but despite the disorientation there was no panic, and most stuck to their posts.

Matty's spine reverberated the way it had at rock concerts when he sat too close to the speaker system for the bass guitars.

Somebody cut off the inside alarms – or was that done automatically after fifteen seconds? Or was it fifteen years? – and after Matty made some major readjustments to his head, he was able to monitor the screen again.

Was he going nuts? Or just hallucinating because of the sirens? The lattice image on the screen was now entirely normal. And there was no indication of an unusual neutron count from any sector of the reactor's core.

Everything, according to the computer, was A-OK.

'It's sector six again,' Ellison said. 'You want us to override? The city's power is cut off and the computer can't find anything wrong with the reactor.'

'Not so fast this time,' Lombardy said. 'And don't switch off the island sirens yet, either.'

'Nobody can get anything done with those things blasting away.'

'I know. Let them sweat. We're okay here in the dome. I want to try a little experiment.'

Lombardy told Ellison what he wanted done. And Ellison set it up.

He informed Lombardy when everything was ready.

'Okay, then let's do it,' Lombardy said.

From the central control board in the dome where they had made some adjustments, they pushed the switches that would neutralize the back-up warning circuit in the alarm panel in sector six. The island sirens shut down immediately.

'One more time,' Lombardy said.

Switches up, sirens on. Switches down, sirens off.

'That's it, then,' Lombardy said. 'Mason was right. It's that back-up circuit that's triggering off the alarms. Which means a sudden drop in liquid sodium pressure. Sabotage, my ass!' He kicked a nearby trash-can savagely. 'There's a leak. Somewhere along the pipeline there's got to be a leak.'

Chapter 21—Geyser

A stream of super-heated liquid sodium poured from the ruptured pipe and worked its way through tons of limestone and sediment toward ground surface. Pockets of air and water trapped within the ground since the pipeline had been laid combined with the sodium explosively, closing and opening various passageways to the surface. Pedestrians in the vicinity felt minute shock waves from these underground explosions but dismissed them as tremors caused by the mounting late Sunday afternoon traffic on the Metairie throughways.

The stream of sodium finally came to rest against an impenetrable obstacle of inert metal. It collected there in a cavity beneath the obstacle and immediately began to transfer its formidable heat to the inert metal. Inside the metal walls of the obstacle, water which was maintained at an average temperature of 160 degrees Fahrenheit rose very quickly beyond its boiling point and became supersteam. An explosion of tremendous force was imminent.

Dell Hebert, manager of the new Howard Johnson's on Veterans Boulevard, had shed his clothes and was preparing to enter the shower stall of his luxurious suite on the fifteenth floor. Then he decided on a shave, first, to eliminate his four o'clock shadow. Halfway through, the electricity went off. Wouldn't you know it? And he was expecting a visitor, too. Someone he'd been working on all week. She had reservations only till Monday morning. Maybe he could persuade her to stay on till after the Fourth. As manager, he could easily juggle things around, even though he was booked full clear through next weekend. Damn, he looked like an ad for Gillette! And somewhere on the premises there had to be a Gillette to finish the job. He'd find it after the shower.

He reached into the stall to turn on and adjust the water. He left it running while he took a leak.

When he got in he noticed a slight difference in temperature. He wondered if the thermostat control for the underground hot-water tanks was malfunctioning. He started to sing, 'What's new, pussycat?' when the first jets of supersteam escaped through the shower head and struck him full across the back. It felt like a sudden blast of ice-cold water. He turned his head and was instantly blinded. The supersteam fused his eyelids to his corneas. He groped and left the skin from his right hand clean down to the bones on the poker-hot shower controls. He was a burnt-up crisp before he hit the tile floor.

Seconds later the hot-water tanks exploded, drilling a volcanic shaft through fifteen floors and spewing debris over a ten-block radius. The steam condensed into a spray of hot water that hissed from the top of the Howard Johnson's for several more minutes till the underground water reserve was exhausted.

Chapter 22—The Howard Johnson's

Slayer had two questions on his mind when he arrived at the hospital: How badly was the boy burned? And why couldn't he stop thinking about that underwater excavation?

He looked for Wolford and the mayor in the halls and alcoves surrounding the emergency ward and decided they must have left the hospital.

When none of the nurses would volunteer any information about the boy's condition, Slayer felt foolish, helpless, and lonely. It hadn't occurred to him how unco-operative hospital bureaucracy could be, especially to people who were not relatives. Coming here was a mistake. It he weren't so emotionally drained and tired, he could maybe take on that emaciated head nurse with the sharp tongue who thought she was a fashion model. As it was, he felt close to tears.

'There you are,' Wolford said.

Slayer couldn't help bursting into a large smile at the sight of her friendly face.

'We're upstairs. The nurse called and said you were here.'

When they got to the hall with the elevators, Wolford told him about the boy.

'I guess I've been trying to fool myself,' Slayer said.

Wolford nodded. 'I saw the look on your face when you

put that Geiger counter against Peter's chest. There's the elevator. Wait up. The mayor asked for some coffee. And you look like you could use some yourself.'

The mayor was pleased to see him. They caught each other up on information. The mayor told him about her plans to reactivate the old power plants and he explained his theory about the Kenner pipeline. 'I'm really on my way to the desalination plant in Kenner now. Maybe I can dig up some evidence out there.'

They hadn't even finished their coffee when the electricity went.

They sat for a few moments in silence, like deactivated automatons. The dim light of late Sunday afternoon fell across the room from the one outside window enhancing their paleness. Their skin glowed with a dull, metallic sheen. The hospital switched to its independent generator and the fluorescent ceiling lights flickered back on.

'Twice in one day?' the mayor said. 'Lombardy would never allow that – if he had control of things. This is real trouble.'

She called up the police department for another chopper. At the same time they informed her about the explosion in Metairie. They even had live transmission from a police car on the scene which they piped into the phone at the mayor's request.

'Slayer. Wolford.'

The mayor motioned them both to the phone receiver.

The voice on the phone was describing a sequence of very odd events at the new Howard Johnson's and trying to make them sound like the consequences of a conventional bomb explosion.

Slayer shook his head. 'I don't think so. The man's a professional. Trained to think in categories which his colleagues can relate to. I don't think he's describing a bomb explosion at all.'

'I don't know much about bombs,' the mayor said. 'But just listen to his voice. The man doesn't believe what he's saying himself.'

'A geyser,' Wolford said. 'The man's describing a geyser.'

'A what?' the mayor said.

'A geyser.' Wolford, chalk-white, turned to Slayer. 'Caused by tremendous underground heat and pressure.'

'The pipeline,' Slayer said. 'Mayor Mathieu . . .'

'I'm way ahead of you,' she said. 'Why do you think I wanted you to hear this? That new Howard Johnson's was built right after they finished laying the pipeline. Built almost right over it, in fact. The experts – ' she almost choked on the words – 'said there was no danger involved. Absolutely no danger at all.'

They split up in the hospital's parking lot.

'Wolford,' the mayor said, 'I want you to stick with Slayer this time. From here on out take good care of one another. You two may be my only allies on the whole GP staff. Don't spend too much time in Metairie. Just get the vitals on that Howard Johnson's and get back to the island as fast as you can. Here comes my chopper. Be careful. I'll see you back on the island.'

As Slayer drove away the mayor reflected on her motives for sending Wolford along. They made such a good pair. Why couldn't they see that for themselves? If only they both weren't so goddamn cerebral! Keep them together and sooner or later they would have to look at one another. Even scientists came in male and female varieties. If Al were here, he'd tell her not to meddle. But Al wasn't Creole and didn't have the gift for seeing things the way they *should* be. Keep them together. And sooner or later they'd contemplate something a trifle more mundane than the laws of nuclear physics.

When all of this was over she thought she might get the two of them to spend some time at the fishing camp in Little Woods which had belonged to her father. She still kept the old place as a sort of monument. It was there she and Al had made love for the first time. And it was there that, to her utter amazement, he had asked her to be his wife.

She had never thought he was going to ask her that. He was a graduate-school teaching assistant and she was just a little freshman right out of Ursuline Academy, where they cultivated girls as if they were Easter lilies. He was her teacher for 'A Survey of Western Philosophy,' a required course for all freshmen at Louisiana State. And she had become hopelessly infatuated with him by the second week of school. In the meanderings of her mind, as she sat at the front of her class, watching him, she broke every statute of morality that had been drummed into her little conscience by the admonishing priests and consentaneous nuns at Ursuline. She played the coquette through the first quarter and scarcely caught a word he said. On campus he was a hot item. He was slim, handsome, and so irreverent. Everybody thought he'd get in trouble for his outspokenness. He ballyhooed religion and politicians and even the sacred establishment of the university itself. But when nobody came to cart him away, they all thought he was an Albert Einstein secure in the vastness of his intellect and untouchable.

He called her in at the end of the quarter to discuss the weakness of her grades and she managed to finagle a date. By Christmas they were seeing each other regularly. And by spring vacation she was sure she was hopelessly in love. Al never talked about marriage and she would never quite allow them to become intimate without it. It was hopeless. Hopeless. And when her father entered the picture, it became a situation fraught with despair.

By mid-term she was sure her father knew about the affair. After all, he was a man of considerable power in the state and had spies even in Baton Rouge. What she didn't realize at the time was how her father might misconstrue what was happening and how vengeful he might become over the imagined compromise of his daughter's honour.

During Easter vacation she brought Al into the lion's den.

She had heard the week before from sources of her own that the dropping of Philosphy 108 from next fall's roster of required courses along with the name of its current teacher was in the offing. She went to see the dean of philosophy behind Al's back and sensed in the man's little smiles and rudenesses the overwhelming presence of her father.

She believed that to know Al was to love him, or at least – in her father's case – to like him immensely. And so her plan was to bring Al home with her for Easter.

It turned out to be a complete disaster.

Even Al, who was a total political ingenue, sensed something was wrong when he met the mayor of New Orleans. Later he asked her in private if he had bungled some social amenity. 'It's just his way sometimes,' she said, 'when he's overworked and tired. He'll be different tomorrow. You'll see.'

To ensure that it would be so, she confronted her father late in his study after Al was safely asleep in his room for the night.

It was then she discovered how little her father thought of her.

He was beside himself with rage. He accused her of every immorality. He called her stupid and impressionable, easy to subvert and seduce. He shouted about the plans he had made to oust a degenerate rebel from his daughter's life. Al would be blackballed from every university in the country and she would be returned to New Orleans to finish her career in college at Loyola University under the watchful eyes of the Jesuit Fathers.

She was humiliated and speechless and powerless to bend her father's indomitable will. All she could think about was Al and the thickness of the walls. Thank God for these old French-provincial walls. They could withstand the force of hurricanes and shield the weary from the sound and fury of shameful and unfounded vituperations.

The next day all she could think about was Al and escape. She had her key to the old fishing camp. She would take Al there; and for the rest of Easter vacation she would pamper him and please him and do everything in her power to make it up to him. She felt like a cretin who had brought him down and ruined his life, and only because she had found him appealing.

She had not planned the love-making. But she was angry at her father, and she *was* in love with Al. It was as if some tie

94

with her father had been broken. She wanted to give Al
everything, before it was too late, because she had a sudden
feeling he was being drawn inexorably from her, and she
wanted to hold him.

They had been walking on the beach. The moon was
enormous and jack-o'-lantern yellow. The water was
inviting and rough and they decided to swim, though they
had no suits.

'Come on,' Al said. 'I'll turn my head. We'll meet in the
water where it starts to get deep.' Without further ado he
started removing his clothes.

She found it harder to do, and, in fact, cheated. She kept
glancing over her shoulder to make sure he wasn't looking.
When he started into the water with his back toward her, she
followed, unable to discard her panties and bra.

When he got waist-deep and started to turn around she
ducked into a wave, keeping herself covered from the neck
down.

'Come on,' he said gently. 'Stand up. You don't have to be
ashamed.'

She shook her head and backed into deeper water, still
crouching low.

He didn't press her but began to dive into the whitecaps.
He ducked and jumped at the waves. And she caught
glimpses in the moonlight of things she had dreamed about
but never seen before, and that excited her.

The waves were pounding the beach hard and tossing her
around. She was knocked over, and before she could regain
her balance and ward him off, he was there at her side giving
her a hand.

'Why, you little cheat!' he said, discovering her bra. 'And
I suppose . . .' She felt his hand on her rump. 'Stand up,' he
commanded in a firm voice. And she, like an obedient slave,
complied.

He walked her into shallower waters and turned her
around to face him. She tried to keep her eyes fixed on a
point somewhere over his right shoulder. He laughed and
completed undressing her, removing her bra and sliding her

panties down her long, thin legs.

Later, as they lay on the moonlit beach in each other's arms, he proposed. She hadn't known it at the time, but it was the start of her upward climb. If he could love her that much, then she wasn't the cretin, after all. Her father was wrong. She was somebody. She would grow in strength till she could have a showdown with her father and get her way. By the time she and Al were married with her father's reluctant approval, she was already well along in her political career.

She thought fondly of the fishing camp in Little Woods as she watched Slayer and Wolford drive away. She would surely have to get them out there. A little wine, a little music, a full moon, and breakers on the beach . . .

She chided herself for playing matchmaker at a time like this.

Was she so incorrigibly the Frenchwoman?

They had clearance to get through the barricades which the Metairie police and fire department had set up to cordon off the area around the Howard Johnson's. On her way to the dome by helicopter, the mayor had radioed the police to be on the lookout for them and to let them through right away. She also instructed the police to give them any assistance they needed.

When Slayer and Wolford got to the scene, they found the police were still acting on the premise that a bomb had exploded. Slayer's first hardcore evidence that the police were wrong was the reading on his Geiger counter. Wolford had it sitting on her lap as the truck pulled inside the first of the barricades on Veterans Boulevard. She jostled Slayer's arm and pointed to the dial.

'Yeah,' Slayer said. 'Just out of the normal range. And we're still a couple of blocks away. I don't like this at all.'

They parked the truck and Slayer got his larger counter from its crate in the truck's bed.

'This will give us audio, too.' He turned it on and immediately it began to click with increased frequency.

'It looks like there's been a dispersion of radioactive material over the whole area,' Wolford said. 'George, I don't think it's a good idea for all these people to be lingering here.'

'I agree,' Slayer said, 'and not just because of the radiation.'

They found the Metairie chief inside the lobby of the hotel. The explosion had demolished the entire west wing. The rest of the building appeared structurally sound. And because the Howard Johnson's had its own independent generators, which had remained undamaged, there now was electricity.

Emergency medical teams had established temporary first-aid stations in the lobby and on several other floors where there was a steady flow of wounded. The dead were being carried down to the parking lots on the bottom level.

Slayer told the chief about the pipeline, explaining how it ran straight from the dome to the desalination plant in Kenner. 'Liquid sodium is a coolant. Think of it like the cooling system in your car. The desalination plants act like giant radiators. By boiling sea water at the plants, the sodium liberates its heat and is returned to the reactor by a cool pipeline. The one under this building is hot and it's ruptured. You've got to evacuate this building right away. You've got to evacuate this whole area.'

The chief played with Slayer's Geiger counter.

'This thing isn't pointing to the red,' the chief said. 'What's the big hurry? Besides, these people are better off here, where there's power.'

'There's power here, all right. Listen.' Slayer's voice was suddenly firm and angry. 'You don't understand. The immediate problem is not from radiation. The chemical properties of sodium, that's the problem. It explodes on contact with water or air. There could be another explosion any time. Only this one could take out the whole building. And a few more city blocks to boot. You think you got problems now. That first explosion was just a preview. From the small amount of damage, I'd say the big one's yet to come. This was mainly just a steam explosion. You got water tanks under this building? Ten to one they're not there any more Except for their base or platform foundation or whatever else is left. Something's keeping that liquid sodium from touching off. But it won't for long. Believe me, this stuff is unstable and unpredictable. And when it goes, it goes like TNT.' Slayer gestured around the lobby. 'You want to be responsible for all these people getting killed?'

'All right,' the chief said, 'I'm hearing what you're saying. You're an expert in your field. I've got experts, too. And they're telling me somebody set off a bomb. You flash this thing around and because it ticks a little more than usual, you tell me there's going to be another explosion. I need more proof than that. In a little while it's going to be dark out there. No lights anywhere. Burglar alarms not working. And you want me to use the lion's share of my force to supervise an evacuation here? Okay. You get me some more proof. You go down in that hole we found in the west wing and you make sure you know what you're talking about. You do that for me. And I'll start vacating this place pronto.'

Circles of white light glided over the dark walls, ceilings, and floors in the west wing. Slayer had a flashlight, too, which he aimed at Wolford, in back of him. He held out his hand and she took it, tucking herself in tight behind him.

'This is crazy,' she whispered into his shoulder. 'The chief had no right to talk you into this. It's dangerous.'

'Seems I've heard those words before,' he whispered back. 'Why the hell didn't you stay behind?'

'I'm supposed to take care of you. Mayor's orders. Remember?'

'What are you two whispering for?' The Metairie chief had come back from down the hall. His flashlight swept quickly over their faces. 'It's getting pretty hairy. Half the floor's completely gone up ahead. Miss Wolford, why don't you please wait for us back in the lobby?'

'I'm staying.'

'Suit yourself, dammit. But I won't be responsible if anything happens to you.'

'Nobody asked you to be,' Wolford said. Her tone was

caustic. 'Besides, if something happens it will happen to all of us. You won't even know what hit you.'

The Metairie chief, who was not used to women talking back, snorted. He addressed the rest of his remarks to Slayer. 'This hallway looks passable. And we shouldn't be too far from the shaft the explosion made. What I don't like is we're seven floors up. We're going to have to lower you by rope. I've already told Langsley.'

Slayer nodded.

Langsley was one of the chief's bomb experts. And Slayer's job was to convince Langsley of the true cause of the explosion.

A number of the chief's men stood at the edge of the shaft. Beyond the hole in the roof eight storeys above stars twinkled, though outside it was still dusk and no stars were yet visible. The chief's men shined their flashlights up and down the shaft. Then, one after the other, beams were aimed straight down at the feet and held there.

'Four, maybe five floors down,' one of the men said. 'Beyond that you can't see a damn thing. We could get a searchlight up here in about twenty minutes.'

The chief looked at Slayer before answering. 'Ten minutes. We're getting our asses out of here in ten minutes.'

They set up the ropes and pulleys for lowering the two men. Wolford attached a shoulder strap to the audio counter and looped it over Slayer's head.

'Listen good to this thing,' she said. 'You don't know how radioactive it is down there.'

'Don't worry,' Slayer answered. 'My instinct for self-preservation is very strong.'

Langsley and Slayer went over the brim simultaneously. They felt the heat right away.

'Damn!' Langsley said. 'It must be an oven down there.'

Slayer signalled to the men on the pulleys with his light. 'Hold it,' he said.

The words had a trembling quality which he felt everyone could perceive. He regretted having to halt the descent, but his nerves were attacking him and he needed a minute to get himself back under control. That goddamn fear of heights. It's only seven storeys down, he told himself. About sixty feet, that's all. Keep your eyes focused along the sides and don't look straight down into the abyss. Come on, you can do it. You have to do it. People's lives are at stake. Wolford's life.

He reached into his pocket and withdrew a handkerchief. Another action he regretted. Everyone's eyes were on him. He took several deep breaths and instead of putting his terror of heights on public display by mopping his drecnhed brow, he carefully unfolded the handkerchief and held it out towards the centre of the shaft in the flashlight crossfire. Let their minds go to work on this little demonstration.

Everybody watched the handkerchief leave Slayer's hand. Instead of falling it remained suspended and then began to levitate. Momentarily, it climbed very swiftly up towards the top of the shaft.

'A hot-air up-draught,' Wolford said to the chief. 'Something's happening at the bottom of the shaft. You ever seen a bomb cause an effect like this?'

Some of the officers were tossing handkerchiefs and pieces of paper into the shaft and watching then climb, making exclamatory remarks.

'Stop that!' the chief snapped. Then to Wolford, dryly: 'Langsley's the bomb expert.'

Slayer and Langsley continued their descent.

They encountered obstructions from walls and floors. After the pressure that had torn them loose had passed, they had collapsed from the force of gravity. There were pieces of pipe and metal beams sticking out. At points the two men had to kick and fight their way through, sending debris crashing and clanging down the shaft. The heat grew more intense. Breathing became difficult. Their hands grew slippery with sweat. They had to take time-outs, and they were using up precious time.

Langsley wiped the sweat from his face with a sweep of his arm. He peered down through the remaining levels of the shaft, following the beam of his flashlight. Slayer checked the reading on his Geiger counter.

'Increased radioactivity,' Slayer said. 'I don't know how much further down we can go.'

'To hell with the radioactivity,' Langsley said. 'I don't know how much more of this heat I can stand.'

They descended another level. Kicked away more debris. Langsley spotted it first. Moved his flashlight slowly over its surface.

'Slayer,' he said, almost in a whisper, 'there it is. The bottom of the shaft. It's covered by a metal slab.' He wanted a better view and swung himself over to a beam which jutted out from the side of the shaft near his feet.

Slayer illuminated the base of the beam with his flashlight. It was metal and it was touching the slab at the bottom of the shaft.

'Don't touch that!' he shouted.

Langsley looked up in surprise. 'What?'

He brought his foot down on the beam for support. It slipped off as if it were coated with butter. He brought the other foot down and smelled burned rubber as that foot slipped, too. 'What the . . .' It hit him in a flash what was happening. The superheated metal beam was melting the soles of his boots on contact. He had to keep his flesh from touching that beam. He used his feet to kick himself away. But again they slipped. He swung feebly out towards the centre of the shaft, came to a stop, and helplessly started the return swing back into the beam. He twisted and contorted his body, trying to avoid the inevitable. At the last minute he felt a hand grab him by the belt and pull him aside.

He clutched Slayer's body, trembling. 'Christ! I believe you!' he said. 'This isn't any bomb! Let's get the hell out of here!'

The chief listened to Slayer in silence.

'There's a metal slab down there, probably all that's left of the water tanks. It's superheated and it's the only barrier between the liquid sodium and the air. I don't know how much longer it's going to hold. Get everybody out of the building. Then start evacuating the area. If you can arrange

101

it, get a fleet of cement trucks here as fast as you can. Flood the whole bottom level of this building with wet cement. It might keep the sodium from getting through. I just don't know.' Slayer remembered about the underwater excavation near the Metairie beaches. Jagged rocks and limestone. That's what had been bothering him all day. The water would have worn those edges smooth after only a few weeks' time. 'You got another problem, too. There was a liquid-sodium explosion near the causeway early this morning. The explosion blew out the base of the levee and fused a lot of rock together. It sealed the leak at that point. But I don't know for how long. Better get all the residents out of that area, too.'

When they got outside it was as pitch-black as the west wing of the Howard Johnson's.

'You'd think there could at least be a moon,' the chief said.

'I've never seen so many stars before,' one of his men said, 'It's kind of spooky.'

The chief grunted. 'Looters. Burglars. Murderers. And maybe more explosions. If they don't get the power back on, it's going to be a damn long night.'

Chapter 23—Recommendations

'Procedures to deactivate the Kenner pipeline have already begun,' Lombardy told the mayor. The four members of the mayor's Nuclear Advisory Board were present, along with Ellison, other top scientists, and island managers. 'I knew there had to be a rupture as soon as we determined positively what circuit system was setting off the alarms. Our radio tower is monitoring the Metairie police calls. Apparently, the Howard Johnson's was demolished by a steam explosion caused by hot liquid sodium superheating the underground water tanks. The police are evacuating the area now since a sodium explosion will very likely take place within the hour. The body count – ' his voice trembled – 'is thirty so far. The wounded number in the hundreds. We have to make some very heavy decisions in the next few minutes about the future of the Super Reactor.'

As he spoke a part of Lombardy's mind operated on an entirely different plane. When this was all over, people were going to speculate and speculate on the chain of events and causes leading up to the death of so many people. It wouldn't matter what they decided on in the end. Lombardy already knew the causes: Carlleston, who had hedged and dodged and planted the idea of sabotage in an effort to lessen GP's guilt and responsibility; and Lombardy, himself, who had allowed Carlleston to mislead and manipulate him into procrastination. If only he had gone with Mason's hunch. If only he had deactivated the Kenner pipeline this morning. All those people. They might still be alive. He saw the actions of Carlleston and himself as part of the general character flaw of 'Pop' Wilson's company. Somewhere in the interstices of General Power, Inc., somewhere in the flow of ideas and passions up and down the chain of command, the spirit of old man Wilson was alive and well. Everyone was tainted. No one survived unscathed. He had come to General Power because that's where the action was. And he had stayed for the same reason. Did it take the death of thirty people to reveal the full extent of his fall? When this was over he would leave 'Pop' Wilson's forever. But in the meantime, could he make some small retribution? Lift himself from the mire? Place his foot on the road to redemption?

Ellison had taken the floor.

'The reactor can operate, even at full power, as long as one of the two pipelines is functioning properly. We have no reason to believe the New Orleans East pipeline is damaged in any way, and there is absolutely nothing wrong with the reactor itself.'

'Then you vote to keep the reactor going?' the mayor said.

Ellison appeared surprised and somewhat perplexed. 'I

didn't know shutting it down was at issue,' he said. 'The reactor is in perfectly sound condition. I was talking about restoring power to the city.'

Harris, from the mayor's Advisory Board, intervened. 'Professor Ellison is being a little misleading. You can't consider the reactor as an entity apart. Those two pipelines are an integral part of a whole – shall I say *organism?* The reactor complex *has* been damaged, and seriously so. All risk factors in its operation have been doubled with the rupture of this pipeline. At least one desalination plant must be flawlessly working along with the heat exchangers in sector six to sufficiently cool the reactor core.'

Ellison jumped back in. 'That's only when the reactor is operating at full power. We could cut it to ten per cent of its capacity output and still supply electricity to the city.'

The mayor addressed herself to Lombardy.

'If it's at all feasible I'd like to restore power to the city at least till noon tomorrow.' She then disclosed her plan to switch the city's electrical supply back to the old power plants.

Ellison, mouth agape, stood up and gestured toward the floor of the dome. 'You mean to shut down the reactor entirely, then?'

'That's exactly what I mean,' the mayor said.

One of Lombardy's junior managers raised his voice heatedly. 'You'll be in violation of contract.'

The mayor turned on him savagely.

'Mayor Mathieu,' Lombardy said, reaching out, touching her shoulder lightly, 'I apologize for Mr Prospero's un-thinking remark.'

Mayor Mathieu spun around, glared, and waited.

Lombardy cleared his throat and addressed all of them.

'With the death of thirty or more people, everything has been changed. We can no longer operate here according to old plans and commitments. All agreements and contracts are suspended, cancelled – at least till we know more about what's going on here. I believe the mayor's plan to switch to the old power plants is the only sane approach. And I want

104

everybody on my staff to co-operate with her to their fullest capacity. I don't care what disagreements there have been in the past, what enemies have been made, whose feelings have been hurt. What I want now is a united effort to do everything in our power to ensure the safety of the people in the Greater New Orleans area. Everything we do here in the next few hours, days, months, or however long it takes, must be subordinated to this effort. It may well be the case that what happened at the Howard Johnson's was a fluke, a million-to-one long shot. I know that's what the majority of you believe. I'm inclined to that opinion myself. In all likelihood the reactor is in perfectly sound condition and will remain so for the next fifty years. However, we cannot gamble people's lives on our belief that the reactor is safe. I want proof. Incontrovertible proof. With this end in mind I make the following recommendations, which are in accord with the mayor's wishes. One, reduce the heat output of the reactor to ten per cent. Two, restore power to the Greater New Orleans area until such time as the conventional power plants can resume operation. Three, shut down the reactor at the earliest opportunity. Four, launch an investigation with the aid of the NRC to determine the cause of the Kenner pipeline rupture. And five' – he looked directly at the mayor – 'submit Dr Slayer's report to the best minds in nuclear physics for a re-evaluation of the whole Super Reactor programme.'

Chapter 24—Emissary

The mayor conferred with her husband in the dome's staff lounge.

'How did you get in?' she said. 'In all this excitement I forgot to leave word you were coming.'

'I didn't have any trouble at all,' Al said. 'I told the guard at Post One who I was. He called Lombardy, and Lombardy gave me clearance right away. I've been here for quite some time.'

The mayor frowned thoughtfully.

'What's wrong?' Al said.

'Oh, nothing. I was just wondering why Lombardy is being so co-operative.'

Lombardy's little speech, completely backing her position, had left her flabbergasted. While exiting the glass office where their meeting had been held, she had overheard a pair of mumbling GP officials. 'What's Lombardy up to?'

'Company suicide, if you ask me. Lombardy's got power. But not that much power. Company heads will never go along with it. What he's proposing is bankruptcy for GP.' Those mumbling youngsters were right, of course. Lombardy spoke as if GP didn't matter any more. As if his own career didn't matter. Both were completely tied to the success of the Super Reactor, and Lombardy had done all but deliver an elegy. What was the man up to?

Slayer's report . . .

Fr Donahue . . .

Insurance companies . . .

She was only half-listening to Al. Whatever else Lombardy was, he was no fool. And he wasn't weak. In her dealing with him she had never seen him show fear or back down under pressure. He was a talented leader. Wolford respected him, too, called him intellectually honest. Was this a manifestation of that honesty? Lombardy sounded sincere, even moved by the death of all those people. Why couldn't she take his words at face value?

He said he believed in the safety of the reactor, said he thought the accident was a fluke, a million-to-one shot. Yet he acquiesced. Gave in to her demands. Would a talented leader do that? Capitulate? To pressure resulting from a million-to-one shot?

Inch by inch a new interpretation of Lombardy's words worked its way into her mind.

Lombardy's whole pitch was for unanimity. He had called for a suspension of squabbling, a putting aside of differences

106

in outlooks and objectives, a truce in the everyday war between human being and human being. As if they all must now unite against a common enemy.

She felt suddenly very frail. A woman at the mercy of a murderous assailant. An assailant that wasn't even human and had no right to exist on this planet. An invader. Who had inveigled its way into existence with empty promises of a better, more leisure-oriented way of life for mankind. Foolishly, she had taken the bait. And the very future of her people hung in the balance.

'Al,' she said, 'would you do me a tremendous favour? What Fr Donahue said makes sense. We should look into this question of insurance. But all the people to see are in Baton Rouge. They should be consulted in person and not by phone, and I can't get away. Al, could you be my personal emissary?'

The state capital was ninety miles away. There, surely, Al would be safe.

His expression was one of perplexity, and he began protesting. One by one she fielded his arguments, taking care not to reveal her true motive for getting him out of the city. Finally, he relented, as she knew he would. Had he ever refused her any favour? After all these years he could still be moved by her smile. She wanted to embrace him but refrained for fear of giving herself away.

He must leave tonight, not wait till morning. She gave him a list of people he must see. She insisted his mission was urgent. He should be on his way. For the first time in her life she thanked God their two daughters, who had long since married, lived out of state. And she repented for holding a mother's grudge against the Almighty all these years.

After Al left she remained in the lounge, which was white and clean and sparse like a chapel. Thoughts of Al floated in her mind, of their love and how huge it was; how small it was in the face of an apocalypse. Life was a pawn in a chess game of catastrophes and she prayed. When Lombardy came for her she was ready, physically and spiritually.

'Mayor Mathieu,' he said, 'there have been some new

107

developments.' Once again his face was the colour of ash. 'Will you accompany me to the top of the dome?'

She nodded and preceded him through the doorway to the interior of the dome itself.

Chapter 25—The Warning

Just before the lights went out for the last time all over the city, the radio operator at the Coast Guard base in West End received a weak and broken signal coming off Lake Pontchartrain. It was a message of distress in Morse code, and it sounded like it was being sent from the island. The message repeated twice and then went off the air:

MAYDAY . . . MAY . . . REQUEST IMMEDI . . . SISTANCE . . . MUST WARN . . . STRONG FERRO . . . FECT . . . ALL WAR . . . SYSTEMS OUT . . . WARN CITY . . . NOT ATTEMP . . . LAND EVAC . . . WARN CITY.

'I pieced everything from the two broadcasts together and that's what I got,' the radio operator told Commander Higgins.

'And you think this message came from the island?' Commander Higgins frowned. 'They've got a very powerful transmitter out there. Why was this signal so weak and in Morse? Somebody's playing games.'

'You think it's a hoax?'

Commander Higgins picked up the phone. 'They've had trouble out at the dome all day. A lot of people monitoring the waves know that. This could be some jackass's idea of fun.'

At that point the lights went out. Nobody said a word till the independent generator came on. The commander, still holding the phone to his ear said, 'Damn!' and ordered his officer of the watch to verify the number he had dialled in the book of emergency listings. The officer called the numbers out while the commander dialled again.

The expression of annoyance on Commander Higgins's face changed to bewilderment. 'That's funny,' he said. 'The phones are on a different circuit. They should still be working.' He motioned for the radio operator. 'What do you make of this?'

The line was filled with a strange humming noise that rose and fell in random octaves and half-octaves. It was like something alive and had the qualities of a human voice in terrible anguish. It sent chills down the radio operator's spine.

'I've never heard anything like this before,' he whispered.

'What would make the phones go dead, too?' the commander said.

'This is the island number?'

The commander nodded.

'Let me try something.' The radio operator hung up and dialled again. 'I thought so,' he said. 'The phones aren't dead at all. "At the sound of the tone the time will be eleven-fifty-eight, p.m." There's just something wrong with the phones out on the island.'

'Warren,' the commander said to his officer of the watch, 'get hold of the city police. They have a special hotline to the island. Tell them what's happening. Let me know if they get through. I'll be in the radio shack.'

For several minutes the radio operator tried contacting the island with the commander standing by.

'I didn't think it would work,' the commander finally said. 'Take a look at this. I've been extrapolating on the message you received.'

The radio operator took the piece of paper the commander handed him. But before he could finish reading it, a disaster alert blasted over the air waves. It was a call for help from New Orleans International Airport, Delta Flight 722 from New Orleans to Jackson, Memphis, and St Louis was down over the lake. Three minutes into its flight, which roughly placed it at an altitude of four thousand feet above the steel dome, its instruments went berserk and its engines died. The airport authority wanted the Coast Guard to begin an immediate search for possible survivors.

The Coast Guard commander took up the radio mike and instructed his operator to broadcast on all channels.

'To all boats and aircraft in the vicinity of Lake Pontchartrain, this is a directive from Coast Guard command. Effect immediate withdrawal from all sectors within a ten-mile radius of the steel dome. Do not attempt a rescue operation. I repeat, do not attempt a rescue operation. Aircraft and boats on the north shore are to seek immediate refuge in Covington. Do not attempt a lake crossing. I repeat, do not attempt a lake crossing. This is a directive from Coast Guard command.'

The radio operator looked at his commander, agog.

'But what about survivors?' he said. 'You're sentencing them all to certain death!'

'Survivors? After a four-thousand-feet crash? Besides, it can't be helped.' The commander's voice was shaky.

The radio operator picked up the piece of paper with the island message and read it aloud with the additions pencilled in by the commander.

'Mayday. Mayday. Request immediate assistance. Must warn city. Strong ferromagnetic effect. All warning systems out. Warn city. Do not attempt island evacuation. Warn city.'

The radio operator whistled under his breath. 'Ferromagnetism. So that's what knocked out the phones.'

'And their radio gear,' the commander said. 'And, God help them, Delta Flight 722. "Don't attempt an island evacuation." They know what would happen, all right. Cars, planes, boats – anything with engines will be knocked out. Something's going on out there on the island and those people are stranded. They know it, too. And unless we can pull a rabbit out of the hat, they might as well be stranded on an island a million miles away.'

110

Chapter 26—Stranded

Al cruised along I-10 towards Baton Rouge at the speed limit and flirted with the idea of taking his Corvette up to ninety miles an hour. The powerful engine and trim body lines were built for speed and it was almost a crime against nature to hold the car back. He did nudge it up to seventy-five – at this late hour the super-highway was almost deserted – but no more. It would not do for the husband of the mayor to be arrested for speeding.

Of course, he did enjoy a certain amount of anonymity, since his wife had chosen to showcase her talents under her maiden name. What parish sheriff or state trooper would associate *Jaffe* with *Mathieu*? Of course, a shrewd small-town traffic judge might. And the rest of the state was notoriously anti-New Orleanian.

Indeed, it had been no mean feat, what his wife had done to bring together the various power elements in the state – north and south, Orleanian and non-Orleanian – to make the Super Reactor a reality. Nobody had ever been able to do that kind of politicking before with any degree of success. Huey Long had united the state but had never won the hearts of the people of New Orleans. Already there was plenty of talk about Mathieu for governor.

It wasn't fair, what was happening. The moronic masses would blame Dottie for the scientists' errors and they would deny themselves the best governor in the history of the state.

If only the damn thing had worked the way it was supposed to. Cheap power and clean water. Unpolluted sea water, desalted by the reactor's tremendous heat. No more drinking from the Mississippi, which had become the sewer of the whole Midwest. No more ingestion of carcinogenic wastes. If only the damn thing had worked. Already the powerful clergy bloc in New Orleans was thinking of Dottie as another Joan of Arc. She would have been governor by next year.

But wasn't it just like her to put all considerations of her political future aside. She would never hedge a bet or lie. She would never lie. She got that from her mother. 'A person who will lie will steal.' Dottie, too, lived her life by that maxim. And now she would probably perish by it. Well, let the damn fools set Lousiana politics back twenty years. Let them have their stump orators and their two-ring front-runners. 'I got me my Knights of Columbus ring for that New Orleans crowd and my Mason ring for when I'm north of Baton Rouge.'

To hell with them all!

Al's car radio was still picking up New Orleans stations sixty miles out, and he knew the exact time the city lost its power.

'Damn, Dottie!' he said to himself. 'You don't lie, but you're as crafty as your old man.'

He had a hunch he was being sent out of town at such short notice for a hidden reason. Things were still wrong out on that island. And Dottie was doing her damnedest to save his hide.

At the next I-10 exit he swapped directions and barrelled southward at one hundred and ten. No cop would even try.

In twenty minutes he was swinging his Corvette on to Causeway Boulevard. Later, he would find out how well his car had performed, getting as far out on the causeway as it did. At the time, though, he screamed and swore and kicked the tyres before starting his long trek back toward the south shore.

What had happened? It was almost like some giant invisible hand had gripped the front of the hood, slowing the car to a stop. And there was no getting it started after that. The radio had stopped working and he even had trouble getting his key out of the lock.

By what he thought was coincidence, his watch had stopped, too. And he could only guess at the time he lost plodding back over the eight miles or so to the south shore entrance. God, was he out of shape!

He had hoped to hitch a ride and thought it odd that no cars were passing him either direction. After a mile he came upon a Volkswagen stalled out with its owner absent. Later, he was overtaken by two long-haired kids who had gotten farther up toward the north shore before it happened to them. They said it was happening to all the cars and that some of the people they had passed were freaking out. They wanted to know if Al had any ideas about what was going on He told them he didn't trying not to sound frightened. Wishing him luck, they quickened their pace once again. He could still hear the clacking of their sandals on the cement long after he had lost sight of them. It was that quiet and that dark.

What *was* happening?

By the time he was nearing the south shore, hours had passed and he was thoroughly bushed. All he could think about was Dottie out on that island. What was keeping him from reaching her? Was there some connection between the island and what had happened to the cars? He racked his brain for a clue and cursed the fact that his background in the applied sciences was inadequate.

He had to rest more frequently now and a notion began to grow in his mind. Maybe he didn't have the stamina to make it back to shore. Surely they would be sending out rescue parties when they discovered what had happened. As a matter of fact, what was taking them so long! Surely they must know by now. Nobody seemed concerned about his plight.

He felt a sense of accomplishment when he overtook the owner of the Volkswagen. The man was younger than himself but grossly overweight. He was gasping for breath and holding his chest with one hand and the railing with the other.

'You okay?' Al said. His sense of accomplishment was replaced by a genuine concern.

The man nodded. When he got his breath back he asked Al what was happening.

'I don't know,' Al said. 'All the cars on the causeway are stalled out.'

'I mean out there,' the man said. 'I know about the cars. Everything's magnetized. But look out there.'

Far in the distance in the direction of West End a string of lights paraded across the lake. The two men watched as the string grew longer as more lights joined the parade at its rear.

'There must be dozens of them,' Al said. 'They're sailboats from the marina in West End. And it looks like . . . they're on their way to the steel dome.'

Chapter 27—The Furnace

Just when Lombardy had thought he was out of the woods, things began happening fast. Not two minutes after his meeting with the mayor had been concluded, a very tired science technician named Matty Bushnell confronted him with a pocket calculator that wasn't working properly.

'I was on the main computer when the sirens went off,' Matty began. 'I got so rattled Dr Ellison had me relieved. I didn't say anything about what I saw on the monitor screen because I thought my mind was making it up. But this got me to thinking it all through again.' He held up the pocket calculator. 'I play around with this for relaxation back in my room. As you can see it's displaying nothing but gibberish. That's because the battery's weak and the circuits aren't getting enough juice. Well, I think something like this may have happened to the main computer. Right before the electricity went off I got a real strange reading from the monitor. After we went on back-up power, the readings went back to normal. I know this isn't supposed to happen, but maybe in the power switch-over the juice going to the main computer dropped too low. That could even damage some computer circuits. You know how sensitive they are.

The thing that bothers me most is that maybe some circuits got damaged in the first power switch-over early this morning. That would mean the readings. I've been taking all day long – the normal readings – are unreliable.'

'What part of the reactor are you assigned to monitor?' Lombardy asked.

'That's what's got me really scared.' Matty's upper lip twitched nervously. 'I guess I should have come to you about this earlier, as soon as it happened, even though I thought I was hallucinating. My job today was the biggie. I was monitoring the plutonium fuel-core lattice.'

'I wish people on the science staff would go through the proper channels,' Dr Ellison said. 'Bushnell should have come to me first about this. I would have put him straight in a minute.'

'Then how do you account for the neutron readings he got?' Lombardy said.

Ellison shrugged. 'Bushnell said it himself. He was very fatigued. He only *thought* he saw abnormal readings.'

'You think there's no chance the computer is malfunctioning?'

'Bushnell has halfway convinced himself he saw abnormal readings because of that story he's concocted.' Ellison chuckled. 'Comparing the main computer to a pocket calculator. That in itself is the work of a very tired mind.'

Lombardy had quit relying on his science staff to tell him what was possible and impossible. He already had an investigative team at work on the computer circuits and power supply systems. And procedures had commenced to bring the heat of the Super Reactor down to a mere fraction of its total output. Surely, that would take the punch out of any fission process that had started to run wild.

Meanwhile, a problem had developed in Security. In all the excitement over the Howard Johnson's incident, nobody had noticed the absence of Assistant Chief Englebrecht. His team should have reported in on the conditions of the New

Orleans East pipeline hours ago.

Chief Warner, in the radar tower, tried to raise the boat by radio. With characteristic impatience, Warner had pushed aside the regular operator and was adjusting dials and pushing buttons for himself.

'Recon East, this is Island Tower. Come in. Recon East, please come in for Island Tower.'

Warner kept calling for fifteen minutes and then had the regular operator do it for fifteen more.

'Why don't they answer?' Warner snapped.

The operator called again and once again they listened to the silent air waves, silent except for a crackling noise which occurred with increased regularity.

'What is that noise, Hubbard?' Warner said.

The radio operator shook his head. 'It sounds like a thunderstorm moving in over the lake. Only there are no blips on the radar screen. I don't know what it is. Something somewhere is causing interference.'

Warner drummed his fingers on the edge of the radio console and came to a decision. He would get a boat crew together and go looking for Englebrecht himself.

Down in a sub-level of the dome, where all the back-up power systems were contained to make the dome self-sufficient during blackouts, electrical engineers studied diagrams, tested circuits, scratched their heads, and cursed Lombardy.

'Another wild-goose chase,' one engineer remarked. 'What the hell are we looking for this time?'

'Problems in the back-up systems feeding the computer,' said another. 'That's all I know.'

'We're not on back-up power now. Are they expecting more trouble?'

'Just do your job, goddamnit!'

The search for trouble went on without results. And knowing Lombardy, the engineers were sure he would expect answers. If Lombardy had reason to suspect there was trouble, you could never convince him otherwise except on

116

the most rigorous and exhaustive grounds. If they didn't find trouble soon, they could very well be down here the rest of the night.

Jules Dove, an old-timer 'electrician,' who said they could keep their fancy titles, was the one to discover what was wrong. Everything checked out on the circuit testers. But Jules relied more on his common sense and keen eye than on instruments.

It was just that kind of talk that had made Jules a borderline case ever since he started work for GP on the island. He never got promotions, just the annual cost-of-living raise, and he was on the bottom of everybody's sharp-guy list. Everyone knew he was just a 'local boy' who would be let go once GP's commitments on the island had terminated. Nobody bothered to really study his work record or responsibly evaluate his many talents. His bosses took him for granted. And that's why they were inclined to slough off his story of a misplaced staple.

'It's back in the cable tunnel,' he said. 'Too much slack in the wires. Somebody just bunched them all together, tied 'em up with cord, and stapled 'em to the wall. Those wires should've been stretched taut and run through conduit. Somebody saved themselves a couple of days' work.'

When he saw nobody was listening, he got a young apprentice electrician to give him a hand. Jules was not a heavy man and the shoulders of the apprentice worked just fine. He spent several minutes eyeballing the wires and the staple and pounding on the wall with the handle of his screwdriver. When the young apprentice started squirming and complaining, Jules relented and worked the staple free with a pair of needle-nose pliers.

Simultaneously, on the electrical engineer's board and on the main sensor panel in the top tier of the dome, a red warning light clicked on. And only Jules Dove, who 'never trusted a circuit-tester in my life,' could tell them why.

Jules explained it to Lombardy in person:

'Somebody wasn't watching what they was doing. If they wasn't going to go through the bother of shortening the

117

wires to the right length, they should of just left 'em hanging down. That staple cut through two small sensor wires. That's right. And it was a T-700 staple. Went right through the wood panel and smacked up against metal conduit on the other side. Those two cut wires have been shorted out since that staple was put in and no telling how long that's been.'

The function of the two cut wires was vital. During blackouts, before the independent generators had time to come on, the power to keep the main computer running was supplied by a system of large wet-cell storage batteries. The proper level of charge in the batteries was maintained on information supplied by a sensor system of which the two shorted wires were components.

'We know one thing for sure,' Jules concluded. 'When I pulled out that staple, you got a red light warning, right? Well, one or more of the wet-cell batteries must be dead. Maybe all of 'em are. How long you think that staple's been in the wall?' He held his age-worn prize up for all to see. 'Well, that's how long it's been since those batteries have had a good charge.'

It only took minutes to confirm that three of the back-up batteries were completely dead. Lombardy asked Jules what he thought that would do to the main computer during a blackout.

'It could damage the computer, all right,' Jules said. 'That thing's like a brain and it feeds on electricity the way our brains feed on oxygen. Take away its food supply and, well, part of it could die.'

'Jules Dove's manner of speech is very figurative,' Ellison said, 'but not entirely inaccurate. Programme and memory circuits could be entirely fouled up. Of course, we have no direct corroborating evidence from the computer itself. Some of your engineers and my technicians are running tests on it now. So far we've got nothing.'

'We've got Matty Bushnell's "hallucination," ' Lombardy said testily. 'Are you still telling me you think that damn machine is reporting information accurately?'

'When you asked me about the computer before, you didn't tell me there were three dead batteries in the back-up power system. Certainly the machine could be feeding us misinformation.'

'I'm going down to the staff lounge. I'm going to bring the mayor back up here. When I return I want to see all the top men on the science staff. And all the senior technicians, too. I want to commence procedures for a total shut-down. Tell them. A *total* shut-down. And I want those procedures to begin immediately.'

'Mr Lombardy,' Dr Ellison said.

'Later, Doctor. I'll hear arguments later. I have the final authority here and I'm giving you an order.'

'I just wanted to tell you that I think you're doing the right thing. Being the one man solely responsible for everything that happens on this island can't be easy. I'm sure Mr Carlleston and the board will know you've done the best job you could. Speaking for the entire science staff, I want to know whatever you decide, we're behind you a hundred per cent.'

Lombardy smiled a smile that showed all his teeth. 'Ellison,' he said, 'if you're going to be standing behind me from here on out, I'm going to start pinning mistletoe to my shirt-tails.'

Chief Warner didn't like the feel of strange coincidences. Three out of four security boats wouldn't start. And nobody could figure out why. The one that did start hadn't been sitting in the dock for very long but had just returned from making the routine ten-thirty security cruise around the perimeter of the island. Without switching off the engine, Warner had his men gas up the tanks. Then, with a crew of five, he set out on the same course which his assistant chief had pursued earlier.

One of the crewmen stayed at the radio trying to raise the missing boat as they sped along. Warner kept one ear cocked in the direction of the receiver, listening to the silent responses, wondering at that strange crackling noise which seemed to diminish as they got farther out from the island.

Searchlights on the bow provided adequate illumination across the dark, calm water. But all they spotted after the first twelve miles was one fishing troller. Its captain was gruff with them and complained they were scaring away all the fish. He said he hadn't seen another boat all night and wished to God he hadn't seen theirs, either. Warner asked him to leave the area and the captain told Warner he knew what he could do. Ten minutes later, with the troller far behind, Warner was still red-faced and muttering oaths.

As they neared the area of the cypress swamps, however, Warner's mood changed. He thought they would have certainly spotted Englebrecht's boat by now, becalmed, out of gas, with waving figures on deck waiting to be rescued. The idea kept occurring to him that maybe they had gone ashore. But why would Englebrecht do that? Boat trouble? *And* radio trouble? Then why hadn't he phoned the island from shore to let security know what had happened? It just wasn't like Englebrecht to deviate from rule-book procedures.

Warner examined the pipeline chart and the compass reading.

'You sure you stayed right on course the whole time?' he asked his helmsman.

'Yes, sir. Right on the mark.'

'Hmm,' Warner said. 'Muggy night. As a matter of fact, it's goddamn hot.' He realized suddenly he was dripping with sweat. And it was getting hard to breathe.

The first hard thump against the boat's hull knocked them all off balance.

'Well, Louis, goddamnit,' Warner complained, 'don't take us into the damn swamp. This isn't a pirogue, you know.'

'That wasn't a cypress and it wasn't bottom,' the helmsman said. 'The swamp don't begin for another two hundred yards.'

Another thump rocked the boat in the other direction.

'Chief! Look at this!'

One of the men on the searchlights had something in his

beam. A third thump nearly pitched him off the bow and into the water. But he clung to the searchlight housing for dear life.

'What is it!' Warner shouted. 'What did you see?'

The man re-aimed his beam off the port.

At first Warner didn't understand what was happening. Near the edge of the swamp the lake was erupting in huge air bubbles that exploded on contact with the surface. Luckily their boat lay just at the edge of the whole turbulent area and was not struck in force. Scalding spray from the bubbles swept over the men on the boat and brought cries of agony.

'Turn your heads the other way!' Warner shouted. 'Don't look or you could get blinded! Helmsman, get us out of here fast!'

When they got to a safer distance they tried contacting the island by radio and found they weren't getting through.

'What's happening, Chief?'

'Superheat from the pipeline. It's boiling the water. If we had gotten in any closer . . . we were almost capsized as it was.'

'You think that's what happened to Chief Englebrecht?'

'We've got to get news of this back to the island. It's spreading. The whole pipeline is starting to superheat. It could explode any minute.'

'We're never going to get through by radio.'

'Make for shore fast,' the chief said. 'We'll reach them by telephone.'

The radio operator in the island tower scrutinized the radar screen worriedly.

'Jack,' he said to the radar man, 'you're sure this equipment is functioning properly?'

'Nothing wrong with *my* equipment,' Jack said. 'Well, hell, look out the window, Hubbard. You see any clouds? You see any flashes of lightning?'

Jack was right, of course. It was a gloriously starry night. Not a cloud anywhere. And yet *something* was causing interference on the air waves. Something close and strong and getting stronger every minute.

'You got snow here, Jack,' the radio operator said.

'Snow? What are you talking about, man?' Jack strolled over to confront the radar screen. 'Oh, that. Just some static from somewhere.'

'Maybe your equipment's picking it up, too.'

'If you're so worried about *it*, maybe you'd better put a call through to the man.'

'Maybe I will, Jack. Maybe I will.'

The radio operator went back to his console and sat down. He gave his co-worker the finger to his back and donned his headset. He flipped some filter switches on the console, adjusted the volume, and leaned back in his swivel chair. And for several minutes all he did was listen.

The noise on the air waves made his skin crawl. It was a high-pitched wail alternating with an incredibly strong pounding, like something trapped behind a door. It wanted out. It was in pain. It was becoming hysterical. Finally, he couldn't stand it anymore. He pulled his headset off and went to the observation windows. His eyes moved nervously over the calm panorama of a clear summer night. Something was out there, all right. But what? What could cause such powerful electro-magnetic disturbances? If sheer terror and chaos had a voice, that was what was buzzing through the earphones.

'You really got the willies, don't you?' Jack said. 'Put it back on the speakers. It don't bother me none.'

The radio operator said he'd rather not.

'Well, hell.'

Jack shook his head disgustedly and walked over to the radio to listen for himself. He held one of the earphones to his ear for several seconds. When he spoke again his voice was edgy.

'You picking this thing up on all frequencies?'

The radio operator nodded.

Jack turned the frequency-control knob on the console.

'Man,' he said, 'if this stuff gets any stronger . . . I think you better call Lombardy.'

'Jack,' the radio operator said, 'is it just my imagination, or is it getting darker in here?'

Jack reached for the telephone. 'Are you holding out because of what I said a while ago? I'm calling Lombardy before we get in a mess of trouble. I don't know what this stuff is, but it's knocking out the radio gear, man.'

Jack put the receiver to his ear and froze.

'Jack?'

Jack started shaking his head. He held the receiver out in front of him, staring at it uncomprehendingly. 'The telephone!' he said. 'It's in the goddamn telephone!'

The radio operator started for him.

So did everything metallic that wasn't heavy or nailed down. Jack let out a yell and ducked behind the console as an ashtray and screwdriver went sailing by his head.

Lombardy was explaining the shutdown procedure to a very concerned mayor.

'It's not like a kitchen oven or house furnace, where it's just a small step from turning the fire low to turning it off completely. We've got the reactor on low now, but it will be some time before it's completely shut down. An entirely different configuration of Boron inserts must be decided on and employed. Usually the main computer decides on which rods to use, but under the present circumstances . . . Don't worry. If I have to, I'll order the technicians to insert all the Boron rods, even if it causes irreparable damage to the core.'

For the first twenty minutes the procedure went on without any hitches. On the uppermost tier of the dome they watched monitor screen renditions of the fuel core lattice as the Boron rods were inserted. The computer's evaluation of the fission process at each point of entry by the rods was well within the predicted limits. And Lombardy, Ellison, all of them started wondering if they were wrong about the computer, after all. The rods were absorbing neutrons, the chain reaction was slowing to a halt, and the computer was accurately monitoring the whole process. Could the computer perform so impeccably with damaged circuits?

But when a technician from the bottom floor of the dome reached the top tier, out of breath, and pointed an accusing finger at the computer readouts, they knew they were in serious trouble.

'I tried reaching you,' the technician said. He held his walkie-talkie up disgustedly. 'Nothing but static. It's the same with the phones. I thought you stopped the shutdown procedure. That computer's lying. No Boron rods have penetrated the reactor core for fifteen minutes, or more.' The technician was looking at his watch and shaking his head. 'This damn thing has stopped.'

Lombardy read the man's name tag. 'Johnson.'

'Jensen, sir.'

'Jensen, are you sure you know what you're talking about?'

'I'm a technical observer on the bottom tier. I watch over the control rod operations and supply visual confirmation that the rods are operating properly. Well, they're not – operating, I mean.'

One of the scientists had taken Jensen's walkie-talkie and was listening to the static.

'This is absolutely amazing,' the scientist said.

Everybody with walkie-talkies was doing the same.

'Have you people lost your minds!' Lombardy snapped.

'Mr Lombardy,' the scientist said, 'look at your watch.'

'It's stopped.'

'So has everybody's else's. All at the same time. Something strange is happening, something very strange.'

The scientist was handing back Jensen's walkie-talkie. The small metal box left the technician's hand and sped toward the ceiling of the dome.

They were on auxiliary lighting again, battery lighting. Even the back-up generators were knocked out. And they had a limited amount of time to complete their work – if, indeed, they could complete it, Lombardy thought. There was only one man on the island who could supply the answers and tell them if they had any chance at all: the man who had designed the Super Reactor and who knew more about controlled nuclear fission than anybody else on the planet – Nichols. A nervous man, possibly a madman, was now their only hope for survival.

Lombardy wondered how he could break the news to Nichols without pushing him over the brink. Would he even be able to get through to Nichols? The man's condition had probably deteriorated since the morning. And there wasn't even time for psychiatric consultation. Lombardy, however, had one ace up his sleeve. He knew what made Nichols tick. The man was an androphile through and through. Nichols believed in the basic goodness of humanity. He believed that man had a destiny. According to Nichols, that destiny was to surmount a harsh and chaotic environment, to establish harmony and order, to live ultimately in peace with a Nature he had subdued and humanized. Man was an instrument of God placed in Nature to further God's creative work. Years ago Lombardy had learned it was these naïve beliefs that had kept Nichols first at Wilson's, then at General Power.

Nichols's state of mind during the years could explain his breakdown. Enrico Fermi was a modern-day messiah. And Nichols was a disciple. Nichols was, therefore, a special instrument of God. A man with a mission. A man whose task was to engineer a device that could place limitless power at humanity's disposal. Power to feed the hungry and shelter the homeless. Power to mould a hostile world in the image of God.

Nichols had taken upon his shoulders the burden of the world's future. In failing in his task, he had committed the ultimate failure.

Lombardy's plan was to make Nichols see things the way they really were. Maybe then Nichols's guilt would be dissipated. And he could function once again.

Nichols, motionless, lay on his bed in the dim light of battery back-up power while Lombardy poured his guts out. Wolford and Dr Miller, the staff psychiatrist, stood in a shadowed corner of the room, looking on. Wolford had expressed anxiety and Miller professional disapproval over what Lombardy was doing. But they had to acquiesce. What else could they do? It was a life-or-death situation.

After Lombardy had finished, Nichols continued to lie motionless, staring at the ceiling. Lombardy started wondering if anybody was home.

'Professor Nichols,' he said. 'Dennis.' Finally he sighed and stood up.

'Where's Slayer?' Nichols said. 'On the island?'

Lombardy, Wolford, Miller: they all did a double-take. Lombardy put his head down close to Nichols.

'You want to see Slayer?' he whispered.

'I want all the best minds on the island. At the dome. Right away. I need help.'

When Mason and Slayer entered the dome, they were greeted with the grim and frightened faces of the men and women technicians on the lower tiers. Some of them, like caged animals awaiting slaughter, seemed too terrified even to move. The lighting was bad and getting worse by the minute.

'Oh, shit, I'm seeing things,' he whispered to Slayer. 'There's mushrooms growing on the ceiling.'

'They're not mushrooms,' Slayer said.

'You mean you see them, too?'

'There's all kinds of stuff up there. Metal stuff. Somehow the dome has become a giant magnet.'

When they reached the top tier they found that everybody was waiting for them. Nichols, who seemed a lot older and more frail, prompted Slayer to speculate. His questioning was keen and sane. He seemed to have most of the answers already and was querying Slayer chiefly to fortify his own opinions. For the first time since his arrival on the island, Slayer felt like he was part of the science team.

'All the atoms in the steel girders which comprise the dome's skeletal structure are lining up pole to pole,' Nichols said. 'What does that say to you?'

126

'A very powerful magnetic field,' Slayer answered. 'Unbelievably powerful.'

'Yes,' Nichols said. 'And everything that's ferromagnetic is lining up. Slayer, you're the speculator, the man with the imagination. How is the reactor bringing this off?'

Slayer shook his head. 'We could kick that one around for months. Somehow the reactor is coverting heat energy to atomic spin. Angular momentum. I don't know. The important thing is to turn it off. We can speculate on the whys and wherefores at the post-mortem. Wait a minute. You can't turn it off. That's what you're saying. That's what this is all about.'

'Any machinery with ferromagnetic parts is knocked out,' Nichols said. 'Steel gears are used to insert the Boron rods. The gears have become magnetized and are locked up solid. The strongest man here can't even crank the rods in manually as long as those gears are frozen. And they'll stay frozen till the reactor is turned off by some other means.'

'Why haven't you gotten everybody out of the dome?' Slayer said. 'Without the rods, you've got no control. The reactor will go critical. Then it's a meltdown. Explosions. The dome itself could rupture. You've got to evacuate the whole island.'

'Think,' Nichols said. 'Think it all through. Nothing works. No vehicles. We're trapped here. Everything metallic is magnetized and will remain so till the reactor is turned off. Not with the rods. By some other means.'

'What other means? Listen. All the warning circuits will be affected by this field. Have you thought of that? Damnit, have you realized yet we can't even alert the city to the danger it's in?'

'We tried to get a message out by radio. We don't know if we got through. We used Morse. It had a better chance than voice through all the static. We didn't get a reply. And we won't be broadcasting again till the reactor is turned off *by some other means.*'

'Why do you keep saying that?' He looked Nichols in the eye and read something there. 'Yes . . . There may be an-

127

other way. We could take the rods off their tracks, or if you've got extra rods or even just chunks of Boron alloy, we could use that. The liquid sodium can be pumped out of the reactor for a few seconds. Then somebody can enter the fuel core through the service portal in a Widmark radiation suit. He can plant the Boron in position between the fuel rods by hand. Who do you have in mind for the job? Somebody you don't like, since it's almost certain death. Those Widmark suits can't perform miracles. I'm beginning to understand why you sent for me and where all this has been leading.'

'No,' said Nichols. 'You're wrong.' He turned to Mason. 'This is a job for a metallurgist, not a theoretical physicist.'

The whole idea was insane. What was worse, Mason was going to go along with it. Frantically, Slayer tried to dissuade his friend. But Mason wasn't listening. He was off on a trip, one of his danger trips. Did they know that about Dan? Have it conveniently on file some place? Dan loved to gamble with death. They knew it and were using it.

'Dan, listen to me. I must have been crazy to even suggest it was possible. Nobody can go into a reactor while it's on. The heat, Dan. Nothing can survive that heat. You'll be burned to a cinder.'

'You've seen the figures on the new Widmark suits,' Dan said. 'I got a good chance. Besides, how can I pass up an opportunity like this? The only human to walk right into a live nuclear super furnace? Not even Evel could follow an act like that.'

Were they all crazy? That, Slayer thought, could just possibly be the case. Magnetic fields of this intensity were a rarity on earth. Except for the most rudimentary physical properties, little about them was really understood. Prolonged exposure might affect biological processes, especially thought processes, which were electro-chemical in essence.

Nichols was explaining how Mason was going to beat the heat problem.

'We're not going to drain the liquid sodium coolant from the reactor core. That would only give you seconds for a job that will take you several minutes to complete. The Widmark suit is completely self-contained. It's like a diving bell with its own atmosphere. You should be able to move about through the liquid sodium the way you would through any fluid. That way the sodium can keep the outside temperature of your suit down just as it helps keep down the skin temperature of the fuel rods.'

The Widmark suit was an engineering wonder. Comprised of multiple heat and radiation shields, it weighed in at just over three tons. It was more robot than suit, a type of wrap-around machine with telescoping arms and legs. Inside, a man could extend his limbs to twenty feet or more. Though its weight was formidable, it operated on bionic principles of muscle amplification and could be easily manoeuvred by an eighty-pound weakling. All a man had to do was move his arms and legs in regular fashion; the machine did the rest. It walked, and stooped, and knelt, and reached. It was a mechanical extension of the body, with incredible strength.

Marvel though it was, the suit had never been tested under these terrifying conditions. And it was not specifically designed to operate in a liquid medium.

Still, Mason was prepared to carry it off.

The plan was simple in conception, and not much different from what Slayer had outlined under Nichols's prompting. Inside the suit and armed with a variety of Boron inserts, Mason would enter the top of the reactor through the service portal. He would then descend on wall staves parallel to the fuel lattice, examining the rods visually as he went along. At specified areas and at hot trouble spots he would place a Boron insert into the lattice structure and secure it to the fuel rods themselves with zirconium alloy clamps. Wherever placed, the Boron inserts would absorb the neutron emissions and bring the chain reaction to a stop. If it went well, the entire reactor could be shut down in less than thirty minutes.

Already, on the floor of the dome, they had the Widmark suit standing near the service portal. It was a cross between a medieval knight and something right out of a flying saucer. Its highly polished heat-reflective surface shot yellow rays of back-up lighting to all tiers and corners of the dome.

Technicians, acting like tailors, took measurements of Mason's arms, legs, and torso, and made adjustments inside the suit with special tools.

The success of the whole operation depended, from the very start, on a basic point of physics.

After the adjustments had been made on the suit, Mason got inside and found that he couldn't budge it an inch.

'Unfortunately, there are components in the bionic system that are ferromagnetic,' a suit technician said. He shrugged. 'Who could have foreseen this problem?'

'This *is* crazy,' Mason said.

'We thought so, too,' the technician admitted. 'When Professor Nichols ordered the suit's preparation even though it wasn't working, we thought . . . well, you know. But we were wrong. Nichols saw far in advance what nobody else saw. Maybe it takes a crazy man to be a genuis. We forgot about the Curie Point. Once we get you inside the service portal and the suit starts to heat up, the bionic components will shed their magnetism.'

'Yes,' Slayer added, 'but in the meantime, before the temperatures of those metal components reach their Curie Points and disrupt the magnetic alignments, you'll be helpless, entombed. If anything goes wrong . . . Dan, reconsider.'

'I will,' Mason said, 'if you can tell me what other chance we've got.'

Behind the service portal was an air lock with a second hatchway that opened directly into the reactor core. Because the reactor coolant combined violently with oxygen, atmospheres inside the air lock had to be swapped before that second hatchway could be opened.

Mason could feel and he could hear. He heard the service portal close and the hiss of the gas jets. It was just like Nichols had said:

'The sound vibrations will carry well through the metal parts of the suit so you'll be able to hear the portal close.' Nichols had spelled it all out, in advance, so there wouldn't be any surprises. 'After the air lock is filled with argon, the reactor hatchway will slide open and directly expose the Widmark suit to reactor heat. The surface of the suit will start to warm up rapidly. As soon as the photo-sensitive plates on the outside of the helmet become demagnetized, you will start receiving visual data on the small TV screen positioned in front of your eyes. You will get voice contact next with Slayer and the rest of us who will be standing by right outside the service portal. We'll be at the other end of this insulated telephone cable. It unwinds from the rear of your suit as you move along.'

While Mason waited for the second hatchway, he kept mixing Slayer's words in with Nichols's.

'You'll be helpless, entombed. If anything should happen . . . '

Something did. Mason heard the opening of the second hatchway and was immediately struck down by a force of tremendous magnitude. His head was jostled by the fall; he thought he might even have blacked out for a time. What had happened? It was as if he had been hit by a tidal wave. He lay on his back, trying to think. He was still alive; he was breathing; his heart was racing. Slayer was right. It was like a tomb! He was completely immobilized, in total darkness, cut off absolutely from the outside world. For the first time in his life he felt thoroughly helpless. He was trapped. His destiny was out of his hands. If he was going to die, he could at least use whatever time remaining to figure out what had killed him.

Could he actually feel the suit getting warmer? And what was this strange sensation in his arms and legs? The hair on his limbs was actually tingling, as if he were bathed in a turbulent fluid. Was it the increased air flow in the suit's internal cooling system? Or could he sense, in some mysterious empathetic manner, what was happening to the outer skin of the Widmark suit?

His ears kept popping. He felt he was being subjected to tremendous pressure. And he had to swallow constantly to alleviate the pain. His ears were filled with a crackling noise which gradually subsided enough for him to hear a human voice.

'Dan . . . Dan, are you all right? What's happening?'

It was Slayer's voice.

'Hello, George?'

'Dan!'

'Well, at least the damn phone is working.'

'Dan, what do you mean? What's the matter?'

'I'm flat on my ass. Something knocked me over. And I can't see. Maybe the suit got damaged.'

'We'll get you out right away.'

'No,' Mason said. He tried to sound calm, nonchalant. More the way Slayer would expect him to sound. 'I think I know what happened. And if I'm right, you can't open that service portal. It's a lot hotter in here than we anticipated. The fuel core must be pretty close to meltdown and the coolant has started to boil. The pressure is terrific. Wait a minute. My suit has just started to go visual.'

Slayer, Mathieu, Wolford, Lombardy, Nichols, Ellison: there were more than a dozen scientists and personnel staring silently at the phone box, listening to the static, waiting for Mason's voice to break through. Nichols put his hands out toward the service portal, like a man warming himself before a fire. He tested the surface with a fleeting touch. 'Hot,' he mumbled. 'It's far too hot.'

'Hello, George?'

'Yes, Dan, I'm here.'

'I can see – sort of, anyway. There's a lot of snow on my screen. The air lock is full of liquid sodium. That's what knocked me over. It shot in when the reactor hatchway opened up. The pressure is building again. I don't know how long that service portal can hold.'

'It will hold,' Nichols said. 'What about the bionic components? Have you got any movement yet?'

'I'm up on my knees. And I can feel my arms getting stronger.'

'Can you complete the mission?'

'I can't walk out of here through the service portal till I do.'

Nichols nodded his head and for the first time smiled. There was a general feeling of relief among the scientists and technicians, as if, till now, they hadn't allowed themselves the luxury of hope.

But Mason wasn't telling them the complete truth. He projected positive thinking over the phone while he struggled with a suit that was only seventy per cent functional.

Components must have been damaged in the fall. He could only lift his right arm to chin's height. And his left leg wouldn't bend at the knee. He had to drag it along the floor of the air lock like a lame man. And there was something else wrong, too.

The tingling sensation in his limbs had gotten stronger. It numbed his fingertips and toes. It was irritating, even distracting, and could interfere with his own effectiveness. He wondered if some malfunction in the machine's life-support system was responsible and whether that system would hold out for the duration.

Despite the suit's massiveness and bionic strength, he was being buffeted about by the extreme turbulence of the liquid sodium. He tottered on the brink of the reactor's maw and almost fell over the side as he placed his foot on the first wall stave. If he had gone over he would have fallen into the fuel core lattice, all three tons of him. Fuel rods would have bent and torn loose under his weight. He could have triggered off chemical explosions that would have ruptured the reactor's shielding, killing everybody in the dome. He could even have mangled the rods into a different geometrical configuration that would have created spontaneously an atom bomb explosion. For that was the secret of controlled nuclear fission: precise geometrical placement of the rods. When scientists said reactors couldn't blow up, what was always understood and seldom mentioned to the layman was the proviso: *as long as a correct geometrical spacing of the fuel rods is maintained.* Sudden close proximity of as little as one one-hundredth of one per cent of the plutonium in the reactor's core could produce a spontaneous nuclear chain reaction. Mason trembled as he considered the momentous implications of every step of his descent down the wall staves. Then he employed the trick used by every man accustomed to facing extreme and ultimate danger: he put it all out of mind. He had a task to perform. He would concentrate on that and only on that. He would break it down into steps, simplify it, get it done with consummate skill and accuracy. There was nothing else in the world to think about.

Much the same thoughts were going through Slayer's head, only he couldn't put them aside so readily. He saw fear and even open terror on the faces of his colleagues. But at last, he thought, the masquerade was over. They could no longer view themselves as keepers of the great Benevolent Angel. For what had held the image of a godsend had now revealed its true face. Incubating beneath the lead shielding under their feet was an ecological nightmare. An enemy of mankind and all things earthly. Anti-life.

Why couldn't man imitate nature? Fission material existed there only in a most rarefied and diluted quantity and form. It was as if a higher wisdom, the product of four billion years of evolution and experimentation in survival, had conspired to rid the planet of a monstrosity. But man had counter-plotted to open a door to that monstrosity. And a thing of indescribable horror, a monster which belonged in another time and place, an entity that could annihilate the world, waited.

'George?'

'Here, Dan.'

'I'm at the top of the fuel lattice now. It's not too bad here. I can see okay but visibility gets worse farther down. I'm going to position a Boron insert for practice. Also, I've got a numbing sensation in my extremities. Could it be a suit malfunction? Ask Nichols. I'd like to correct it if I could.'

The suit technicians conferred with Nichols. They shook their heads, shrugged their shoulders.

Mason came back on the phone.

'There. That was easy enough. This is a pretty fantastic suit. It seems to read my mind. I'm ready to move on to the next level. Got anything on this numbing sensation?'

Slayer looked at Nichols, who shook his head.

'We're still working on it,' Slayer said. 'Is the numbing becoming a problem?'

'No,' Mason lied. 'Just a discomfort. Don't worry about it.'

In fact, the numbness had become an intense electrical shock that spread throughout his whole body and made him grit his teeth in pain. The next time Mason's voice came over the phone box, everybody knew it was the end of everything.

'This is no good,' Mason said. 'I can't make it. I thought I could, but I can't. My head's about to bust open. I'm being electrocuted. Eddies, George. You got that? Charged eddies in the liquid sodium. The damn pumps are working so hard they're making whirlpools all around me. The whirlpools are acting like solenoids. Generating a tremendous electrical field. The suit's not insulating me enough. Liquid solenoids, George. A tremendous electrical field. That's the source of your magnetism.'

Slayer started shouting into the phone box.

'Get out of there, Dan! Get back to the air lock! We'll figure a way to get you out!'

'No good, George. You get out. Get out of the dome. Everybody. Get out of the dome! This reactor is going to blow the roof off and nothing can stop it!'

For several seconds nobody moved a muscle. Then, like a clap of thunder out of the blue, the panic began.

People started running for the dome exits. Hysterically. In droves, wide-eyed animals with fire at their heels.

'Keep you heads!' Lombardy shouted. 'Get to the fall-out shelters!' He turned to Nichols, Wolford, the essential science staff who were dumbstruck by this sudden turn of events. 'What the hell are you waiting for!' he yelled at them. 'You people, more than anybody, have to survive.' He started shoving bodies. He called for his security men by

135

name. 'Hank! Stan! Get these people to a fall-out shelter! Move it, goddamnit!'

It all happened so fast. Wolford was gone. The mayor was gone. Herded away like cattle. In the end, Slayer was left alone by the phone box with no one else in the entire dome except Lombardy.

Lombardy grabbed Slayer by the shoulders.

'Call him,' Lombardy ordered. 'Call him!'

'Dan. Dan, can you hear me?'

There was a long silence before the weak response.

'George . . . get out.'

Lombardy butted in.

'No, Dan. George is staying. He's staying till you finish your job.'

Slayer started for Lombardy, his face twisted by disbelief and hatred. Lombardy stiff-armed him.

'He's got to finish the job,' Lombardy hissed. 'He's still the only chance.'

'Can't,' Mason was saying. 'Can't do it.'

'You can do it,' Lombardy said.

'The pain's too much.'

'Oh, God!' Slayer yelled. His eyes were black with fury, and his angular face under the wild black hair was illuminated by rage.

'Listen!' Lombardy shouted. 'Wherever you are now, it doesn't matter. Take the Boron inserts from your pouch and throw them into the lattice. Come on, Dan. Move your arm! Take the inserts and throw them in!'

Mason was almost unconscious. In sheer reflex obedience, his arm started moving before he could piece the sounds of Lombardy's command together. He grabbed a handful of inserts and sent them flying. At the same time he lost his grip on the wall stave. He gouged out chunks of metal from the wall of the reactor core on his quick descent. He stretched his leg muscles and the feet of his suit telescoped out to meet the floor four yards ahead of his body. The extended limbs worked like shock absorbers and broke his fall.

Here on the bottom of the reactor core the turbulence was

at its peak. He was smashed into sections of the wall and carried around and around by a maelstrom. Centrifugal force had drawn the liquid sodium away from the fuel lattice and the heat build-up was incredible. The alloy jackets of the fuel rods bulged and bubbled and glowed with sun-like brilliance. Neutron emissions had run wild. The base of the fuel core was seconds away from meltdown.

Mason's body shook with the realization of what was about to happen. Several hundred pounds of plutonium were going to melt out of the fuel rods, pour down the throat of the maelstrom, and refreeze on contract with the liquid sodium. An instantaneous chain reaction would result which would take out the entire lower Mississippi Basin.

He had to stop it from happening. Before he died he had to stop it. He reached into his pouch and withdrew a variety of Boron inserts which he held in the talons of his suit like clusters of thunderbolts. He stepped forward into the maelstrom, planting his feet over the drain at its base and jamming his arms through the open spaces in the fuel core lattice. The steel skin of his suit started to bubble and melt away.

He tightened his leg and arm muscles to make sure the suit would remain rigid and in position after he was dead.

His final thoughts placed him miles away. A cool, gentle hand brushed the hair from his eyes. Sweet lips kissed away his tears. A loving caress enveloped his tired limbs.

'Kathy,' he said.

For a long time after, Slayer listened on the phone box, resigned, knowing that the end had come for his friend. Knowing that very soon it would be his turn.

Lombardy gently put his hand on Slayer's shoulder.

'I'm sorry,' he said. 'Very, very sorry. But I had to make him try.'

Slayer looked into his eyes.

Together they sat down on the floor of the dome and waited.

Chapter 28—Rescue

Al continued to observe the fleet of sailboats on his long causeway trek. They appeared in the dark waters like a string of Christmas tree lights unravelling from the marina in West End and nearing the steel dome. On board the lead craft, Coast Guard Commander Higgins watched the dome loom larger on the horizon, blocking out more and more stars. There was something about its massive presence, playing dead, like an extinct volcanic mountain having second thoughts. His blood ran cold. He did not move any closer to the dome. The boats would help Dottie better than he could. Now he could only wait.

Right after Coast Guard headquarters had received the warning from the island and Higgins had realized that a conventional rescue operation was not feasible, his junior officer had hit upon an idea. Sailboats.

'This is the weekend,' the officer had said. 'You've got all those yachtsmen sitting on their butts drinking beer down at the marina.'

Watching the dome now and feeling endless shivers take hold of his body, Higgins realized that half of them would be having second thoughts, as well: these weekend enthusiasts who had so magnanimously volunteered for a mission of mercy.

Higgins understood enough about human nature under stress to foresee an eleventh-hour copout. That was why he had placed a Coast Guardsman aboard every boat with orders to assume command, to threaten, abuse, or do whatever necessary to ensure that the crew and boat stayed on course.

But as the dome got nearer and his own anxiety grew, Higgins fretted that even that would not be enough. The dome was too foreboding.

The lead boats hadn't even neared the dock end of the island when the panic started. It was too dark to see what was happening. All Higgins and his crew could do was hear the sounds.

One of the crew said, 'We must have woken up the whole island population of seagulls!'

They listened hard as the boat got nearer.

'That's people!' Higgins said.

And nobody had to add 'terror-stricken.' The cries and shouts were unmistakable And the fear they conveyed was virile and contagious

Pale yellow light bled out of the dome at points of exit, exhibiting running, hysterical figures

'Christ!' somebody said.

The captain of the sailing yacht approached Higgins aft.

'Listen,' he said. 'Something pretty bad is going on here. I never bargained for this. I got a sixty-thousand dollar boat here. And my son-in-law is on board.'

'Stow it,' Higgins snapped. 'We're going to do what we came to do.'

People were hurling themselves off the edge of the island, smacking the water and thrashing widly.

'Damn,' Higgins said. 'They see our lights. They're taking a short-cut.'

'Lights out!' someone shouted.

'No!' Higgins countermanded. 'Lights on! All the lights! As many as we can get! Hard a' starboard. Let them see we're making a run for the docks.'

Higgins's plan was partially successful. People stopped jumping. But then there was a mad rush to get to the docks first.

The owner of the sailing yacht argued bitterly. He said they couldn't dock up under these conditions. A stampede on to the boat would capsize it. The sane thing to do was turn back.

Higgins ordered the boat to lay off the docks while he thought hard and hoped for a miracle.

*

The numbness in Wolford's head was replaced by a searing pain. She went down on one knee and felt those hands pulling her up and forward. She tried running and managed only to stumble along while an arm reached around her waist to give her falling body support. Her vision was severely blurred; the sounds she heard were chaotic and meaningless. She couldn't remember why she was running or even where she was. Only an overwhelming sense of impending peril kept her feet moving. Finally, she went down again. Her mind was inundated with terrifying images. She saw herself being pushed and squeezed through a narrow aperture by a wall of human flesh. She could not breathe. Her nostrils were flared. The air was thick with the aroma of human fear. She felt sick to her stomach. She clawed and fought her way to the outside. In the process she was knocked to the ground by a two-hundred-pound man who trampled across her as if she were not there at all. She felt the searing pain again in her head and found herself lying on the steps to the dome before an avalanche of people. She tried to stand but couldn't. She shouted and pleaded. No one noticed her as the avalanche descended. Feet rushed over her with bone-crushing blows. She cried out in agony and threw her arms up over her face. She called upon a deity in whom she did not believe and waited for the pain to be over.

Her life did not flash before her, as she had heard it might. Instead, a sense of frustration and utter loss took hold of her. She was to die without ever having really lived.

Hands reached under her arms, firm and gentle hands which she clutched to her chest. She was being urged by those hands, urged to her knees, to her feet, urged to move onward. Strength came into her limbs with the knowledge that someone was going to remain with her, go down with her, if she did not help herself. Those hands were there to stay.

'You,' Wolford sighed. 'It's you. Somehow I knew.'

The mayor tugged helplessly at Wolford's arms. She was so exhausted herself by now she could scarcely talk.

'Mary, get up. We're almost at the docks. There are boats. Get up! Mary!'

Wolford tried, then shook her head. 'It's no use.' She cringed at the sight of people running past. She felt pain in her chest as she spoke. 'You've done all you could. You've got to save yourself. Get to a fall-out shelter. The boats are no good. They'll be capsized. You can't stop this panic.'

'I'll stop it.'

More people came running by them. A man collided with the mayor and knocked her down.

'Noooooo!'

Wolford's scream was a shrill banshee wail which stopped the man in his tracks. He looked down at the woman he had struck.

'Help us,' Mayor Mathieu pleaded.

The man seemed to come out of a trance. He put his hand to his head and surveyed the chaos. He looked back in the direction of the dome and stammered, 'It's going to . . . blow!'

'Help us,' the mayor repeated. 'Help us get to the docks.'

Slowly the man started nodding his head.

'Yes.' he said. 'Yes, I'll help.'

'Commander, that group of people at eleven o'clock.'

'I got them, Lieutenant. What does it look like to you?'

'Two men carrying a woman.'

'Ten o'clock. More of the same. They're bringing up their wounded to get them on the boats first. That's it, Lieutenant. Let's get in there!'

Professor Nichols saw Wolford being helped aboard the sailing yacht. Then he stumbled away from the dock area to the seclusion of a narrow alley between two storage buildings. He sat down on the concrete and pushed his back against the wall.

The evacuation was taking too long. Maybe the first few boats could get out of range before it happened. But even that wasn't likely. He sighed deeply. Yesterday he would have believed implicitly in the steel dome's ability to withstand rupture from any explosion.

'Believed implicitly,' he said out loud.

He was condemned by his own words. He had believed too much about too many things. If he didn't *know* what the reactor was capable of doing, who on God's earth did? The computers? They had always verified his figures, backed him up, showed through model construction and analysis that the Super Reactor was a perfectly safe machine. His allies, the computers. His mirror image. All they had to go on was the data he supplied; the sum total of their mentality was the programmes *he* had designed. All they could ever do was make explicit his *beliefs*.

'Parrots,' he said aloud. 'For years the genius has been listening and nodding to the mindless squawking of parrots.'

He started laughing and found he couldn't stop. He was like two people. The spectator lamented that he had not become a crazy old man years ago.

Inside the dome Lombardy and Slayer came to the same realization at about the same time.

'How long has it been now?' Lombardy said.

'Yeah,' said Slayer.

They both stood up. If something was going to happen, it should have by now.

Lombardy put his hands against the service portal and withdrew them quickly.

'You can't go by that,' Slayer said. 'It'll take a long time for that much heat to dissipate.'

He began strolling around the floor of the dome, eyeing objects which clung to the ceiling. As the time passed, his hopes grew. Could it be that Dan had somehow accomplished the impossible? He spotted a large metal trash-can suspended near the very centre of the ceiling. It had to be one of the heavier objects up there. He sat back down, Indian fashion, and put all of his concentration on that can. Lombardy caught on and started his own systematic scanning of the clinging bric-a-brac. When the can finally began to move, they both came to attention.

'It's not my imagination?' Lombardy said.

'I saw it, too,' Slayer answered. 'It moved, all right.'

Very slowly the can detached half the perimeter of its brim from a steel girder. It tottered, rolled, lost its grip. Two seconds later it crashed into the concrete floor. A flashlight was next, then an ashtray. A rain of metal objects commenced as the magnetic field rapidly diminshed in strength.

'He did it,' Lombardy said incredulously. 'Dan Mason did it. He shut down the reactor!'

Chapter 29—Post-Mortem

'We came that close,' one of the reactor technicians said. With help he freed one arm from the Widmark suit and held his forefinger and thumb a half-inch apart for all to see. 'That close.' Suit technicians worked to free his other limbs.

Close by, in another Widmark suit, Slayer stood silently, awaiting his turn at divestment. He and the reactor technician had gone into the core to look things over and to retrieve Mason's body. They had returned empty-handed.

Lombardy assisted the suit technicians, whom he thought were taking too long, in getting Slayer out. Slayer's face was grim and Lombardy did not start the debriefing till after Slayer's third cup of coffee in the staff lounge.

'What will it take to get Dan out of there?' Lombardy said.

Slayer didn't answer right away. He was trying to control his resentment towards Lombardy, resentment which was aggravated by Lombardy's use of Dan's first name. At least Lombardy was not asking about the condition of the reactor core first.

'I don't know what it will take,' Slayer said finally. 'I'm not even sure Dan's still there. All we found was a melted lump with a pseudopod holding up a cluster of Boron inserts. Parts of the pod are enmeshed in the fuel core lattice. I'm almost sure the suit was ruptured while it was melting. If it did, flesh and bone would have boiled away in a matter of seconds.'

Lombardy nodded. The muscles in his face went lax. Slayer saw the sorrow in his eyes.

Slayer's mind began to work on two levels. He continued to answer Lombardy's questions; he supplied data about the condition of the reactor core; he corroborated statements made by the reactor technician; but all the while another part of him brooded. A man was dead. Perhaps the only man he loved. A man who said he cared nothing for other men, but had given his life to save them.

He wanted to get away. From the dome, from Lombardy, from his work. He wanted to shake off the dust he had accumulated these past several years. It was as if a lengthy experiment had finally terminated. He wanted to close up shop, call it a day, go home. He wanted to return to his own people. He looked down at his arm, at the chestnut skin which suddenly seemed too pale. He was remembering how tawny he was as a boy under the heat of the desert.

Now that the crisis was over, Professor Nichols was again preoccupied with vague misgivings which had something to do with Slayer and which made his right hand shake in involuntary spasms. He had to hide his hand in his lap from time to time so as not to attract attention. The staff psychiatrist, who would like nothing better than to return him to his rooms and put him back on sedatives flitted about the top tier of the dome like a mosquito.

When Slayer left the dome, Nichols watched him out of the corner of his eye. He continued his calculations with the aid of a hand computer. And the results of the calculations continued to be puzzling. Nichols would have liked Slayer to stay for more questioning on what he had seen down there in the reactor core: Slayer was a better source of information than the reactor technician, a better observer, and something he might say might provide an answer to these riddles

144

the calculator was spitting out. Still, Slayer was tired and mourning for his friend and probably past the stage of being able to think acutely. Weren't they all?

Also, there was Nichols's nervous hand, which got worse when Slayer was around. The shaking hand was accompanied by a deep, dark, seething, irrational panic. Why did he fear Slayer? He turned the thought around in his head until he was dizzy.

Slayer's equations imposed limitations. In tapping energy from the nucleus, you can only go so far; that's what the equations really said. You can only go so far.

Chapter 30—Union

She was asleep and didn't appear to be hurt very badly. But he remained anxious until Mary Wolford sighed and tossed her head, showing by the smile on her face that she was having pleasant dreams.

His plan had been to go straight to Jackson from the island. He had made Dan Mason a promise which he intended to keep, no matter what the cost to his own sanity. Kathy had a right to know what had happened and she had a right to hear it from him. He had decided he would tell her everything. She had a right to learn how even Slayer had aided and abetted the death of his friend. Then he would leave the island behind. He would go back to the deserts of New Mexico, to his roots, and never return to New Orleans.

But someone had mentioned *Wolford's* name.

His mind had not been thinking too clearly, his ears not hearing very well. What did that man say? What did he say about Mary Wolford? He collared a co-worker like a madman and demanded to be told. They grabbed his arms and calmed him down and said last night there had been a panic.

How he had found his way to the St Tammany Parish Hospital or driven his truck through the heart of Covington without killing someone, he could not say. He was like a poor dog, demented and blinded with disease, crashing headlong into objects in its path. He had smashed his truck into railings and a tree and demolished a fire hydrant before reaching the hospital.

And only now, with the vision of her sleeping form before him, had he begun to return to his senses. He was standing back from the open doorway to her room near the opposite wall and watching her chest rise and fall with reassuring regularity. Then she had tossed and smiled and he knew she was going to be all right. When she smiled it seemed his very life came back to him.

Someone – perhaps she had been well enough to do it herself – had brushed her raven-black hair straight back. He had not seen her widow's peak before, nor appreciated fully the elegance of her oval face. Her thick hair blanketed the pillow, and a few strands, like wisps of clouds, fell across her smile. Her face was a pale moon glowing evenly, lovingly in a charcoal sky.

It was then that she opened her fire-blue eyes. He paused briefly to close the door behind him, then he was at her side, bending over her, wondering why he had never noticed the eyes before when now their deep blue was stealing all his thoughts.

He kissed her. At first she thought it was a part of her dream, for the act blended so well with her fantasies. She clung to his lips, needy and searching. When they parted, the mind of the scientist returned, and she became reticent and matter-of-fact.

'Hello! It's so good of you to come.'

Her brain was back on automatic pilot, keeping him at a distance, though another part of her struggled desperately to draw him to her . . .

'I was sorry to hear you were hurt,' he said.

She shrugged and tried not to look at his eyes. 'I'll be out of here in two or three days. Just a couple of cracked ribs.

No concussion. I don't know why they're keeping me at all.'

She was perspiring. She could not stop thinking about wanting him. Suddenly they were kissing again, and she drew back.

'Why fight against it?' he was saying. 'Something has happened to us.'

She knew it was true. Even before she had awakened she had been in his arms. His presence had seemed so natural, as if he were meant to be there. Something had happened. Yet she could not bring herself to tell him it was true.

'Well, what about you?' she said, desperately seeking neutral ground. 'Are you okay?'

When he nodded she went on about how she was malingering. He really shouldn't have bothered coming to see her. She would be back on the island in no time. She mumbled about how awful she looked and finally excused herself, saying she had to brush her hair, it was all knots. In the bathroom she closed the door before he could protest.

She looked at herself in the full-length mirror on the inside of the door, demanding to know if she was really a hopeless case.

And then a strange calm came over her, a calm that was as natural as her life and her attraction to Slayer. She opened the door to the bathroom and went back to him . . .

Chapter 31—Analysis

By noon, investigative teams of scientists and technicians, working independently, presented Lombardy with two reports. Each report purported to explain, in a preliminary fashion, the demise of the Super Reactor by placing yesterday's events in their proper cause – effect relationships.

Report #1 commenced with the rupture of the Kenner pipeline at approximately 5.58 a.m. of 2 July and proceeded chronologically:

'This rupture caused a sizeable quantity of liquid sodium coolant to escape, thus triggering several events both inside and outside the reactor core: (1) deprived of sufficient coolant, the fuel lattice began to superheat; (2) the drop in coolant pressure set off the alarm system and cut off the prime generators in the power plant of sector six; (3) the switch-over to back-up power damaged electrical circuits in the main computer system; (4) the damaged computer circuits masked the true condition of the fuel core lattice; (5) the drop in coolant pressure coupled with the superheating of the lattice activated special safety devices within the coolant system; these devices augment the speed of the coolant pumps; (6) the increased speed of the pumps caused eddies in the coolant enveloping the lattice core; (7) these eddies, through a combination of their centrifugal and centripetal forces, drew additional quantities of coolant away from the lattice core, thus compelling the lattice to overheat further; (8) these eddies of liquid metal became solenoids manufacturing a magnetic field in a manner analogous to the manner in which the north and south magentic poles are generated by rotational eddies within the molten-iron core of the earth; (9) the magnetic field produced by the eddies caused ferromagnetism in steel components of the reactor's shutdown system; (10) the reactor became unable to be shut down by conventional means; (11) human intervention became necessary for prevention of meltdown; (12) meltdown was prevented by a human agent implanting a Widmark suit over one of the three main coolant drains and allowing it to melt; (13) blockage of the drain by the melted suit disrupted the formation of eddies and returned geometrical distribution of reactor coolant to normal; (14) Boron insertion by human agent dampered chain reaction and reduced heat output of fuel core lattice; (15) reduction of heat output further disrupted the formation of eddies, thus reducing the strength of the magnetic field; (16) reduction in strength of magnetic field allowed reactor shutdown system to partially refunction; (17) shutdown was effected in part by the refunctioning of conventional system and in part by Boron inserts positioned in the fuel core lattice by a human agent.'

Report #2 read much the same, except that it began by postulation maverick neutron emissions which caused the coolant to superheat in the first place, in turn causing the Kenner pipeline to rupture. The conclusion of Report #2 smacked of Slayerism and was disturbing.

'We feel there is an uncertainty principle governing the behaviour of highly fissionable material in large quantities, making it all but impossible to predict the occurrences of dangerous events such as maverick neutron emissions. It may also be that this uncertainty principle governs the behaviour of the machinery designed to control and derive beneficial results from highly fissionable material. In this respect we note that safety devices themselves helped drive the reactor towards meltdown, thus effecting the very results they were designed to prevent.'

Lombardy read the reports again. He was very much aware of Nichols's presence and glanced repeatedly at his seated form. Whenever Lombardy thought of Nichols, whenever he pictured Nichols in his mind, it was always in this manner: a man seated, back hunched and head bent over a table filled with formulae and calculations; a man apart, whose only soul-mates and friends were the computers. (Whom else could Nichols really talk to?) He wondered briefly whether Nichols felt a sense of loss, now that the main computer was silenced. The hand computer to which Nichols had been forced to resort was hardly a worthy substitute. It was rather like replacing one's child prodigy with an infant Mongoloid.

In many ways the reports were an indictment of Nichols and his invention by his peers. And Lombardy had reservations about showing them to him. Still, Nichols's opinion was invaluable and he needed his support once again.

'Well?' Lombardy said after Nichols had perused the reports.

'Poppycock!' Nichols said.

Lombardy sighed, exasperated. 'You have a better theory

about what happened?'

'This *appears* to be what happened. But I've been doing some figuring. Things just don't equal out. We don't have the whole story yet. Too much time elapsed between the start of the eddies and their disruption. We should have had a meltdown. I just don't understand it. My equations don't balance. Something is very wrong. There were huge amounts of heat liberated by the fuel core, still unaccounted for. Where did it go? Something's very, very wrong.'

Lombardy squinted down at the tremorous hand which Nichols was trying to conceal in his lap.

'I'm not imagining things,' Nichols said.

'I didn't say you were,' Lombardy answered.

Chapter 32—Black Tags

TV reporters with a portable mini-camera were being held at bay in the administration building's foyer. Lombardy had hoped to placate them with junior officers of GP who had been freed to tell all regarding their hair-raising narrow escape during the night in the face of disaster. The junior officers Lombardy had picked for the job were low-brow administrative appendages, practically errand boys, who had no real knowledge of yesterday's events from a science point of view. They could tell little more than what the reporters would already know. But they were talkers, every one of them, hypochondriacs and martyrs, who would embellish last night's events with their little hardships. Their stories might contain some human interest angles and so distract the reporters from honing in on the more profound issues. Lombardy knew he was only buying time. Sooner or later he would have to face public scrutiny. He just wanted to put it off till he got his head together, sorted out some things, took care of the more pressing problems. But it was hot and everybody was irritable. He got the word on the reporters.

They were howling for him. His little ploy wasn't working.

As unobtrusively as possible, Lombardy cornered Miller, the psychiatrist.

'I'm very worried about Professor Nichols,' Lombardy said. 'He's done an extraordinary job. We couldn't have made it without him. But he's tired. Nervous. I don't want to do him harm by keeping him here.' Lombardy refrained from mentioning the uncontrollable hand.

'I'll have him off the island in fifteen minutes,' Dr Miller said.

'I already have a car waiting. Get him a hotel. I don't want him in a hospital. Take whatever help you need.'

'You're being very sensible. I think Professor Nichols is on the verge of hysteria.'

'Can a man be that disturbed and still remain fully rational?'

'Professor Nichols's rationality has never been at issue.'

Later, Lombardy approached Ellison, again in charge of science.

'All that heat,' Lombardy said. 'All that time. How do you suppose we avoided a meltdown?'

Ellison was sullen.

'Damn lucky.' He said nothing more.

Other scientists Lombardy queried either concurred with Ellison or hadn't given it any thought at all.

'What are you getting at?' one of them asked.

Lombardy shrugged.

'Probably nothing,' he answered.

Ferromagnetic problems still lingered in the island's switchboard. And Lombardy had to do all his phoning from the pay phone in the dome's staff lounge. The connections he got were weak and crackled with interference, but they were discernible. He had been calling Wilson, Nevada, all morning, trying to get in touch with Carlleston, Carlleston was conveniently indisposed. So were all of the six vice-presidents. Lombardy couldn't even get hold of an executive secretary. All of Wilson must be an angry anthill by now, he thought. Ten to one they're having a round-the-clock closed meeting

151

for all division heads trying to decide on a plan of action. It was an insult of the highest order that they had not returned his calls. He was top man at the dome, even if he wasn't going to be in the future.

Finally he decided to place the call he dreaded most. This time he dialled the downtown New Orleans number which he had extracted from Mason's personnel file. Somebody had to tell Mason's girl about what had happened.

Repeatedly he got no answer. At last a nosy and very annoyed landlady who was not above using her pass key picked up the phone and wanted to know who was disturbing all her tenants. He explained there was an emergency situation. She grunted and read him the note Kathy had left for her room-mate.

Dan had been so worried about the reactor that he'd talked his girl into going up to Jackson. Lombardy wagered that Slayer knew about this. It would certainly explain Slayer's absence from the island all morning, and, dammit, he needed Slayer back here. The things that Nichols had been saying were puzzling and worrisome. If Slayer had gone up to Jackson, it would take him a good six hours to make the round-trip. Maybe more. He wouldn't get back till late afternoon.

When Lombardy returned to his glass office on the top tier of the dome, he found it had been invaded, stealthily and swiftly by twenty or more Black Tags from Wilson. He found, too, that he was no longer in charge.

A smug Ellison was conferring with three Black Tags at the computer control board. Inside the glass office three more Black Tags were raking Security Chief Warner over the coals.

Lombardy tried entering and found the door to his own office locked. The Black Tags looked at him through the glass wall. There was a momentary respite in Warner's interrogation while one of the Black Tags came forward. He opened the door a crack and smiled amiably. 'We'll be finished in a minute, Mr Lombardy,' he said. 'Then we

152

would like to confer with you.' The door reclosed and Lombardy was left speechless.

Black Tags were like bank auditors. They could examine anything and everything. And they had final and absolute power subject only to Carlleston. They were, in fact, Carlleston's private secret police force.

When Warner came out of the office he was flushed. He glanced furtively at Lombardy as he passed and muttered, 'They're hungry for blood.'

'Mr Lombardy, come in, please. And close the door behind you.'

Stiffly, Lombardy did as ordered.

'We took the liberty of turning the air conditioning back on,' one of the Black Tags said. He introduced himself as Barry Blume. 'How can you stand working in this heat? How can you think straight?'

Barry Blume was Carlleston's number-one hatchet man. Lombardy knew him by reputation only.

'The heat up here is nothing compared to the lower levels,' Lombardy said. 'The reactor is still radiating even though it has been shut down. The independent generators can only do so much. I channelled all available power on the island to the air-conditioning units on the lower tiers. Most of the work is being done there and I don't want my men to have heat strokes.'

'Well, there's work to be done up here, too,' Blume said dryly. 'Thinking-type work.'

Lombardy sat while Blume paced. Blume had just finished reading through the two reactor reports Lombardy had prepared. He turned back a page or two, thumped his brow, and frowned.

'Let me get a few things straight,' he said. 'How many people were killed in the Howard Johnson's explosion?'

'The final count was forty-two,' Lombardy said.

'Forty-two. And Sam Webre, the causeway attendant; and we'll count that boy who was swimming. That's forty-four. Then there was Assistant Security Chief Englebrecht and his four-man boat crew. And, of course, Dan Mason.

153

That brings the total casualty list to fifty. Yet, here in the report summation, you state that the reactor is responsible for one hundred and thirty-two deaths?'

'That's right,' Lombardy said. 'Delta Flight 722 had seventy-four passengers and eight crewmen. Eighty-two people. Plus fifty: One hundred and thirty-two.'

'Nobody knows what made that plane go down.'

'Everybody knows what made that plane go down. The magnetic field generated by the reactor was enormous. Everything electrical was knocked out for miles.'

'The plane's flight recorder has not been recovered.'

'That's besides the point.'

'Oh?' said Blume. 'I should think that was very much to the point, indeed. It's bad scientific – and legal – practice to jump to conclusions. Now, as for the list of wounded, are these figures completely accurate?'

'To the best of my knowledge,' Lombardy said.

'One hundred and sixty-three people wounded at the Howard Johnson's. And another twenty-six people . . . right here on the island? That must have been some evacuation. Haven't you people been complying with safety regulations, having practice hazard drills, and so forth?'

'You know we have,' Lombardy said.

'That brings the total of wounded to one hundred and eighty-nine. Plus fifty dead. We'll suspend judgement on that plane. The burden of proof is on the airline. You know, that's not a bad figure.'

'Since you're doing this by figures,' Lombardy said, 'let me mention a few. There are almost ten tons of plutonium in the fuel core lattice and breeding chambers of the reactor. And we've been running the reactor at various test levels for the past six months. For the last two days we were running it at maximum capacity. There are more radioactive waste products and fissionable material in this dome than in all the atomic and hydrogen bombs exploded on or under the earth since the start of the atomic age. And early this morning we were seconds away from unleashing that power and poison on the people of the southern Mississippi Basin. We were just seconds away from annihilating the human race for a hundred-miles radius. No manipulation of casualty figures can mask that reality.'

'Nobody's trying to mask anything,' Blume said. 'Let's move on.' He flipped through several more pages of the report. 'Some of these comments sound like the work of George Slayer. How much of this report is he responsible for?'

'He didn't write any of it. As a matter of fact, he isn't even here.'

'Nowhere on the island?' Blume said. 'Strange he would leave at his moment of triumph, so to speak.'

'Slayer's not like that,' Lombardy said. 'As a matter of fact, he's performing a personal obligation. He blames himself for Dan Mason's death.'

'Oh?' said Blume, 'How so?'

'I'm not sure. He probably feels that if he hadn't written up his ideas about the Super Reactor, we wouldn't have had a test run and Mason would still be alive.'

'I understand that Professor Nichols is absent from the island, as well.'

'Yes.'

'What is his problem?'

'He's a very tired man.'

'I understand, from some members of your staff, it goes deeper than that. Why didn't you mention Professor Nichols's condition yesterday when Mr Carlleston called?'

'What condition is that?'

Blume smiled. 'Come now, Mr Lombardy. Are you saying that everybody on the island knew about Nichols's neurosis except you?'

'I'm not an expert on mental health. Neither are the members of my staff. You'll have to ask Dr Miller about Professor Nichols's frame of mind.'

'Yes,' Blume said, 'Dr Miller, the company psychiatrist, who is also absent from the island.'

Lombardy said nothing.

'Now,' Blume continued, 'about Chief Warner. I have my

155

doubts about the man. Not about his loyalty to this company, of course – his loyalty is beyond reproach. I'm concerned about his competency.'

'Chief Warner is entirely competent,' Lombardy said.

'As chief security officer it was Warner's job to find the man or men responsible for the reactor breakdown. I came here expecting positive results. And what do I find? An investigation that is practically nonexistent. He couldn't even supply a list of suspects. I told him we suspected infiltration of our company by one of our competitors. I asked if he had at least investigated personnel records to establish who might possibly have mixed loyalties. And do you know what he said? That he could only remember one name right off. Yours. He said, "Mr Lombardy came to us from Westinghouse." What do you think about that?'

Lombardy stood up.

'You're doing a great disservice to this company,' Lombardy said. 'And so is Carlleston. You might save face by pushing the idea that a saboteur is responsible for what happened here, but only for a time. Meanwhile, the point of our failure here will be lost. General Power or Westinghouse or somebody else will build another Super Reactor or maybe even reactivate this one. Then it will happen again. But next time we might not be so lucky. In the wink of an eye we could kill over ten million people. Don't try to find a scapegoat. Don't polish the company emblem at the expense of truth. In the end you'll be found out. And at a terrible cost to yourselves and the rest of humanity.'

Chapter 33—Simon Says

RAY WATKINS, of WWL-TV: 'Mr Lombardy, how soon were you notified about the plane crash this morning?'

LOMBARDY: 'As soon as our radio equipment started working again. I believe around four-thirty this morning.'

WATKINS: 'You were incommunicado all that time? Starting from about midnight you had no idea what was happening to the outside world?'

LOMBARDY: 'We had no knowledge of specifics. But we had a good idea of what must have been happening.'

SARA TREBEL, of WDSU-TV: 'Could you elaborate on that, please?'

LOMBARDY: 'We knew what effects the magnetic field was producing on the island, and it wasn't hard for our scientists to calculate its strength. We knew, for example, that all boats and cars would be inoperable for several miles beyond the perimeter of the island.'

LYNN ABEL, of the *States-Item*: 'And that's why you radioed the Coast Guard not to attempt an evacuation? Because you thought any attempt would fail?'

LOMBARDY: 'That's right.'

ABEL: 'I bet you were glad to see all those sailing vessels. Did it come as a surprise?'

LOMBARDY: 'Yes. We had completely overlooked that possibility.'

ABEL: 'I guess even scientists can fail to see the obvious.'

LOMBARDY: 'Yes, Miss Trebel?'

TREBEL: 'Wouldn't it be more accurate to say not that you overlooked a possible rescue by sailboats, but that you thought it unfeasible under the circumstances? I mean you really didn't think you had that much time left, did you?'

LOMBARDY: 'No, I just think nobody here on the island thought about sailboats.'

ABEL: 'There's talk about awarding the Medal for Merit to the men of the New Orleans Yacht Club for their part in the rescue operations. Would you like to see them get such an award?'

LOMBARDY: 'I certainly would. I think what those men did took a lot of courage.'

TREBEL: 'Mr Lombardy, what does the "Chinese Effect" mean to you?'

LOMBARDY: 'I believe you mean the "China Effect." Physicists use that term to describe the inability of all earthly

157

substances to contain plutonium in a molten state. Theoretically, molten plutonium could eat its way through the earth itself – right though to China.'

TREBEL: 'Then under certain conditions things could get totally out of hand and there would be nothing you could do to avoid a serious accident.'

LOMBARDY: 'I think that's true of any human undertaking.'

DEXTER MORPHY, of Associated Press: 'Mr Lombardy, you don't know me. I'm down here from New York to report on the official unveiling of General Power's Super Reactor, which was supposed to be tomorrow. Two questions. Why was the reactor already operating at full power? And how long will the unveiling be delayed by yesterday's unfortunate accident?'

LOMBARDY: 'We were operating the reactor at full power as part of a test programme to better determine safety parameters prior to delivery of the reactor to Louisiana Power and Light. And as for your second question. I don't know the answer.'

TREBEL: 'Mr Lombardy!'

ABEL: 'Mr Lombardy!'

LOMBARDY: 'Mr Watkins.'

WATKINS: 'You're staring to make my skin crawl. I get the feeling something enormous happened here last night. Are you going to start levelling with us?'

TREBEL: 'Your people here. Scientists and technicians. All professionals. What made them panic like that? What made them almost trample one another to death trying to get off this island?'

LOMBARDY: 'Up till last night very few people on the island would have believed the Super Reactor was anything but one hundred per cent safe. Last night the reactor started to show its true colours. Special alloys we had thought incapable of melting in all foreseeable circumstances melted. Machinery for shutting down the reactor in an emergency situation failed to operate. Safety devices designed to prevent nuclear catastrophe behaved unpredictably. We came within seconds of a disaster that would have made Hiroshima and

158

Nagasaki look like child's play. You people here today would either be dead by now or walking dead men. There's going to be a lot of red-hot debate in the next few weeks over when this complex should ever be reactivated. Most of my superiors will be disagreeing with me; I probably won't be around. That's why I want to give it to you straight. I don't ever want to see this complex reactivated. I don't ever want to see General Power or any of its competitors build another Super Reactor. I don't think they are safe or reliable machines, and I don't think they can ever be made safe. There are too many unknowns involved. I did not come to this conviction quickly, and my superiors do not share it. They will try to convince you I am wrong. When they do, I want you to remember one thing. They were not on the island last night. I was.'

Chapter 34—Ally

The mayor knew why there was so much traffic on the down-town streets and boulevards. And the knowledge made her uneasy.

A faded Buick convertible pulled even with her at the stoplight on St Charles and Jackson. The five youths in the car were restless and impatient for the light to change. They were in the same hurry as the score of other cars that had passed her since she left the Loyola campus, doing five, ten, fifteen miles better than the speed limit. They didn't care where they went; they had to get away.

It was because of the heat. The air was still and oppressive. There were no air conditioners, no cold water. When people got hot they became disturbed, belligerent. And the first sign of the mounting tension was the traffic. Trapped and nervous, people turned to their cars, though they were hurting themselves more than helping. The engine and friction heat, the hot fumes: they all took their toll. And on a day like today, with nothing moving . . . Damn, she said to herself, why did people have such short-range vision!

Commerical buildings, except for hotels, were largely empty. Not all businesses had closed for the Third, but enough to increase the mayor's uneasiness. People at work, performing tasks, giving and taking orders, would still suffer from the heat, but they would have less time to brood.

When the mayor got to Lee Circle, she turned left for City Hall. She had a premonition of what the Hall would be like when she arrived. Everyone would be up in arms, from the water commissioner to the chief city councilmen. They would be clamouring for her, as if she could somehow make things right. And if she couldn't, then at least they could blame her.

She knew, too, there would be reporters. But she hadn't expected them in such profusion. When she got to Perdido Street, she spotted a camera truck from Channel 6. She drove her car past the promenades so she could get a better view of the parking areas. There were three more camera trucks and an assortment of bright red, orange, and yellow automobiles. Reporters were always loud. A seasoned politician could spot them in a crowd just by their dress, or, as now, by the gaudiness of their cars.

Many of the reporters' cars either had out-of-state licence plates or were leased. And this she found puzzling, till she remembered. Her already pale face turned white and her mouth twisted in a grimace of realization. The city was playing host to newsmen from all parts of the country who had come to see General Power's Super Reactor go into operation on the Fourth. The eyes and ears of the entire world were on her city. And suddenly she felt the full weight of yesterday's events.

How was she going to explain what had happened? The city was without power on the eve of what was supposed to be the greatest day in the history of power development. Not only that. She had to make a complete about-face. She had to go before a public she had cajoled and wooed on behalf of nuclear energy and convince them she had been wrong.

How was she going to do that and remain credible? In their eyes she would be a fickle, unreliable woman, the stereotype she'd fought against, or worse. She'd just be one more lying, conniving politician who had sold them down the river.

She couldn't allow that to happen. The future of her city was in danger. GP was going to do everything in its power to patch up its Super Reactor and cram it down the people's throats. She had to find a way to stop the inevitable tragedy. She had to.

Shirley, her secretary, looked up at her with surprise and relief when she strolled through the door to the outer office.

'Everybody in the world is looking for you,' Shirley said. 'And aren't you the calm one! Not a hair out of place. No sweaty brow. Not a loose thread on your dress. How did you avoid getting torn to shreds by those reporters?'

Shirley modelled her dishevelled state.

'You should have taken the back way up,' the mayor said.

'Secret way, you mean. I've never been able to figure out that route of yours.'

'Try the fire escape outside the window of the ladies' room on the first floor.'

Shirley humphed and presented her boss with a list of names.

'You've got Carlleston underlined and circled in red,' the mayor said.

'His secretary called a half-dozen times. Sounds urgent.' And when the mayor didn't respond, Shirley added, 'Want me to return the call?'

The mayor shook her head. 'But put him through when he calls again. Meanwhile . . . ' – she scanned the list – '. . . get me Chuck Harper.'

Harper was the city's public relations man for the dome. The Fourth of July unveiling had been his brain child. No doubt he had a dozen tricks in his Madison Avenue briefcase to save face. And she supposed she should talk to him first. There might be something in his bag of tricks for her.

But on the phone he sounded panicky. He was ill-informed

and had been trying to reach *her* for help. He just couldn't believe it when the mayor confirmed the rumour he had heard.

'But surely there's still a chance the dome could go into operation,' he said. 'Maybe later on this week. Like maybe for the weekend?'

'No way,' the mayor said. 'Even if it could, I wouldn't allow it.'

They argued for ten minutes. Harper could not understand her position at all. He accused her of inconsistency. He recited all the aspirations they had shared about Unveiling Week. He tried using tuneful and catchy phraseology on her. She could not make him see that everything had changed. If this was any sort of preview . . . how was she going to reach the general public?

'Okay, okay,' Harper said finally. He paused for a moment and became submissive. 'We'll do it your way right down the line. How do you want to handle it?'

'I don't know,' the mayor said. 'I haven't had time to think it through.'

There was another pause. 'You were calling to see if I had any ideas, right? Okay. I take it you haven't talked to the reporters yet, right? Well, some way we have to placate those people.'

Harper suggested a banquet for all newsmen concerned to be arranged for that evening at a swanky restaurant on the north shore of the lake, where they still had electric power.

'It's a stalling tactic,' the mayor said.

'Of course it's a stalling tactic. I'll get my staff together on a speech you can deliver there tonight. In the meantime, don't say a word. Don't even make a public appearance. My boys can do wonders with the spoken word. You know that. We'll get you out of this somehow. You'll see.'

'No,' the mayor said. 'No banquet and no speech.'

'What do you want from me?' Harper said angrily. 'Blood?'

'A miracle, I guess.' She hung up. '*Ciao.*'

She went down the list of people who had been trying to

reach her. She returned their calls and initiated some calls of her own. And no one offered her advice she could live with. It was either concede to evasiveness and half-truths or stand alone. And alone, what chance did she stand? She would lose the people's confidence and GP would topple her position. Bulldozer versus dandelion.

She turned herself inside out, trying to think of a plan. Every course of action entailed a checkmate. And by the time Carlleston called again she was on the verge of tears.

She had Shirley put him on hold while she composed herself.

'What can I say,' Carlleston begun, 'except that these things happen? They happen to even the best of security forces. And believe me, that security force on the island is among the very best. Of course, it's a young staff and local. But nobody's finding fault. Let's just chalk it up to lack of experience.'

The mayor listened uncomprehendingly. Then she cut Carlleston off in mid-sentence.

'I don't know what you're talking about,' she said.

'Oh, of course,' Carlleston said amiably. 'I guess things are still pretty confused down there. There's probably been a foul-up in information flow. They were supposed to keep you up to date on all developments in our investigation.'

'Investigation?'

'Yes,' Carlleston said, with an overtone of shock and surprise. 'You mean you didn't even know we had launched an investigation? I'll have to really get on some asses. I want you to know everything that goes on. We've been aware for some time that our company has been infiltrated by agents working for some of our competitors. It's just a matter of time before we identify the saboteurs and put the blame for what happened yesterday where it really belongs. Also, I wanted you to put your mind at rest. I know what you must be going through. People down there, reporters, even friends, must be trying to make you look like the village idiot. Am I right? You have been one of the Super Reactor's most ardent supporters. And then to have all this eleventh-hour trouble. You must be worried about your credibility. Without that, where's a politician these days? So, I wanted to tell you that you won't be on the spot for long. Preliminary reports from my technicians are very optimistic. Minimal damage has been done to the reactor core. As soon as the pipeline ruptures in the cooling system have been repaired, the Super Reactor will be back in business. That city of yours can be back on cheap and efficient nuclear power within a month at the outside. And we can all breathe easy.'

When dealing with a snake, be cunning, and cautious. How many times had she heard her father say that? Don't make any noise. Don't beat the bushes and don't grab him by the tail. The one predictable thing about a snake is that he'll twist himself a full 360 degrees just so he can bite you out of pure meanness. Her father had always been able to play dead before a political reptile only to counterstrike at an opportune moment with one decisive blow.

She listened to everything Carlleston had to say, waging an inner struggle to keep her anger down at his every word. And when he hung up, she waited ten seconds before slamming down the receiver.

Shirley poked her head through the doorway and asked if she should get in touch with the telephone company again. The mayor picked the receiver up again, made some test dials, and shook her head.

'It's okay, Shirley,' she said.

'I'm going down the hall for some coffee. Want some?'

'About a gallon.'

She made up her mind, then, to confront the reporters head-on – not because she knew what to say, but because she felt that her resolve to tell the truth was weakening. Carlleston's words were getting to her. That frightened her more than her imminent political downfall.

Her own personal destruction did not matter. The city's welfare mattered. If only she had a strong and competent successor, someone who could carry on the fight and rock GP back on its heels. If such a person existed in the political arena, she would not have to flirt with these notions of self-

164

compromise. She could make her stand, lose her support, be impeached, or whatever. It was just that with her out of the way, GP was almost sure to win. Maybe if she went along with Carlleston just halfway . . . But the idea made her sick to her stomach.

When Shirley returned, she told her to set up a press conference for noon.

'What are you going to do ?' Shirley asked.

'I wish I knew.'

At eleven-thirty the mayor began to set her house in order. She phoned the Public Service and used all of her clout – something she might soon be sorely lacking – to get them in gear. They promised her delivery of two of the old power plants by midnight, supplying electricity to sixty per cent of the residents in Orleans Parish. Then she got in touch with LeRoy Stroud, the water commissioner. Stroud informed her in his conservative manner that the water situation was fair to middling, which meant that Stroud was on top of things and there would be no problems with the city's water reserves. She thanked God they hadn't switched the water system over to the nuclear desalination plants early, as they had originally intended. Being without water and electricity in all this heat would have been too much for the people to bear.

Finally, she studied the list of dead which she had compiled from the Delta flight's passenger list which the airline had sent over, from the Howard Johnson's list, and from the names she herself had written down while at the dome.

One hundred and thirty-two names in all.

After a while she dried her cheeks with her handkerchief, frowned at her reflection in the small compact mirror, and applied powder under her eyes. How tired and old she looked! Had she aged so much in the last twenty-four hours ? Or was it just for the first time in years she was seeing herself with unalloyed vision ? She had no pretences left, there was in her no lingering youthfulness, no indefatigable stamina, no unfaltering courage. She was just an exhausted and frightened middle-aged lady who was prone to high blood pressure and occasional choking spells from an inoperable hernia. Here she was, drained of her life force, about to undertake the most arduous of ordeals. How could such a commonplace bundle of weaknesses succeed in the endeavour?

She got out her personal cheque-book and wrote out a cheque for three hundred dollars to the Society of Jesus. She would have Shirley mail it directly to Fr Donahue, who would protest. She would, however, insist that the money be kept as stipend for the one hundred and thirty-two Masses she had requested from Fr Donahue that morning. She could at least honour the dead.

'You don't look so good anymore,' Shirley told her at noon.

'Thanks.'

'What I mean is you look like you could use a rest. When was the last time you slept? Why don't I go down to the lobby and call off this press conference or at least postpone it till tomorrow?'

'Just ply me with another cup of that coffee if it's still hot. And tell me truthfully if I've got too much powder on my face. I didn't want to be photographed with two red eyes.'

She rode the emergency elevator down to the second floor. Then she got off and walked the last flight of stairs. That way she could make her entrance into the lobby as unobtrusively as possible and at the same time get an unobserved look at the reporters' moods.

They looked sullen and angry and hot. They were congregated near the elevator lobby. Some of them kept glancing at their wrist-watches.

A little voice kept telling her to co-operate with Carlleston. Compromise. Compromise. It's the only way out.

She took a deep breath and opened the stairwell door. She was spotted at once.

'Mayor Mathieu!'

'Mayor Mathieu!'

They rushed her, crowded her, and pushed against her with waving microphones. She pressed forward towards the conference room. She wished she had the limbs of an

166

octopus to extricate herself from this maze of human forms.

The conference room was jammed. The din of voices and the cacophony of questions that accompanied her down the corridor subsided as she took her place behind the speaker's podium.

She surmised, from this sudden acquiescence to law and order on the part of the reporters, how grave her expression must appear.

She opened her mouth to speak and no words came forth.

Compromise, said the little voice. You have to!

'Ladies and gentlemen,' she got out before Ray Watkins of Channel 4 stood up and asked for her indulgence. He was acting as spokesman for the entire audience of newsmen. A move which portended the announcement of an occurrence immense enough to overcome reporters' already immense egos.

He presented her with several pages of mimeo-copy.

'Transcript of a press interview,' he said. 'Some of us were out at the dome this morning. Everybody here has a copy.'

She took several minutes to read through the transcript.

Lombardy, she said to herself, you beautiful man!

Dead silence prevailed in the conference room as she read. When she finished and looked up, Watkins's eyes were riveted to hers. His features bespoke a challenge. Go on, they said, deny any statement there. At that moment she knew that she had won. The city had won. Carlleston and General Power were finished. Because of a man who put truth and humanity before his own welfare.

'Ladies and gentlemen,' the mayor said, 'Simon Lombardy is the most honest man I know. Everything he tells you here is the truth. Let me go over yesterday's events in my own words in order to corroborate his statements.'

Chapter 35—Explosion

'Weingardner,' Ellison said, 'who's down in the reactor now?'

'No one,' Weingardner answered.

'Well, we have to get somebody back in there to take a look around now that we know what to look for.'

'What do you expect to find?' Blume said. For the first time there was uncertainty in his voice.

'Cracks or bumps in the graphite cladding,' Ellison said. 'You see, graphite swells as it absorbs heat. The reactor walls in the core may be pushed in, diminishing its volume. Someone will have to take measurements. Aicklen, we got a couple of Widmark suits ready to go?'

'Listen,' Lombardy said, 'there are documents here in the dome, charts, records, that are invaluable to this company. We'd better start getting them all together. I'll handle the administrative stuff. Ellison, you or somebody from your staff will have to take care of the science end.'

'Hold on,' said Blume. 'We're not just going to turn tail and run. We're going to identify the problem – if, indeed, there is a problem – and then find a solution.'

'Ellison, you tell him,' Lombardy said.

'Mr Blume,' Ellison said, 'if our problem is a possible Wigner Release, then there isn't any solution. Short of dismantling the entire reactor core and removing the graphite layer – which would take at least several months – there just isn't anything we can do. If the heat is still there in the graphite, then it's finished, over. And the best we can do is save whatever we can and get as far away from this dome as possible.'

Lombardy was in the glass office with Blume, getting company records together, when it happened.

Ellison and Aicklen were down on ground-floor level with two reactor technicians who were suited up and standing before the reactor's service portal.

Ellison had just given the order to open the portal when he got a call over the intercom from a general-conditions observer countermanding the order.

'Dr Ellison,' the observer said, 'something's happening. I've got confirmation at this post that the coolant pumps have just come on automatically.'

'Quickly!' Ellison snapped. 'Your readings on the liquid sodium levels.'

'Affirmative, sir. The reactor core is being flooded with liquid sodium from our back-up cooling system. Heat levels are rising off the scales.'

Ellison's next words were silenced by the deafening clangs of thick steel and lead panels sliding shut to cover all exit corridors. Ellison jerked his head in the direction of each resounding boom. Aicklen wet his pants and fell to his knees, saying, 'Jesus, my saviour,' over and over.

Up in the glass office Blume said, 'What's those noises?'

'For once the damn machinery's working,' Lombardy answered.

The shrill whistle of the fast air pumps registered vaguely in everyone's ears.

'What's happening?' Blume shrieked. 'Those men out there – they're choking to death!'

'Suffocating,' Lombardy said. 'Now you know the reason for this glass office. But it won't save us.'

There was a blinding flash of light from the floor of the dome. The service portal blew out of its frame and demolished the men in the Widmark suits. Another, and greater, explosion followed immediately. Glass shattered around Lombardy and shards flew everywhere. The tier collapsed and hung suspended by a thread of steel girder at a forty-five-degree angle.

Lombardy, unable to move, lay bleeding and lacerated at the edge of the tier.

At least the dome didn't rupture, was Lombardy's final thought. For he found he was not just bleeding, but suffocating, to death.

Chapter 36—Tomb

The nurse came back into the room with a packaged chest bandage which she handed to Dr Beroni. The doctor opened the package, took the bandage out, and gestured towards it with exasperation.

'Nurse Gries,' he said, 'I know the patient is little, but she's not *that* little.'

Mary Wolford blushed.

Nurse Gries looked puzzled.

Dr Beroni tossed up his hands.

'Please return this bandage to the supply room and come back with a *female* model.'

The doctor put Wolford through some minor exercises while the nurse was gone. She found she could not twist her torso without a sharp stab of pain.

Dr Beroni looked at her over the top of his glasses.

'I can't keep you here against your will,' he said.

'Please Dr Beroni,' Wolford interrupted, 'we've been through all that already.'

'Try to touch your left shoulder with your left hand, please.'

Again she winced.

'Umm-hmm,' Beroni said. 'You haven't been doing anything to aggravate your condition, have you?'

'Uh, no,' Wolford said.

'Well, the chest bandage will help you some. Let me take another look at that bump on your head.'

'Ouch!'

'Tell me, young lady, how can someone so young be so indispensable to that island out there?'

'I just can't stay here,' Wolford said very emphatically.

'All right. All right.'

Beroni made her stand up.

'Don't do any stretching or bending over. I'll write you out a prescription for the pain. You can fill it at the pharmacy across the street. How are you getting back to the island?'

'I've rented a car. They said on the phone they would bring over. It should be here any minute.'

'Not that Henry Joe's Rent-a-Chariot?' Beroni said.

'Why? Do they have a bad reputation?'

The doctor shrugged. 'They have their own towing service, too.'

Chapter 37—The Menace

Professor Nichols had protested wildly when they forced him to leave the island. And Dr Miller, to avoid further agitation of his patient, which, he believed, could bring on fits of hysteria, agreed to let Nichols partially have his way. Nichols had insisted on ransacking his living quarters before they left the island in order to assemble an array of scientific papers, calculations, charts, and diagrams, which he stuffed into two large suitcases. After they arrived at the New Orleans Royal Sonesta, it took Nichols only a matter of minutes to transform his plush suite of eighteenth-century Spanish decor into a cluttered, stuffy set of rooms akin to those of his island abode.

Dr Miller shook his head and argued with himself, back and forth, over the necessity of administering tranquillisers. Maybe this work fixation was good therapy. Maybe, too, Nichols was on to something. There was wildness and desperation in Nichols's growing insistence that the island was still in danger. But there was also a look of cold, ordered rationality in his eyes. Time and again during the past twenty-four hours Nichols had demonstrated the accuracy of his rational mind. Miller was too good of a psychiatrist to dismiss a man's thinking ability merely because he had become disturbed emotionally. In addition, there could be many lives at stake.

'What makes you think there's still something wrong out there?' Miller said.

'The answer is somewhere right here,' Nichols responded.

Draped over the couch was a four-by-six schematic diagram of the reactor complex inside the dome. Nichols had plucked it from the wall of his island study to bring with the rest of his booty.

Over Nichols's shoulder Miller studied the diagram with little comprehension. Then he limped with the help of his cane to the large twenty-first-storey window facing lakeward. He drew back the drapes. From this vantage point he could see all of New Orleans, from the French Quarter to the Coast Guard lighthouse at West End. Beyond the lighthouse was the great expanse of grey lake water with the dome embedded there like a pearl in its oyster. It appeared so tiny and remote. It was hard to think of it as a possible threat.

Maybe Professor Nichols's imagination was starting to run wild. Maybe his rationality was finally getting tainted by his emotional state.

'Professor Nichols,' Miller said, 'how is your hand?'

'What does it matter?' Nichols answered.

'Let me see it,' Miller said.

He held the hand, felt Nichols's pulse, studied the look in Nichols's eyes.

'This . . . problem,' Miller said, 'with the reactor. Don't you think somebody else on the island would have noticed it? Every one of those scientists out there is a genius in his own right.'

Nichols said nothing, but continued going over the diagram.

'I have something,' Miller went on, 'that would calm your nerves, help you think.'

'No drugs!'

Nichols's voice was suddenly full of explosive anger. It convinced Miller that something had to be done.

'No drugs, of course,' Miller said quietly. He hobbled into

the bathroom, where he filled one of his syringes with a Thorazine derivative that would put Nichols out for twenty hours.

When he re-entered the living-room with the syringe behind his back, Nichols was still consumed by that diagram.

He's on the brink, Miller told himself. He's right at the edge of violence.

Miller picked his spot from across the room: the throbbing artery on the left side of the neck. Then he hobbled closer, closer.

Nichols shrieked.

'Miller, you fool! You goddamn fool!'

Nichols pulled the syringe from his neck with one arm, and with a swinging blow from the other he sent the psychiatrist flying across the room. Miller's assistant came running in from an adjacent bedroom, tried restraint, and shortly found himself sprawled out on the floor next to his boss.

'Watch out! Here he comes again!' Miller shouted.

But before he could reach them, Nichols was down on his knees and losing consciousness rapidly.

'I knew it,' Miller said with righteousness. 'I knew he was becoming violent. Did you see how strong he was?'

Miller's assistant got to his feet and helped Miller up.

'He's still not out completely,' the assistant said. 'He's trying to tell us something.'

Miller, very cautiously, approached his felled patient and put his head down close enough to hear the strained words.

'I know the answer,' Nichols whispered. 'Call the island. Tell Lombardy. Tell Lombardy the heat went into the graphite. It's a menace. The graphite. Tell him. Tell him!'

'He's out, Dr Miller,' the assistant said.

'Yes. What do you suppose he meant?'

The assistant picked the syringe up off the floor.

'Barbitone?' he asked.

'Thorazine.'

'Well, he won't be telling us what he meant for quite some time.'

Miller studied the diagram of the reactor once again.

'You know about that stuff?' the assistant said.

'I know very little about that stuff,' Miller answered. 'But I know one thing. Well, see for yourself. These fast-breeder reactors have no graphite moderators. Professor Nichols's mind must be more confused than I thought.'

The assistant shrugged. 'Could be.'

Dr Miller saw his patient to bed and then considered the question of whether or not to call the island.

Chapter 38—The Wigner Release

Before leaving the island, one of the reporters presented Lombardy with a passenger list for the Delta flight 722 that had gone down in the lake. The island's teleprinter was still on the blink, along with most of the sensitive electronic gear in the island's radio tower; and Lombardy had been unable to obtain any detailed information on the Delta flight. The reporter was only too glad to oblige the man who had, through his press interview, leaked one of the year's biggest news stories.

'You seem very anxious to see this list,' the reporter said, having fished a crumpled sheet of paper from one of his pockets. 'You didn't know anybody on that plane, did you? What I mean is I hope this terrible tragedy hasn't touched your personal life, as well.'

Lombardy thanked the man and quickly scanned the bottom third of the alphabetical list.

His heart skipped several beats, and for a moment he felt as though he'd been kicked in the head.

'You do know somebody on that list,' the reporter said.

Lombardy nodded.

The reporter placed a sympathetic hand on Lombardy's shoulder. 'You're a good man, Mr Lombardy. And I hope you don't blame yourself for what has happened.'

A good man, Lombardy repeated to himself.

Since mid-morning Lombardy had been disturbed by a hunch. It was as if a curse hung over this project. Good invariably brought forth evil results.

It had never been his *modus operandi* to wax philosophical or to let himself become preoccupied with moral and religious considerations. But this morning he had felt .... could words really explain the feeling? He felt as if he were looking into the face of death. No doubt a mood, a frame of mind, a variety of acute hypochondria brought on by a shattered career and lack of prospects. A feeling to be dismissed, but one not readily dismissed.

These preoccupations, he told himself, were absurd. I am forty-three years old and in the prime of health. I am not close to death. And these notions of good and evil should be set aside for old age, when the impotency they inflict upon those who seriously entertain them is a state of nature, as well. I am still a young man. And while I have the ability to act and get the job done, I'll leave it to the old and feeble to weigh and lament the consequences of my actions. I am too young to be a moralist.

But the hunch was there. Does good invariably end in evil? And if it does, what kind of a perverted creature is man? For man professes, and it is his highest aspiration, to act for the good.

To shake himself of these morbid considerations, Lombardy constructed a little experiment. What greater good than for a man to lay down his life for his fellow man? Very well, then. He would consider the case of Dan Mason. And the experiment was this: find the evil embedded in Mason's acts. And if there was none, then so much for a stupid fixation. And good does not end in evil invariably, after all.

For a while his little experiment had worked, sufficiently, at least, for him to set aside his new-found scruples. And that was certainly a good, for the course ahead was full of hurdles. And a crippled man had no business being in the race.

But a co-worker had set his mind in turmoil once again. Bill Aicklen, a scientist and sometime friend of Slayer's, told Lombardy, yes, Slayer might have gone up to Jackson to see Mason's girl. And then he had added, 'Maybe he's flying up and you could still catch him at the airport.'

Lombardy had reminded Aicklen how terrified of heights Slayer was and how Mason had gotten Slayer to go up on his kite only once. 'Slayer has never taken a plane anywhere at any time in his life.'

And at that moment the devastating thought had occurred to Lombardy for the first time.

What if Kathy Raffer had decided to fly up to Jackson?

Delta flight 722: Jackson, Memphis, St Louis, Chicago.

What if Kathy Raffer had been on that plane? Then, Mason, for all his self-sacrificing, had accomplished what? He couldn't even save the woman he loved. And, in fact, by his insistence that she flee the city, he was an accomplice to her death. How can man lift his hand when the result lies so far from the resolve?

Lombardy was paralyzed by these thoughts. And back at the dome after his press interview, he became remote and listless. He did not resist Blume and his pack of Black Tags as they carried on their petty investigations. He withdrew to the staff lounge and quietly sat upon its veranda watching the seagulls catch their dinner. He surprised even himself. Hadn't he always believed in the basic depravity of man? Weren't these events just one more proof in a long chain that his cynicism was well founded? Why, then, was he depressed and filled with dread?

He was still sitting on the veranda when they paged him on his walkie-talkie. Get to a phone, they said. Dr Miller was calling him from New Orleans.

Miller explained that Nichols's condition had deteriorated and he had had to sedate him.

'I'm sorry to hear that,' Lombardy said.

'He wanted me to give you a message.'

'Oh?'

176

'He wasn't being very coherent, I'm afraid. Listen, that reactor doesn't use graphite moderators, does it? That's why it's a fast breeder, right?'

'That's right,' Lombardy said.

'That's what I thought.'

'What's the message?'

'The message doesn't make sense. Nichols said to tell you that the heat went into the graphite, and that the graphite was a menace. I just thought I'd let you know. Of course, since there is no graphite, I suppose his message is meaningless, right? Hello? Lombardy, are you there?'

In his sprint to the top tier of the dome, Lombardy left the phone receiver dangling.

Blume was on a phone, too, speaking to one of its Black Tags, when Lombardy stormed into the glass office. Without a word of explanation, Lombardy proceeded directly to his desk, retrieved a schematic diagram of the reactor core from a bottom drawer, and began spreading it out on the floor.

'I'll get back to you,' Blume said into the phone and hung up. And then to Lombardy: 'Well, you really did it, didn't you? I've just heard about your little escapade over in Administration with the reporters.'

'Where's Dr Ellison?' Lombardy said.

'Aren't you even listening to me?' Blume growled. 'You've just cut your throat with this company!'

'Page Dr Ellison. Aicklen and Weingardner, too. Get them up here on the double. Do it, goddamnit!'

Blume, bemused, complied. He wanted to give Lombardy all the rope he needed. And when the scientists arrived, he suppressed a smile, shrugged, and gave Lombardy the floor.

'Mr Blume seems to think this is some kind of joke,' Lombardy began. 'There's nothing funny about a possible Wigner Release.'

'A Wigner Release!' Ellison exclaimed. He had been seated. Shot up. 'What . . . how . . .'

'Okay,' Lombardy said, 'everybody just listen.'

When he had finished explaining about Professor Nichols,

Blume practically laughed out loud.

'Just a minute, Mr Blume,' Ellison said. 'You're not a scientist and you don't understand. The reactor core is blanketed by a layer of graphite. It was one of Professor Nichols's more ingenious improvisations. Normally you don't find graphite in a fast breeder. This layer of graphite acts as a neutron shield and increases the reactor's efficiency twofold. It allows more neutron interaction with the uranium in the breeding chambers. The problem is that graphite has the capacity to store huge amounts of heat, which it can suddenly and spontaneously release at any future time. Eugene Wigner discovered this property of graphite years ago and very carefully outlined the hazards of its use in the design of nuclear reactors. Nichols took these hazards into consideration in his design of this particular reactor. The graphite has a special alloy coating which should prevent excessive heat storage. But at this point the situation has been radically altered. There was so much heat liberated in that reactor core that God knows what kind of structural changes may have taken place. Metals, alloys, may have become fatigued and taken on different physical and chemical properties. If Professor Nichols thinks it's possible . . . Lombardy, what were the results of Nichols's calculations? Exactly how much heat did the reactor liberate last night?'

'I don't have his calculations here on the island,' Lombardy said. 'But Nichols thought enough heat was released to melt the reactor three times over.'

'God,' Ellison said. 'Dear God. Then we must assume along with Professor Nichols that most of it went into the graphite layer and that it may be released again at any time. At any time, gentlemen, we could have a Wigner Release that would melt the reactor core and blow us all to hell!'

'Dr Beroni,' Wolford said, 'I'm getting back to that island some way. And you are an impossible man.' She smiled and took his hand. 'Thanks,' she said, 'for not trying any harder to make me stay.' She stretched to give him a light kiss and

178

had to shrink back from another sharp stab. 'Oh, no,' she said.

Beroni shook his head.

'Wolford, Wolford.'

It was a pretty sleazy car, with a rip in the roof lining, a missing sun visor, and an ashtray full of cigarette butts. But it ran. And she didn't have to resort to a tow truck. At least Dr Beroni was wrong about that. As for the pain . . .

The pills he had prescribed did help a little. She had taken two of them in the drugstore right away. The chest bandage helped, too. But they weren't nearly adequate. Maybe she should have taken Beroni's advice and stayed in the hospital for a couple of days, at least.

Oh, well, too late now.

Besides, she had to be back on the island by the time Slayer returned from Mississippi. There were some things they had to straighten out that couldn't wait. After they had made love, he had told her about Dan and Kathy, and she had tried to talk him out of driving up to Jackson – not because she felt someone else should break the news to Kathy, but because in his state of mind an accident could easily happen. He had told her how important Dan's friendship had been during his stay on the island. How he felt he was largely responsible for Dan's death. And then she broke her promise to Simon.

She told Slayer that he had another friend he didn't even know about and described how Lombardy had gone to great trouble and risk to get him hired at GP. He1 purpose was to talk him into returning to the island, where he was needed. Lombardy would be under GP fire now and would need all the assistance and brain power and friendship, too, that he could get.

She had not expected his reaction. Suddenly he couldn't get away from her fast enough. He said he was going to Jackson and would stop by tomorrow to see her. His voice had sounded distant, insincere. She couldn't understand why he was being so insensitive. What had just happened between them, what had meant everything to her, had, possibly, meant nothing to him. It was the only way to explain it.

Later, when he was gone, she came to realize it might have been her own insensitivity that had driven him away. She had forgotten the rumours about her and Simon! All along Slayer had to have been thinking the worst. But surely he couldn't believe that she would go so far as to sleep with him just to win Lombardy his support! It was such an absurd idea, given the situation. But it brought home one fact she had not realized. Her chronic reluctance to become involved had not only belated the loss of her virginity; it had actually retarded her understanding of the complexities of human nature.

Henceforth, she stated to herself with bravado, it would not be so! And she pushed her foot hard against the accelerator.

The guard at the gate stepped out from his guard post and made her show her ID.

'Come on,' Jackie,' she said, 'you know who I am.'

'Sorry, Dr Wolford, but I'm going to have to look in your trunk, too.'

'What's up, Jackie?'

He leaned close to her ear.

'Black Tags. A whole flock of them in from Nevada. We're on a security alert right now. Keys.'

He checked out her trunk and gave her the okay.

'Hey, Jackie,' she said, 'has George Slayer been through here this afternoon?'

'I just came on ten minutes ago.'

'Okay, thanks.'

She drove through the staff parking area and scanned the rows of cars, but she didn't see Slayer's old truck. Then she took the throughway to the dome. She parked in front, checked the cars that were there, and noticed that some of them were from Avis. Black Tags. Still no sign of an old green truck.

180

She walked up the concrete steps to the main entrance. Her discomfort was both physical and psychological. There were still splotches of dried blood where people had been trampled. She couldn't remember the spot where she had gone down and spent a couple of minutes examining this splotch and that. She found what she thought was the place and bent down to recreate her surroundings and her memory. What she got was a sharp reminder from her ribs to be careful and a chill of masochistic pleasure from her warped psyche. Sick, Wolford, she told herself. Sick.

Beyond the glass entrance doors to the dome was a short dead-end corridor, created by a thick steel slab which fit so snugly to the walls, roof, and floor that it looked like a permanent fixture.

So, they're testing the safety devices, Wolford said to herself. Looks like they've got some of the machinery working again.

She lingered for a while, deciding they were going to piddle around in there for longer than she had anticipated, because the dome was still locked tight as a drum.

What were they doing in there, anyway? Too bad there was no doorbell on that thick steel panel, she laughed.

The air in the corridor was very warm and she had begun to perspire. 'Come on, guys,' she said, 'open up.'

She pressed her finger to an imaginary doorbell on the steel slab and withdrew it quickly in pain. The skin on her finger tip sizzled.

She backed away, saying to herself, over and over, Simon! Then she turned and ran.

The car almost started, but after two or three more grinds – nothing!

And now she noticed that her watch had stopped. It was a ghastly replay of last night.

She tried telling herself there had to be some other explanation.

She skirted the perimeter of the dome on foot as fast as she could. Down one of the streets was a scurrying go-cart manned by a security cop. She hollered and waved and finally got the cop's attention.

He turned the cart and started towards her when all she had wanted was for him to stop till she could catch up.

'Don't!' she yelled. 'Stay where you are! Stop! Stop!'

Fifty yards from her the cart's engine went dead.

'Forget it,' she said when she reached the spot. 'It won't start. Let's push it back about ten yards and try it there.'

They did and the engine rumbled to life.

'What's going on?' the security cop said.

'What's the matter with you people!' Big tears were forming in her eyes.

'Say, lady, I . . .'

'Didn't you hear anything? Didn't you feel the island shake? Didn't it make you wonder at all!'

'I don't know what you're talking about.'

'The dome,' she wailed. 'They're all dead inside the dome! And you didn't even know it. You didn't even know it!'

By the time they reached the Administration area, she had gotten herself together. She knew what they had to do. They had to evacuate before the magnetic field got strong enough to paralyze all their transportation. Somebody knowledgeable had to take charge; and she might well be the only scientist left alive on the island.

'Simon,' she said quietly, 'I'll do the best I can.'

She still refused to admit to herself the possibility that Slayer had time to return to the island and was, along with Simon and the others . . . But she could not bring herself even to think the word.

Chapter 39—Operation Watch

By nightfall they still had very little information.

They knew the dome was still intact. There was no radiation leakage. And they knew the magnetic field was much weaker and smaller than its predecessor, encompassing

182

an area of less than half a mile in diameter.

Eight island scientists remained alive out of more than a hundred, and despite lengthy discussions they could not agree on what had happened to the reactor that afternoon or when it had happened. Nor could they forecast what might still be in the cards.

Late that evening Wolford went to the Royal Sonesta. Mayor Mathieu, worried and uncertain about Wolford's health, gave her half an hour's head start, then she left her city council in hot debate at City Hall and followed.

She was waiting in her car at the curb on Bourbon Street when Wolford emerged from the lobby.

'How did it go?' the mayor asked.

'I don't know who is more neurotic,' Wolford said angrily, 'Professor Nichols or Dr Miller!'

There was something in her tone of voice, something fiery in her eyes, that for an instant reminded the mayor of Simon Lombardy.

'That quack has Professor Nichols out cold. I won't be able to talk to him for another twelve hours!'

'What did Miller have to say?'

'Just that Professor Nichols gave him a message to give to Simon this afternoon. And that he and Simon were cut off.'

'Then he spoke to Lombardy this afternoon,' the mayor said. 'Does he remember the exact time?'

'He said it was around two.'

'And you discovered the condition of the dome at four-thirty or thereabouts, right? That gives us some idea of the time. Did you find out anything else?'

'Yes,' Wolford said. 'I think I know what went wrong.'

Wolford explained the properties of graphite and the possibility of a tremendous heat release.

'If only Nichols would have thought it of sooner,' the mayor said.

Wolford shook her head.

'It would have saved those people in the dome. But not Simon. I know he would have still been right there when it happened. It's like a captain who goes down with his ship.

183

That's the way Simon was.'

'Look in my purse,' the mayor said. 'There's a box o
Kleenex.'

'Of course there's no way to stop a Wigner Release. I
would have happened no matter what we did.'

'Well, let's just hope it's finally over.'

'We won't know that till morning. Where are you taking
me? To Coast Guard headquarters?'

'Operation Watch can get along just fine without you,' the
mayor said. 'I'm taking you back to my house, where you're
going to get some rest.'

But Wolford was still awake at midnight. She heard the
phone ring downstairs, and then she heard voices. She got
out of bed, put on the robe the mayor had given her, and
crept down the hallway to the staircase. She paused a
moment and then went down. Dottie and Al were talking in
the kitchen and drinking coffee by candlelight.

'I heard the phone,' Wolford said by way of explanation.

'If I knew you were awake I would have come up and told
you the good news,' the mayor said. 'That was a call from
the Mississippi Highway Patrol on that APB we put out.
They found Slayer's truck on a road a few miles from the
Raffer farm. He wasn't in it and they haven't located him
yet. But now we know for sure he wasn't in that dome. Stop
your crying and come over here. Have a cup of coffee, if you
can stand instant and lukewarm water.'

A hundred observers from a score of different posts along
the perimeter of the lake kept their binoculars trained on the
dome for signs of rupture. But the key to Operation Watch
was the old lighthouse in West End which served as Coast
Guard headquarters. The huge spotlight in the beacon tower
had been dismantled and set aside to make space for the
highly sensitive equipment borrowed from UNO's school of
physics.

Commander Higgins had watched the scientists from the
university set up their infra-red devices and when everything
was ready they invited him to have a look.

He put his eye to a small glass aperture which resembled

the eyepiece on a telescope.

'I don't understand,' he said. 'Is this equipment adjusted properly?'

The image in the eyepiece was so homogeneous he could scarcely distinguish the horizon. The dome, which was the target of study, blended so well with the background it was hardly visible. Everything was a fuzzy red.

'We won't start getting analysable data till the small hours of the morning,' one scientist said. 'There's far too much heat from the sun still trapped within the water. As the water gives it up, we'll get better contrast images of the dome.'

'That won't be till morning?' Higgins asked.

'Right. We should get our best readings between, oh, four a.m. and sunrise. Once the sun comes up the sky will be flooded with heat data and again we won't get good contrast images.'

Commander Higgins nodded and thought for a moment. 'But what exactly are you trying to find out?'

'We've got three different cameras hooked up to this equipment,' the scientist said. 'They'll be snapping pictures at various intervals. We want to find out how hot it is inside that dome.'

'And more importantly,' a second scientist interjected, 'we want to know if it's getting any hotter.'

'And what if it is getting hotter?' Higgins said.

The scientists glanced slyly at one another.

'What if it is?' Higgins repeated.

'Then we'll have to determine the rate of temperature rise and try to predict when the dome will burst open.'

'Oh,' Higgins said. It was an answer to which there was no response.

'Let's go sit on the sea wall,' Al said.

Dottie glanced at the phone receiver.

'You can hear the phone from the sea wall,' Al said. 'Besides, Wolford can catch it. Well, you know she's not asleep up there. Who could sleep? At the first ring I'll come charging back in, okay?'

185

She took Al's hand as they went outside.

'It's a lot hotter than it's been the last few nights,' Al said. 'You'd think that cool spell we were having would have lasted. If it's not one thing, it's ten thousand.'

Dottie began weeping very softly. Al stroked her hair.

After a while she said, 'Al, what if it's not over with yet?'

He did not answer. He rocked her gently back and forth as if she were a child.

She thought how quiet he had been all day, how lost in his thoughts. Sometimes he could become very depressed, and her only clue was these episodes of quietness. She had many regrets in life. Al was not one of them. She felt their love again like a climate that surrounded them. Thirty years ago he was a liberated man before there were such things. And if he was never particularly an asset to her career in politics, he had never been a hindrance. Nor had he ever felt personally threatened by her public image and power. Their marriage had always been her Rock of Gibraltar. Whatever may have happened or might happen in the future, she would always feel her life had been a success because thirty years ago she had met and wooed and captured the one man that could love her, put up with her and make her feel complete. Her father had always thought him weak because he put up with her. But patience took a special kind of talent, a special kind of strength. In truth, over the years, as inevitably she came to compare the two, her husband and her father, she concluded that Al was the better man by far. Al was an honest and moral man without the aid of religion. She could not say that of her father. And she knew it wasn't true about herself. Even now as she fretted over her sins in building the Super Reactor, she knew she could confess and be forgiven. It would take her the strength of a superman to get through life without this escape clause of possible attrition.

'Al?' she said.

'Yes?'

'You remember when Lucia told us she and Dick were moving to St Louis because his chances of success in business were better there? I was like a madwoman because Jane had

186

left New Orleans the year before.'

'I remember,' he said.

'Well, that's when I decided to go ahead and have the damn thing built. I was going to show our daughters that New Orleans could be number one. It was nothing but a sin of pride.'

'Go to sleep.'

'Al? Could we make love? Right here? The way we did the first time . . . at the fishing camp in Little Woods?' In answer he pressed his warm lips on hers, and she felt the battles and chaos of the weekend recede in the pressure of their bodies. Their movements reminded her of the rhythmic lappings of the small, lake waves.

When dawn came, she awoke refreshed. She lay with Al by the sea wall and watched the grey line on the horizon become streaked with yellow.

They had said they would know something by dawn, and yet the phone had not rung.

The seagulls were ravaging the surface of the water, the sky was changing to blue, and the dome was starting to shed its familiar light. Everything seemed peaceful, normal. Someone, somewhere, was shooting off fireworks to herald the start of Independence Day. And still the phone was not ringing.

It was a good omen.

Chapter 40—Hideaway

After he left the Raffer farm, he got only a few miles before he stopped the truck. He ran for the woods, seeking dark shelter like a wounded animal. If he could find a place black enough and foul enough, he could fade into the background, shed his awareness in the wet, rank dirt. The world would never again have to gaze upon his hideous features or cope with his twisted soul.

187

His skin and clothes were scratched and torn from burrs and thorns. There was disorder and chaos in the rampant growth of underbrush. Bush entangled in bush. Vines matted and twisted through branches and ground shrubs. No human had been there all summer, perhaps all year. He was exhausted, overpowered. But he kept up the struggle till darkness. Then he collapsed beneath an old twisted oak and leaned his back against the base of its trunk.

It took several minutes for his breathing to slow. His mind cleared and he perceived in himself the panic and terror that had made him run. He thought it was a delayed action to the panic last night. Perhaps his body had held suspended till now the powerful fluids that impelled his limbs to move at a fantastic speed, subduing all other thoughts except one: run; save your life, run.

He began to weep.

He had not been prepared for the news that awaited him at the Raffer farm. Her parents had just gotten the word themselves. Kathy Raffer was dead. All this time. Even before Dan.

Her mother had had a nervous collapse. Her father could scarcely talk. In his grief her father thought that Slayer was a friend of Kathy's from school. Slayer did not tell him he was his daughter's murderer.

Murderer.

Was he really a murderer?

The deaths of Dan and Kathy were unpremeditated, granted. But he was a skilled meditator by profession, was he not? As were they all.

Murder, unpremeditated, can for some be a double crime.

His tumultuous thoughts and emotions gave way, finally, to sleep. He tossed and turned on the damp ground of the forest and awoke at intervals, sensing a vague apprehension. Before dawn he was wide awake. Somewhat rested, he found he could reason again.

He had to return to the island. His notion that he could go back to the desert was the notion of a fool who only wanted escape. He had to follow the game plan. There was no escape. 'You are part white,' his uncle and adoptive father, Chief George Bonita, had told him on the day he was to leave the reservation for the eastern white schools, 'and because of that I let you go.' They took each other's arms. 'Show them what it means to be Apache. Civilize the white man, for of all the people of the earth he is the most savage. He steals and destroys the land and he is a murderer of women and children. You are welcome in my lodge always, unless you forget you are Apache. You are part white but you are a civilized man. I will know if you become one of them.'

He could not now go back to the desert because he could not bear the scrutiny of his uncle's searching eyes.

Chapter 41—Air Crystals

When he had dislodged himself from the woods and found his way back to the highway, he discovered that his truck was surrounded by police cars and that the Highway Patrol had begun an all-out search with men and dogs and walkie-talkies. They wanted him back on the island. And they wanted him back fast.

The Highway Patrol had a Cessna warmed up and standing by at a small airstrip two miles from headquarters.

'It's a lot slower than a jet,' the captain of the Highway Patrol told Slayer, 'but it would take another hour to get you to Jackson by car. This Cessna will be nearing the outskirts of New Orleans within an hour. Ready, Charlie?'

The pilot nodded his head.

'But . . .' Slayer swallowed, trying to keep down the sick feeling in the pit of his stomach. 'I've never flown before.'

'Nothing to it,' the captain said. 'This is the fastest way to get you back.' He then frowned thoughtfully. 'You're one of those *nuclear* scientists from the big new reactor installation down there, aren't you? There's nothing on the bulletins about any trouble. But they want you back plenty bad. They're keeping their mouths shut.' He shook his head and looked at Slayer with a sadistic glint in his eyes. 'I'm glad it's not me who has to go down there,' he said.

The Cessna's pilot was a young man with a baby face who requested weather data from his transceiver twice before they took off. Five minutes after they were airborne he did it again.

'You got some reason to be so nervous?' Slayer said.

'*Me* nervous!'

'Well, I've got an excuse. This is my first time up.'

'Oh. Yeah. Well, I guess I am a little nervous at that,' the pilot said. 'I need ground visibility to fly this thing. These instruments . . . well . . .' He shook his head. 'I'm just a weekend crop-duster.'

Slayer shrivelled into his seat and gripped his kneecaps till his fingers turned white.

'By the way, name's Charlie Deacon.'

'George Slayer.'

'Well, George, don't you worry none. We got clear skies all the way down. I'll get you there in one piece.'

But as they were nearing their destination something unexpected happened over the lake.

Deacon had received his approach and landing instructions, which included a directive to avoid the centre of the lake and to proceed to the smaller New Orleans Airport East, where he had priority clearance. He did exactly as instructed. And as he was completing his turn over the airport he suddenly lost ground visibility.

He looked incredulously out the window of the plane, then glanced at his passenger for confirmation. But Slayer had his eyes tightly shut.

'Hey, George, something's happened. Or maybe I'm going nuts.'

Slayer opened his eyes to stare down upon a sea of sparkling crystals which reflected the sun like a huge mirror. Nothing else but this homogeneous blinding sheet could be seen for miles in all directions.

The voice of the air-traffic controller became alarmed.

'What's going on up there? You're overshooting the runway!'

'You mean you can see us?' Deacon said.

'Clear as day.'

'Well, we can't see a goddamn thing!'

'Repeat?'

'I said we can't see the ground. It's like the city's been covered by a giant mirror.'

'Okay,' the traffic controller said. 'What you're seeing is thermal inversion. Dust particles, exhaust, chemical wastes, you name it, suspended in the air above the city. It's a common phenomenon this time of year. The effect is like a one-way mirror. We can see you, but you can't see us. You're getting all the sunlight reflected off the particles. Did it happen very suddenly?'

'Yeah.'

'Repeat?'

'Affirmative, affirmative. How am I going to land this thing without ground visibility?'

'Oh, a crop-duster, huh? Keep circling at that altitude and hold on a minute. You can read your altimeter, I presume?'

'Very funny.'

Moments later the traffic controller came back on. His voice was firm.

'We've got to get you down. New Orleans International reports the same phenomenon and they're got some jet jockeys riding a two-hundred-and-twenty-mile-an-hour tail-wind down. Their scheduling is all fouled up and they're rerouting the small traffic over to us. In a few minutes it's going to be very busy where you're at.'

'Terrific.'

'Just calm down. It's a no-sweat situation. You've completed two full circles and you're heading back out over the lake. Straighten yourself out and drop down to a hundred feet. Turn around and come back in to the runway at that altitude. You'll be below the main body of the dust cloud and you should be able to see ground again.'

'That's all there is to it?'

'I told you it was no sweat.'

Deacon dipped the plane down. He flew right into the crystal mirror and it vanished at an altitude of a hundred and twenty feet. Up ahead was the shoreline and the foot of the runway jutting out into the lake.

Deacon breathed a sigh of relief and glanced over at Slayer.

'I guess some problems have a very simple solution,' Deacon said.

He noticed he was holding the stick control so tightly his knuckles had become as white as Slayer's.

Chapter 42—Plan Z

In the Oval Office the President listened gravely to his staff of scientific and military advisors. It was just past dawn in Washington and all the data on the heat levels inside the dome had arrived.

'These photographs taken by Hirschfeld from Tulane are conclusive,' one of the advisors said. 'Moreover, we have additional corroborating evidence from two of our own infra-red spy satellites whose orbits carried them over the southern United States early this morning.'

The President looked over the infra-red prints, then circulated them around the room.

'We know how much heat the dome will withstand,' the advisor continued, 'and we now know the rate of temperature rise. A simple equation of proportion tells us what we need to know. The steel dome will rupture at approximately four-twenty p.m. today. Eastern Daylight Time. Three-twenty in New Orleans. Or about ten hours from now.'

'And you are certain Mayor Mathieu does not have this information yet?' the President said.

'No, sir,' the advisor answered. 'As per your orders, Hirschfeld is withholding his findings till he hears from us.'

'Good,' the President said. He stood up. 'Gentlemen.'

The meeting concluded, the advisors began filing out. Only the President and Robert Tanner, his chief advisor, remained. The President flicked on the intercom and instructed his secretary to get Mayor Mathieu on the phone.

'When you get here, put her on hold, then notify me immediately.' Then he spoke to Tanner. 'I want to tell her the bad news myself and make sure she understands what has to be done. Ten hours. That's not a hell of a lot of time.'

Tanner had gone to one of the wall panels and pushed a button which slid the panel to one side. He pushed several more buttons and the four-by-six-foot computer monitor screen recessed in the wall began to display information which the President could easily read from behind his desk.

'This is Senario Z,' Tanner said, 'with the parameters supplied by Hirschfeld's data.'

The President nodded.

He drummed his fingers on the desk while he waited for his secretary to put his call through to New Orleans. Presently, the secretary buzzed to notify the President that Mayor Mathieu was on hold.

'Mayor Mathieu.'

'Mr President.'

'I hope you managed to get some sleep in during the night.'

'Yes, thank you, Mr President, I did.'

'I'm afraid I have some bad news. Hirschfeld's photographs incontrovertibly establish that the dome is getting hotter.'

'How much time do we have?'

'The dome will rupture at three-twenty, your time, this afternoon.'

'I have the police, fire, and departments of public service standing by to begin immediate evacuation.'

'Yes,' the President said. 'That's what I want to talk to you about. Let me preface my remarks with a reminder. When I spoke with you last evening we agreed to an evacuation postponement till we were sure there would be a need for one. We agreed that a public announcement about the possibility of a rupture and the commencement of a full-scale evacuation would engender a city-wide panic and jeopardize lives. We did not want to inaugurate an evacuation prematurely and perhaps needlessly. I have to tell you now that a full-scale evacuation of your city is not feasible.' The President began consulting the large monitor screen in his office as if it were a teleprompter. 'The factors involved in a grand-scale evacuation have been computed, and the bottom line is this: less than two hours into the evacuation, all the main roadways from your city will be hopelessly clogged. No amount of traffic supervision, police intervention, what-have-you, will alter the figures. It is not logistically possible to move that many people along the spaces provided in the allotted time. Only a fraction of your population will escape, approximately eight-point-two per cent. However, we have a plan. There is a way to dramatically increase the possibility of escape. We can triple or quadruple the percentage of survival. Mayor Mathieu?'

'Yes.'

'You must not alert the general public of the danger. There must be no city-wide panic interfering with our operations. I have here a list of people with skills, talents, real or potential contributions to society.'

'I will not condone a clandestine and selective evacuation.'

'Let me assure you, Madam Mayor, that names were placed on this list without regard to race, colour, or creed. Or without regard to sex, for that matter. There is no prejudice involved. The same criteria which we use to compile the list of Washingtonians who have priority evacuation clearance in the event of nuclear attack were used here, too. Some of the best minds in the country have already been lost inside that dome. We cannot further squander this nation's most important natural resource. The people on this list must be given every opportunity to survive. The

194

alternative is a disorderly, panicky, every-man-for-himself flight from your city, whose outcome will be as disastrous as the event which will occur at three-twenty this afternoon.'

'You remind me how little I have left,' the mayor said, 'so I won't waste it arguing, except to say this. I've always considered it perverted logic that the ones most responsible for bringing disaster to their fellow-men should be the ones best provided with the means of escape. People are responsible for their actions and must be held accountable. If we are going to perish here today, let the businessmen, the scientists, engineers, the people who have built and profited from this dome, perish, too. If I have my way – and I intend to – the ignorant and the innocent are going to have a chance for a change.'

'You're not thinking rationally,' the President said. 'I know you are under tremendous strain.'

'I don't have time to argue.'

'In any event, Plan Z will go forward with or without your assistance.'

'We have one of the old power plants back in operation. We have electricity. In exactly twenty minutes I'm going on the air to announce a city-wide evacuation, and there is nothing you can do to stop me.'

'I'm giving you an executive order not to make that broadcast.'

'Sit on it, Mr President.' Mayor Mathieu did not even remember where she had heard the expression as she said it.

After the President had slammed down his phone, he turned to Tanner. 'How could such an immoral, vulgar person be elected to public office?' he said. 'Did you hear how she spoke to me?'

Tanner was busy querying the computer.

'It doesn't matter,' Tanner said. 'You have the military under your control. Let the mayor do what she wants. Order in the troops to evacuate the people on this list. Give them orders to shoot in the event of local police interference.' He directed the President's attention to a psychological profile on Mayor Mathieu being displayed on the screen. 'As you can see, she'll never leave that city. After three-twenty p.m. she can't file any complaints, give you any guff, or retaliate in any manner. She'll be on the verge of death.'

Chapter 43—Evacuation

'Al.'

Al gently put his hand over Dottie's mouth.

'I'm not one of your innocents,' Al said. 'I was very much in favour of this dome from the beginning. I thought it would benefit the city and further your career. Anyway, do you think I could leave you?'

By mid-morning it was evident that the evacuation of New Orleans had virtually reached a standstill. As predicted by the President, the roadways out of the city were blocked. There was fighting and riots. Cars were being abandoned and people were walking. The effort was fruitless. For even the strongest would scarcely put twenty miles between themselves and the city limits before the deadline.

The mayor surveyed the situation from a police chopper at low altitude.

'What about the one-ten East?' the mayor asked.

'Even worse,' the pilot said. 'I was flying traffic control over there before it became hopeless. Want to have a look?'

'No. I've seen enough already. Get me back to City Hall.'

The chief of police was waiting for her with news about the military.

'They're got air and ship power,' the chief said. 'And they could maintain some semblance of law and order. But when I asked for their help, they said they were fully committed to an evacuation programme of their own. I tried to get more information and they said to talk to you.'

'Let them be, Jerry,' the mayor said. 'They're engaged in an evacuation programme I cannot condone. But I've botched things up so badly myself, I can't help but wish them every success.'

The chief's manner softened.

'I know what they're up to, all right. I've been getting reports from my men all morning. I just wanted you to tell me it wasn't your idea.'

Wolford had long realized what a terrible mistake they had made, summoning Slayer back to the city. Slayer was a clutch hitter, with his brilliant mind and boundless imagination. But there was no way out of this. The dome was going to rupture and they were all going to be killed. Slayer's presence accomplished nothing. Getting him to return was a brutal and selfish act of desperation.

'It's a terrible injustice,' Wolford said on the phone to the mayor. 'If anybody has a right to be spared, it's Slayer.'

'Where are you calling from?' the mayor asked.

'I'm at the lighthouse.'

'Slayer and the others?'

'We're all here.'

'Okay. Get everybody over to my house by twelve. I want to talk to all of you.'

'What about Slayer?' Wolford persisted.

'Don't worry, Mary. It's going to be okay. I promise.'

The mayor had a speech prepared. It was useless for Wolford, Slayer, and the other surviving scientists from the island to remain any longer. Nichols, she had been notified, had been snatched from his Royal Sonesta suite; Hirschfeld and the physicists from Tulane and UNO who might have provided some assistance were long gone. Why jeopardize the lives of her faithful allies beyond a reasonable limit? Besides, they could better serve her interests alive and telling all.

She decided, therefore, to have them take advantage of the

military rescue operation. She would insist that they do so.

She had the pilot of the police chopper fly her home at twelve.

The pilot set the craft down on her back lawn and expressed his reluctance at leaving her there.

'Mayor Mathieu,' he said, 'please, don't stay. I could put you eighty miles from here in thirty minutes.'

'Berney,' she said, 'how many people does this thing carry?'

'I could squeeze in three passengers,' he said.

'Then do it, Berney. You've got time to ferry about ten people to safety.'

'Mayor Mathieu.'

'Berney, when are you going to realize you are not my personal chauffeur?'

Al came out to meet her on the lawn.

'You just got a call from Wolford,' he said.

'You mean they aren't here?'

'They're still at the lighthouse and they want you to go there right away. I've got the engine running in my car. I can get you there in five minutes.'

Chapter 44—Slayer's Solution

Charlie Deacon's words kept popping up in Slayer's head. 'I guess some problems have a simple solution.' Maybe it was the relief that had shown in Deacon's face coupled with that which Slayer felt himself as the plane had taxied to a stop on the runway. Slayer wanted to experience that same sense of relief again, now, right this instant. Maybe that's why he kept reliving that terrifying episode, kept seeing Deacon's face, kept hearing Deacon's words. More to the point, kept hearing, as well, the words of the air-traffic controller. 'Jet jockeys riding a two-hundred-and-twenty-mile-an-hour tail-wind down.' 'A two-hundred-and-twenty-mile-an-hour tail-wind.' 'A tail-wind.' 'Down.'

Weather conditions couldn't be worse for a city about to sustain a nuclear reactor containment sphere rupture. Thermal inversion meant there were no draughts in the atmosphere to aid in blowing the radiation away. The radioactive dust would hang suspended in the air over the city, becoming part of that great mirror cloud of particles that blanketed the whole region.

But high in the troposphere a swift wind blew southward and out to sea. If there was some way of lifting the radiation into the jetstream . . .

His plan was simple. But it filled him with a new terror, as it would his colleagues. It went against all his instincts, and quite possibly his colleagues would think he was mad.

He had to work out all the details. He had to quantify everything to convince especially himself that he was still quite sane.

When the end result of his calculations backed the feasibility of his plan, he still could not bring himself to articulate it. First, his colleagues would have to be prepared. He would have to demonstrate to them that no matter how horrible the end result of his plan might appear, the alternatives to that end result were even more horrible.

Right away the mayor sensed that something was up. The scientists were congregated in the beacon tower. Slayer was in a corner, eclipsed by four or five bodies assuming a protective pose. Wolford was in the foreground, the apparent spokesman for the group. There was a unanimity of mind here and – dare she think the unthinkable? – a spark of hope.

Without preliminaries, Wolford directed the mayor's attention to several of the Hirschfeld photographs.

'There's interesting heat data on the extreme right of the prints,' Wolford said. 'Those bright streaks bleeding into the pictures suggest a secondary heat source beyond the field of camera vision. Nobody paid any attention to it till now. Slayer thought it must be the east pipeline, again, boiling away the water. He was right. The Coast Guard checked it out. That means that when the reactor blew; the back-up coolant system kicked on. And there's liquid sodium circulating around inside that dome. I don't know why we overlooked that possibility. We should have guessed right away from the presence of the renewed magnetic field. Incidentally, that field is getting stronger as the dome gets hotter. When the dome ruptures, the liquid sodium will combine explosively with the water and air. Several things can happen then. And none of them is good.'

Wolford quickly ran through the possibilities, starting with the blanket saturation of the entire Mississippi Delta with extremely lethal radiation, concluding with the possibility of a super-fission explosion that could destroy four states and quite possibly rock the earth out of its orbit.

Slayer stepped forward.

'We can't rule out this last possibility at all,' he said. 'The explosive power of liquid sodium combined with air and water can act like TNT on the plutonium oxide in the reactor core, suddenly compressing large volumes of the substance into critical masses. When twenty pounds can blow up a city, you can imagine what several tons could accomplish.'

'You didn't call me over here just to tell me more bad news,' the mayor said.

Wolford held the mayor's shoulders.

'If there was the slightest chance,' she said, 'no matter what the risk, you would take it to save the city, wouldn't you?'

The mayor glanced from Wolford to Slayer. Both young scientists were studying her carefully.

'Tell me your plan,' she said.

'This is what we have to do,' Slayer began. 'We have to pulverize the plutonium oxide, suddenly, into superheated gases to ensure that none of it can be compressed into large critical masses. Then we have to lift the gases into the troposphere, where a jetstream will blow them out to sea. I've performed all the calculations. My colleagues here have checked and double-checked. The thermal inversion over the city will help keep the heavy plutonium gases aloft till they reach the Gulf of Mexico, where they will descend and dissipate over water. In short, we have to vaporize the entire dome with a man-induced nuclear explosion and use the adverse weather conditions to our advantage. We are of one mind on this. It's risky, but it's logically and mathematically sound. And it's the only chance the city's got. Maybe even the world.'

Chapter 45—The Steel Dome

The majority of Slayer's colleagues did not share his opinion about the likelihood of a super-fission detonation. But then Slayer had been so right about so many things. And the mayor was not prone to take their side of it. They were trained to think in conventional categories. It had been hammered into their heads that a nuclear reactor was not a potential nuclear bomb, no matter what the circumstances. How ironic, the mayor thought, that circumstance had made these people into the very agents who would help perform the dreaded transformation. For they all did agree with Slayer that vaporizing the steel dome was the only way to vault the radiation over the city and out to sea.

'Slayer and I are the ones to do it,' Wolford said. 'Slayer is the youngest and strongest, and I'm the only scientist here with practical training in nuclear assembly and detonation. Nobody else here is really qualified. Our plan consists of four stages. One, return to the island as soon as possible. Commander Higgins has a Coast Guard chopper standing by. Two, enter the steel dome; and, granted our survival in so doing, collect a sufficient quantity of plutonium for assembling the bomb. Three, assemble the bomb, preferably inside the dome, and time it to explode before three-twenty. Four, return by chopper to where you'll be awaiting us with open arms. And there's a fifth stage to our plan. It involves you. Pray like hell for our success?'

Higgins, himself an experienced pilot, flew the chopper. Slayer, en route, kept his eyes shut. Wolford watched Slayer and tried to suppress a premonition that things weren't going to go well at all.

Higgins commented on his compass readings as they approached the island.

'Damn thing's going wild!'

Slayer opened his eyes.

'It's the magnetic field,' he said, 'getting stronger.'

'Think we can make it in?' Higgins said.

'This is one mission we have to make.'

Even before they neared the island's heliport, the engine started missing. The effect was similar to the ups and downs of a roller coaster. Slayer was on the verge of passing out. Wolford knew about his acrophobia and began to panic. Without him the mission could not succeed.

Higgins started shaking his head.

'I don't think I can land this thing without cracking it up! In fact, I know I can't!'

'Get over water,' Wolford ordered. 'Get as close to the docks as you can, but stay over water.'

'What are you going to do?'

'Jump.'

She grabbed Slayer around the waist. Before he could protest, she threw her weight backwards and out of the bubble of the chopper. Slayer felt the nauseous sensation of free-fall for a brief instant before he hit the surface of the water. In this more secure enviroment he got hold of himself. Wolford was gurgling and struggling ten yards off his right shoulder. The fall undid her ribs and she was literally drowning from the pain.

'Got ya!' Slayer said. 'Don't fight me. We're almost to the docks now.'

'Where's Higgins?'

'He didn't jump.'

Slayer got a good grip on the landing and hoisted Wolford up with a grunt. She groaned as if someone had punched her in the stomach.

Up in the sky the helicopter dipped and climbed and careened like a mosquito hawk with one wing. It disappeared behind a warehouse, then shot up like a rocket. Its engine sputtered out the dots and dashes of an unfamiliar code.

'He's got no control at all!' Slayer shouted.

The two scientists watched, at once terrified and fascinated by this bizarre aerial dance.

'Why didn't he jump?' Wolford cried. 'George, he's heading for the dome!'

They gripped one another in horror.

The chopper swayed near the top of the dome as if it were connected to the arm of a pendulum. It plunged down while making a gigantic sweep at the same time and missed the dome by inches. Higgins appeared to regain control momentarily. The chopper climbed straight and true. And just when it seemed he was going to get clear, the engine died. The chopper fell like a stone, struck the side of the dome, exploded in a ball of flame.

For several moments neither Slayer nor Wolford could bring themselves to move.

Finally Slayer got to his feet.

'Come on,' he said. 'We can still do it. The dome hasn't been breached. That thing was designed to take the impact of a seven-forty-seven.'

Wolford tried to stand and doubled over.

'It's my rib bandage,' she gasped.

Slayer laid her down on the landing and opened her shirt. The bandage was loose. He yanked it tight and refastened the Velcro under her breasts, which were high and firm from the pressure. Wolford blushed as he looked at her, and he rebuttoned her shirt and helped her up. How could such delicate frailty, he wondered, hope to confront such raw, destructive power? Impulsively, he stepped forward and kissed her gently. She looked up at him. They were thinking the same thing. It was too late for them. With the expansion of the magnetic field and the crash of the chopper, the mission had become one-hundred per cent suicidal.

They already had worked out how they were going to get inside the dome. In the sub-levels was an access hatch with a combination lock. This hatch served a double purpose. It opened on to the highly restricted plutonium processing labs, which were lead-and-steel-shielded almost as well as the reactor itself. In the eventuality of a radiation accident in the labs, it provided workers with a means of escape. It was also designed to allow entrance into the dome in the event that company inspectors, years following a major reactor accident, would want to investigate the possible causes.

The hatch resembled a huge bank vault, and it opened on an outer corridor beyond the emergency seals. Slayer had seen it only once before. To his knowledge it had never been opened. Lombardy knew the numbers to the combination. And so did Wolford.

'Several of us knew,' Wolford said, as if to explain there was nothing personal in her knowing. That she tried to be delicate touched his heart. Here they were in the last hours of their lives and she was trying to be tender with their new-found relationship.

'Twenty-seven right, forty left, two right, uh . . . ten left.'

Slayer applied all his strength to the turn but it wouldn't budge.

'Damn,' Wolford said. 'Twenty-seven right, forty left, two right, *fifteen* left. Try it now.'

The bolt turned and the hatch opened.

From here on they would have to proceed with extreme caution. Slayer entered the chamber and went to the second hatch, which opened directly on to the plutonium labs.

'It's not hot,' he said. 'We may be in luck.'

It was crucial to their plan that the heavy shield panelling which surrounded the lab area and made it an island separate from the rest of the dome interior had not been breached. If it had, they would not survive beyond the second hatchway.

Slayer turned the bolt and did not feel any pressure forcign the huge door open. Another good sign. He backed Wolford up and pulled the hatch out just enough for them to slip through.

The air inside was as warm as a sauna, but arid. The first few breaths irritated the membranes inside their mouths and throats.

'No bodies piled up near the escape hatch,' Wolford said. It was another good sign that the labs had not been breached. Evidently there had been no one in the area when the reactor blew. If there had been, they would have escaped or would have died here on the floor, a sure sign to any intruder that he would shortly join their ranks.

'I can hardly see,' Slayer said. 'Electricity in the back-up batteries must be down to the dregs.'

Wolford, who knew her way around the sub-levels, led the way. They went immediately to the 'closet' where all the radiation suits were stored, including the new Widmarks. In the dim emergency lighting they worked furiously to get a Widmark operational. Slayer got inside and tried to move the limbs.

'Problems,' he said.

'Magnetized?'

'Partially.'

'We'll have to make do. Help me with mine.'

Wolford's suit worked better and her vision system was ninety per cent functional. The magnetic field was still, thankfully, far weaker than its former self.

Intense white light bled into the corridors from the forward labs. Wolford moved in that direction with Slayer lumbering behind. They were connected by a telephone umbilical.

'Vision any better?' Wolford asked.

'Not really,' Slayer answered.

'Well, once we get into the dome proper . . .'

'I know. There'll be plenty of heat. My problems should clear up.'

Wolford paused before the hatch door of a forward

processing lab. The crystalline glass slot in the door, positioned at eye level, was a white, blazing ribbon. The vision mechanism of the Widmark suit automatically negated the gamma radiation enough for her to see on her screen what was happening inside the lab. The far wall had partially collapsed from the reactor explosion. The light shining through was intense as the sun. There was debris everywhere. The thick glass panelling which divided the lab in two was melting before her eyes. The mechanical arms behind the panelling, used for handling the plutonium, were charred and blackened and limp. There were no containers of processed plutonium in view.

The heat inside this lab was already formidable and it was a good place for Slayer's suit to shed its magnetism while she searched the other labs. As a last resort she could retrieve plutonium oxide from the reactor core. But the bomb she contemplated would be crude and chancy enough. Far better if she could scrounge up enough nuclear-weapons-grade plutonium, which several of these labs were turning out by the pounds daily.

Effortlessly, Wolford opened the lab hatch and guided Slayer inside.

'I'm going to leave you here for a while,' she said. 'When you've got full command of the suit, you can enter the dome interior through a breach in the wall on the other side of the glass panelling. You know what you have to do.'

She detached the telephone umbilical, tapped Slayer's shoulder as if to wish him luck, and made her exit, slamming the lab hatch closed behind her.

After several minutes Slayer felt his suit becoming more agile. His vision apparatus cleared, and he was ready to go.

He stepped to the glass panel, which had melted to the thinness of a window-pane. He raised his arm and brought it down, expecting glass to shatter all around him. Instead, he rent a tear in the gooey substance and had to push it aside as he would the filaments of an elaborate spider web. He kicked out the concrete base of the glass frame with his foot and moved to the breach in the wall.

It was a crack approximately four feet in length and three inches wide through which tremendous quantities of heat and radiant energy from the dome's interior poured. He stood before this crack, like a Frankenstein monster, absorbing the energy that would free his suit of the last traces of magnetism. When he reached full power he hurled himself at the crack; and, after token resistance, he broke through to the other side and found himself standing on the threshold of hell itself.

There wasn't a tier in the dome that hadn't been demolished. Trusses and girders of twisted, melting metal formed bizarre and hideous scupltures everywhere he looked. Huge blocks of concrete lay in piles along the walls, split and charred and pulverized. The floor of the dome had collapsed to form a gigantic funnel sloping down into the reactor, which lay fully exposed and pulsating with tremendous brilliance like a huge demonic heart. A whirlpool of glowing liquid sodium spun around and around the base of the funnel fed by rivulets running down the sloping floor.

At first Slayer couldn't fathom their source. But as he lowered and raised his head, studying first the reactor core and then the ceiling of the dome, he understood.

The liquid sodium enveloping the core boiled away into gases which collected at the top of the dome. These gases condensed into rain which fell in a steady shower, forming and feeding the metallic puddles and rivulets which returned the liquid sodium to the core only to be boiled away again, condensed, and returned. A self-perpetuating process, if it weren't for the fact that the gases, by condensing near the top of the dome, conveyed reactor heat to the walls, melting metals and eroding concrete, making rupture of the dome imminent.

They had to work fast, Slayer didn't know how much time they had left, but from the way things were melting all around . . .

When Wolford came out of the breach in the wall, Slayer

had already completed his task and had selected three or four possible sites for assembling the bomb.

Wolford re-attached their telephone umbilicals and said, 'It's worse in here than I imagined. We have to hurry.'

'Did you get it?' Slayer said.

'Back behind the wall.'

'I've got a sodium bath prepared. And some possible sites. You make the final decision.'

The bomb consisted of two sub-critical masses of processed high-grade plutonium in stainless-steel containers. These were positioned over two pipes of Zirconium 14, a metal with a slightly higher melting point than steel. Below the necks of the pipes was a third container surrounded by the pool of liquid sodium which Slayer had gathered. They planned to position the whole package in a dome hot-spot where reactor heat would melt the steel containers, allowing the two separate masses of plutonium to pour down the two pipes and to refreeze into one critical mass in the third container cooled by the liquid sodium. The predicted end result was an instantaneous nuclear chain reaction.

'I just wish there was a better way of timing it,' Wolford said.

'I know one thing for sure,' Slayer responded. 'Those steel containers will melt as soon as the plutonium becomes molten. And that will happen long before the dome ruptures. Ready?'

'Ready.'

'Then let's get out of here.'

Before inserting himself back through the wall to the lab, Slayer forced himself to look at the devastation. He hadn't upon entering. He hadn't wanted to remember that over a hundred of his colleagues still remained here. It was too much to face all that humanity reduced to bones and charred flesh, soon to be thinned to their elements. Everywhere he turned he found little signs that made him sick to his stomach. He had tried to distract Wolford's attention from the top tier, or what was left of it, and wondered if he had succeeded.

Did she see that obscenity?

That charred, blackened face jutting over the ledge to survey and preside over the workings of the dome with absolute authority even as it did in life?

Chapter 46—Legacy

It was Wolford's suit that gave them hope. If her Widmark had not fully succumbed to the magnetic field, then maybe . . .

They ran for the docks with everything they had. Wolford collapsed halfway there and Slayer carried her. When they got to the landing he propped her against a piling while he tried to start one of the boats. He tried one of the fast security crafts, but he was reduced to yanking the cord on a small outboard used for fishing. He pulled thirty or forty times on the cord and put all his remaining power into one final effort. But the engine would not kick over, and again the lake was silent.

He dragged himself out of the boat and back to Wolford's side. He sat down heavily. He was resigned to fate.

She took his hand in hers. For a time they listened to the gulls, the waves, the silence.

Finally, Wolford spoke.

'I really never knew you very well,' she said. 'Will you tell me something about yourself, something I can hold on to?'

He brushed strands of dark hair from her face, caressed her cheek, studied her dark blue eyes.

'Tell me something. Please?' she persisted.

He leaned back against the piling and stared at the sky. 'When I was eleven years old,' he said, 'my father committed suicide. He jumped from a tenth-storey window of an Albuquerque hotel! I was there and he had it in his mind to kill me, too. I don't know what changed his mind. It's why I've got this fear of heights. I can still see myself looking down from that ledge at his mangled body. You see, we were both part white and he had come to despise that part of himself. He had worked for a time on the plutonium bomb, the one they dropped on Nagasaki, and he could never get that out of his head. It drove him crazy. I think he saw himself in me in those last moments. My purpose was to right the wrong that was done to my father, to demonstrate the shaky foundations of nuclear technology, halt this madness, and somehow make his life meaningful. Maybe when he thought of killing me he had a vision of what I would become. Like him, I'm part of the very technology I despise. The end result of my life is exactly that of my father's. We are both murderers. The Shatterers of Worlds.'

The man with the Jolly Roger tattoo had kept out of sight, for he had thought at first that they were looking for him, and he didn't want to have to fight for his right to remain on the island. He had spotted the helicopter as it approached and hid. He was inside a warehouse when the chopper exploded and was lured outside, where he saw the two figures in the water. His first instinct was to help, but his suspicions prevailed. Why had these people returned? What or who were they after? He watched them swim to safety and waited till they cleared the landing before he followed, always staying carefully hidden.

When they entered the dome he knew they had discovered some way to get to the inside. He went to each sealed corridor and even singed his hands on one trying to push it open. How could they have gotten inside? How could they survive the heat? He ran from corridor to corridor, level to level, until the heat became unbearable and he had to get out.

He was hiding behind a bush on the lawn near the steps when they reappeared. For the first time he recognized the man. And he remembered his promise. 'Wayne,' Simon had said, showing him Slayer's picture, 'I want you to remember this man. You've always had a good memory for faces, Wayne. This man is our friend. I want you to watch out for him, help him if he ever needs help. But I don't want him to know. Don't let on that you're his friend – at least, not yet. Do you understand, Wayne?' When he told Simon he understood – though he didn't, really, at least not everything; he had never been smart like Simon – Simon had made him promise that he would always be Slayer's secret friend.

'I promise, Simon,' he had said. 'I will be Slayer's secret friend.'

And Simon had smiled and given him a big hug.

Did Slayer need help now? He and the girl were running back to the docks where the boats were. Just like those people had done the other night when something terrible was supposed to happen. Was something terrible supposed to happen now?

From behind a stack of crates near the approach to the landing, he watched Slayer's frantic efforts to start the boats. At first the sight tickled him a little. Slayer was playing some kind of game. Perhaps to make the girl laugh. But he slowly realized that something was wrong. Slayer was trying hard and not a single boat would start It hurt him to see his secret friend in trouble. And he thought and thought. How could he help? There had to be some way to get his friend off the island. There had to be some way he could keep his promise to Simon.

Wolford spotted the man from maintenance almost as soon as he stood up from behind the crates. How long had he been watching them? What was he still doing on the island? Had no one remembered, in all the excitement, to see that the poor retarded man got safely away?

'George, look!'

'The Jolly Roger man!'

The Jolly Roger man appeared equally solicitous. He was waving his arms and pointing.

Slayer got to his feet.

'He's trying to tell us something. He wants us to follow him. Can you stand up?'

211

'What is he saying?'

'I think it's "I can help you." '

When Wolford and Slayer got to the foot of the landing, the Jolly Roger man was down the docks, bending over the pilings and extracting Mason's hang-glider from its protective shelter.

'He wants to play games,' Wolford said. 'He doesn't realize . . .'

'No,' Slayer said, 'it's no game. Mary, he's telling us we have a way out. Look where he's pointing. The Pipeline East. Still boiling the water. There's a hot-air updraught along the pipeline all the way to shore. Two people on Mason's kite. They could ride that updraught. All the way in.'

'My friend,' Slayer said, 'why didn't you get off the island when you had the chance?'

The big man grinned.

'You get off the island,' he said.

Slayer turned to Wolford. They were on the roof of the pumping station, strapping themselves to the hang-glider. The Jolly Roger man had pulled the glider's tow cable out of Mason's boat. One end was attached by a clip hook to the glider. The big man started to descend the steel ladder from the roof, carrying the remaining spool of cable under one arm.

'Mary,' Slayer said, 'I don't know if I'm doing the right thing. Maybe I should stay. You might have a better chance by yourself. What if I should pass out on you?'

'If you stay, I stay,' Wolford said. 'I've never been up on this thing. I don't know a thing about it. At least you've seen Dan do his stuff a hundred times. If you don't think we can make it, say so. But I go where you go.'

They were all ready when Slayer was once more overcome with remorse for their benefactor. The big man stood down at ground level, his huge hands gripping the tow cable, his

212

eyes looking up expectantly, fondly, like a child towards a loving parent. Slayer could not abide those loving, innocent eyes. What affection have I ever shown towards him, Slayer asked himself, that I should win such generous friendship? If only the man was not so huge. If only he was agile and knew how to fly the glider. He could have saved himself. He, the wizard premeditator, would have been pulling the cable for the simple-minded. He would have done it, gladly, to appease his agonizing conscience.

'Ready, Slayer? You ready, Slayer?' the man called. Slayer looked back down.

'Ready!' he cried. 'On three!'

The Jolly Roger man ran as fast as he could and pulled as hard as he could. He felt the lift from the glider right away. The cable slipped across his big hands, ripping his flesh, but it didn't slow him down. He had to be like a speedboat. It seemed to him that Slayer was travelling in the wrong direction. If something terrible was about to happen to the dome, then why was Slayer having him pull the kite that way? Slayer should be trying to get over water. But he was used to not understanding things, and Slayer was smart. Anyway, the kite was flying high now. It was just like when he was a kid and used to fly kites with Simon.

The jolt he got when Slayer released the cable hook knocked him flat. He had been straining against the pull of the kite. Then, suddenly, nothing. He fell head over heels and hit his back hard on the cement. The slack cable came snaking down from the sky and almost hit him on the head. The kite was flying under his own power now. What a sight! He waved and waved.

He felt really good inside. And yet he was crying, too. He had never understood how a person could do that. Feel really good and cry. And here he was. Doing it!

He said aloud to himself, 'I kept my promise, Simon.'

He felt a little tickled, too. That Slayer. He was so smart. But he couldn't figure out everything.

'Simon,' he said aloud, 'if I hadn't promised I'd never tell anybody about us, I guess I'd have told that Slayer. He was really worried about me. He didn't understand. You never left your little brother when he was in trouble. How could your little brother leave you?'

Chapter 47—In Balance

They didn't have a chance without great initial altitude. It was fifteen miles to shore. The dome was starting to super-heat, which was good for their altitude. But it also meant their time was running out.

'George,' Wolford said between gritted teeth, 'it could happen any minute now and we're still at ground zero.'

'Shift your weight with me.' Slayer nudged her with his hip. 'To the right. That's it. Now to the left.'

He kept the glider circling the dome, spiralling higher and higher, taking full advantage of the swift air updraught. He had made up his mind to stay over the dome till they reached the top of the hot-air column. The hotter the dome, the higher the column and the better their chances.

'George, we've got to get away from here!'

He didn't answer her but kept nudging her hip with his. All the knowledge was in his brain, the ins and outs, do's and don't's, of making the glider work. It was there from the time he had book-studied for a solid week to impress Dan Mason. What he had to do now was successfully translate that knowledge into action. His debut on a kite had been a disaster. He had to make damn sure this would not be a repeat performance.

As they neared the top of the column, their fast upward acceleration started to drop off. Slayer had no eye for measuring altitude, but the dome appeared incredibly small beneath them, and to the south the great mirror cloud over the city was again visible. This time, however, he was so high he could perceive its boundaries. And the southern horizon beyond the cloud was green. The Gulf. Designed by his plan as the receptacle for radioactive dust, the likes of which the world had never seen. Whatever the far-reaching and ultimate consequences of that dust, at least it would not descend unalloyed and in concentrated form upon the heads of millions of people. If his plan worked . . .

The upward acceleration was rapidly diminishing. Soon it was hard for them to tell if they were still climbing at all.

'That's it,' Slayer said. 'We're at the top of the updraught. Shift your weight forward and brace yourself for a fast descent.'

Slayer was terrified as he moved his body forward across the suspension bar. But it was the anticipated earthward plunge that would propel them shoreward at high speed. But when they shifted their weight nothing happened. Now Slayer found himself caught in the grip of a new, more intense terror. He perceived at once that they were trapped at the top o the updraught, their weight balanced against the force of the rising air like a Ping-Pong ball suspended over a column of vacuum-cleaner exhaust in a department store display. They were stalemated, unable to move, snared by the law of balance. They would be hopelessly bobbing around when it happened. And there was nothing – absolutely nothing – left they could do in order to escape.

Chapter 48—Flight

'You're wrong,' Wolford said. 'We've got manoeuvrability. We're just too close to the centre of the updraught. Let's increase the diameter of our spirals. When we get to the rim of the column we should be able to slip off.'

They swayed their bodies in unison until the glider was sweeping the sky in large circles and tried to angle the nose of the glider downward.

'It's not working, George!' Wolford cried frantically.

Slayer started unstrapping himself from the glider's suspension bar.

'What are you doing?'

'I have to get more of my weight forward.'

Slayer inserted his fingers between the main strut and the kite material and pulled himself forward till his centre of balance extended beyond the suspension bar.

Then realizing how precarious his situation was, he began to freeze up. He felt as he had on that ledge, and he was unable to move a single muscle.

'George!' Wolford whispered. 'George!'

He couldn't even bring himself to answer her. His body was shaking. At any moment he would lose his grip.

Suspended on a ledge. Terror-stricken. A fireman. 'Just give me your hand.' Smiling. Coaxing. 'Just reach out your hand.'

Slayer moved his hand forward on the strut. His knees came over and across the suspension bar. He moved his hand another fraction of an inch.

And the nose tipped downward. The kite had slipped off the column of air and they were on their way.

Chapter 49—Firecracker

The kite took on speed. With Wolford's help, Slayer pulled himself back across the suspension bar and refastened the straps around his waist and shoulders. His heart stopped pounding. He could begin to think about the possibility of outrunning the blast. They were approximately fourteen miles from shore with a ground speed of what? Fifty miles per hour? Forty? It was a speed they could not maintain. As they lost alltitude they would have to keep making passes over the Pipeline East, and getting the lift they needed would slow them up immensely. And they were making mistakes, too. On their first downward plunge they had allowed the kite to spiral, losing precious time and ground. Their watches had stopped, but the sun was past the meridian. With everything going their way and with no more piloting mistakes, it would still take at least twenty-five more minutes to reach shore. Slayer doubted very seriously that they had that much time left. What, except for a quirk of fate, had allowed them to get this far already?

Wolford's thinking had changed. Ever since the crash of the chopper she had been plagued with visions of doom. Nothing would go right. The mission would fail. It went without saying that their lives would be forfeited. But apparently the wheel of fortune had swung around. She thought about Slayer's edifice of equations and her interpretation of them. In a highly complex system the laws of chance are against things running evenly and smoothly. Runs of incredibly good or bad luck are commonplace. Their endeavour to blow up the island and escape could certainly be interpreted as events in a highly complicated game of chance. Perhaps Slayer's equations applied. Perhaps the incredibly good luck would hold.

They had lost most of their altitude and speed and were nearing the outskirts of the cypress swamp in New Orleans East when the sky and earth lit up all around them as if several million flash-cubes had been fired simultaneously. They were blinded and left with an after-image of the swamp up ahead cast in absolute whites and blacks, like as X-ray negative.

After a second or two, Slayer opened his eyes a squint. The momentary blindness passed. The shadows in the swamp fled into corners as the giant fireball, more brilliant than a hundred suns, rapidly rose out of the lake.

It was of some comfort to know that Wolford's bomb had not been too powerful, and that they had survived the heat flash. But what of those tons of air that had been pushed aside by the blast, streaming in all directions, a tidal wave of atmosphere, reaching out, overtaking . . .

Slayer did not have time to finish his train of thought. The

217

glider lurched and pitched and crumpled as if struck by a mighty hammer. At the same instant an excruciating and deafening roar assaulted his ears. He grabbed Wolford's hand. Below them the water over the Pipeline East was a bubbling cauldron. Cast down, Slayer thought. They were going to be cast down and boiled alive.

But the glider, though maimed and crumpled, was catapulted on the leading edge of the air wave up and into the swamp and away from the path of the pipeline at a thirty-degree angle. Everything happened too fast. It was only seconds before Slayer found himself knee-deep in water, clutching Wolford, ridding himself and her of kite debris, and watching the fireball grow and dissipate and transform itself into a column of hot gases that poured towards the stratosphere at tremendous speed.

Chapter 50—The Dark Cloud

The shock wave from the blast shattered the lakeside windows in the beacon tower of the lighthouse in West End. Three scientists sustained cuts from flying glass. The mayor herself received a slight gash on her left shoulder. The explosion was stronger than they had anticipated.

'You all right?' Al said, helping his wife to her feet.

She nodded. 'You?'

They resumed their positions at the broken window.

'Any explosion strong enough to inject the jet-airstream with the radioactive debris and weak enough to cause only minor damage to shore areas is acceptable,' one scientist said, thinking to himself out loud.

The mayor squinted over her shoulder at the cut. 'I would catalogue that as minor damage,' she mumbled. Then, in horror, she gasped, 'What about Wolford and Slayer?'

Already one of the scientists was anxiously re-aiming the four-inch refractor toward the Pipeline East.

'Hurry,' the mayor said.

They had been following the escape, through the observer's running commentary, supplying cheers and exclamations of encouragement like ringside spectators at a championship bout.

'Can't find them,' the scientist said. 'They're down.'

The mayor was on the phone, ordering in police choppers to assist the Coast Guard boat which was already on its way to the cypress swamp.

After she had talked with the chief of police, the mayor went back to the window and put her arm around Al, who marvelled at this sudden public display of affection.

For several minutes they watched the lake in silence. The column of rising gases was a giant exclamation mark which began to flatten at the top into a T.

All that was left of the fireball was a blood-red streak, like the smile of an evil serpent, near the top of the forming mushroom.

The head of the mushroom spread out and thinned and found its way into the jetstream. After two hours the mushroom was gone. In its place was a dark cloud, elongated, in the shape of a teardrop, its tail end pointing southward over the city and out to sea.

On the rooftops of the Marriott, the Shell Building, the Hilton, the International Trade Mart, and a dozen other high-rise buildings in the heart of the city, firemen dressed in protective suits watched the cloud pass over and consulted the readings on Geiger counters. Aided by the bubble of hot air enveloping the city, the heavy plutonium dust remained aloft.

When the police car arrived at the mayor's house on Shore Drive, the mayor was standing on her front lawn, waiting. She greeted the tired and dishevelled Wolford and Slayer, then put her arms around them.

'Let's go in,' she said. 'We're waiting to hear from Pointe La Hache.'

Before they got to the front door they heard the cheer. Al came to the front door.

'We just got the call,' he said. 'The radiation is moving out into the Gulf. Pointe La Hache reports no fallout.' Al looked at Slayer. 'It's working out,' he said, 'exactly according to plan.'

Chapter 51—Initiation

Nobody understood why Slayer was depressed. The other scientists were gratified to see the predictions of their calculations fulfilled by the reality of events. They felt that, after all, they were still in charge of things. Presently, they were studying atmospheric vectors supplied by the Florida Weather Bureau to determine the path of the cloud and to forecast where most of the plutonium dust and other radio-active debris were likely to descend. Their calculations from this data brought them more good news. The greater portion of the cloud would descend over open water. No land mass in the Gulf or Atlantic would be directly touched. It was so much more than they could have reasonably hoped for that they were ecstatic.

Towards dusk the mayor noticed Slayer's absence.

'I'm worried about him,' she said to Al privately. 'He doesn't look like a man who has just saved millions of human lives.'

Al checked the bedrooms upstairs. He found Wolford in one, asleep. Another bedroom was occupied by two more scientists, with four-o'clock shadow, who were snoring loudly.

The mayor was at the foot of the stairs when Al came back down.

'Not there?' she asked.

'I'll look outside.'

Al walked around the house, then went to the sea wall.

Slayer was sitting on a lower step with a Geiger counter between his knees. He was watching the sun set.

'Hi!' Al said. 'Mind if I sit here?'

'Not at all. Please.'

Al looked out towards the centre of the lake. At the grey, unbroken horizon.

'I sure got used to seeing that dome out there,' Al said. When Slayer didn't answer, he went on. 'Picking up any readings on that particle counter?'

'Not yet,' Slayer said. 'But you can bet that lake is plenty hot.'

'Yes,' Al said. 'We're going to have to make a lot of readjustments around here.'

Again Slayer didn't answer, and Al thought he heard a choked-back sob, disguised as a clearing of the throat.

'Slayer?'

'Yes?'

'Is everything okay? Dottie was worried. You look so preoccupied.' He paused. 'We're not still in danger here, are we?'

'Well?' the mayor said when Al returned to the house.

'He's on the sea wall.'

'What did he say?'

'Did you know that Slayer has it all calculated, how many lives will be lost by the release of all that radioactivity into the atmosphere?'

'How many?' the mayor said.

'About ten million.'

'That can't be,' the mayor said. 'Al, it just can't. That's how many people would have been killed if he hadn't exploded the dome.'

'Slayer says all he did was remove the number of casualties from here and now. He says they won't be New Orleanians, necessarily. They won't all die at the same time. Not during the same decade or even the same century. But they'll die just the same, because of what happened here. That radio-

221

active debris will be active for the next hundred thousand years. It's going into the earth's ecology. Its ability to kill hasn't been reduced in the least by being dispersed.'

'Then nothing's really changed. We haven't saved anybody.'

'We've only saved ourselves. At the expense of our children.'

By the sea wall Slayer stared out across Lake Pontchartrain, thinking of the life the unnatural heat of the water would destroy, even now. The world and life itself had taken on a radically different configuration for the future, one that could not be altered. And he had helped to set a nuclear trap that could not be revoked. Civilization had leaped into the future, and the clock was ticking. He understood, now, what it meant to be a shatterer of worlds.

**Give them
the pleasure of choosing**

Book Tokens can be bought
and exchanged at most
bookshops in Great Britain
and Ireland.

NEL BESTSELLERS

T046 133	HOW GREEN WAS MY VALLEY	*Richard Llewellyn*	£1.00
T039 560	I BOUGHT A MOUNTAIN	*Thomas Firbank*	95p
T033 988	IN THE TEETH OF THE EVIDENCE	*Dorothy L. Sayers*	90p
T038 149	THE CARPETBAGGERS	*Harold Robbins*	£1.50
T040 917	TO SIR WITH LOVE	*E.R. Braithwaite*	75p
T041 719	HOW TO LIVE WITH A NEUROTIC DOG	*Stephen Baker*	75p
T040 925	THE PRIZE	*Irving Wallace*	£1.65
T034 755	THE CITADEL	*A.J. Cronin*	£1.10
T042 189	STRANGER IN A STRANGE LAND	*Robert Heinlein*	£1.25
T037 053	79 PARK AVENUE	*Harold Robbins*	£1.25
T042 308	DUNE	*Frank Herbert*	£1.50
T045 137	THE MOON IS A HARSH MISTRESS	*Robert Heinlein*	£1.25
T040 933	THE SEVEN MINUTES	*Irving Wallace*	£1.50
T038 130	THE INHERITORS	*Harold Robbins*	£1.25
T035 689	RICH MAN, POOR MAN	*Irwin Shaw*	£1.50
T037 134	EDGE 27: DEATH DRIVE	*George G. Gilman*	75p
T037 541	DEVIL'S GUARD	*Robert Elford*	£1.25
T042 774	THE RATS	*James Herbert*	80p
T042 340	CARRIE	*Stephen King*	80p
T042 782	THE FOG	*James Herbert*	90p
T033 740	THE MIXED BLESSING	*Helen Van Slyke*	£1.25
T037 061	BLOOD AND MONEY	*Thomas Thompson*	£1.50
T038 629	THIN AIR	*Simpson & Burger*	95p
T038 602	THE APOCALYPSE	*Jeffrey Konvitz*	95p

NEL P.O. BOX 11, FALMOUTH TR10 9EN, CORNWALL

Postage charge:
U.K. Customers. Please allow 25p for the first book plus 10p per copy for each
additional book ordered to a maximum charge of £1.05 to cover the cost of
postage and packing, in addition to cover price.

B.F.P.O. & Eire. Please allow 25p for the first book plus 10p per copy for the next
8 books, thereafter 5p per book, in addition to cover price.

Overseas Customers. Please allow 40p for the first book plus 12p per copy for
each additional book, in addition to cover price.

Please send cheque or postal order (no currency).

Name ....

Address ....

....

Title ....

While every effort is made to keep prices steady, it is sometimes necessary to
increase prices at short netice. New English Library reserve the right to show
on covers and charge new retail prices which may differ from those advertised
in the text or elsewhere.